STRONGSIDE

STRONG SIDE

AN MM SAND VOLLEYBALL ROMANCE

PALM UNIVERSITY
BOOK 1

S.R. CLARK

TILLY RIDGE

COPYRIGHT

Edited by Sadie with Dot The I Edit

Book Cover by Aliyah with Forever Star Cover Design

Formatting Images by SR Clark

Formatting by Tilly Ridge

First edition 2024

DEDICATION

For all the people who want a man who can both sweep you off your feet and bring you to your knees, sweet baby Clay is written just for you.

-S.R Clark

For all the people who want a boss in the streets and a sub in the sheets. Rockman is waiting on his knees for you.

-Tilly Ridge

And to Sadie... this one's for you, babe.

-Sadie's Psychos

AUTHOR'S NOTE

Welcome to the world of Palm University! It is a fictional College based in Pensacola, Florida. We hope you enjoy The Palm University Panthers. And if you're coming here from either of our previous books, be warned, this is a full-on romcom.

We tried keeping the story true to the rules of sand volleyball and the timeline, but there may be some discrepancies. We are aware mens sand volleyball is not currently a NCAA sanctioned sport, but a girl can dream, right?

This book was written after the name, image, and likeness (NIL) rule for the NCAA was put into place. It does vary state by state, but for the fictional purposes of this story, Palm University in Florida participates in NIL for its collegiate players.

CONTENT WARNINGS

Use of alcohol
Talk of non-MMC getting kicked off the team for SA
Anxiety
Anxiety attacks
Verbal abuse from a parent
Explicit on-page sexual acts
Degradation
Praise
Exhibitionism
Audio recording sexual acts without the other party knowing
Spanking
Snowballing
Use of sex toys

CONTENTS

PLAYLIST

As you read, you will find footnotes throughout the book. The footnotes will indicate which song is playing at the time of specific scenes. You can play the song until the next footnote indicates a song change or until the chapter ends. The playlist is linked below.

Candy (feat. Trippie Redd) - MGK, Trippie Redd
Feel Invincible - Skillet
Limits - Bad Omens
pretty toxic revolver - mgk
Lust - Chase Atlantic
Roses - Awaken I Am
Pretty Girl Rock - Keri Hilson
Dirty Little Secret - The All-American Rejects

Doomed - Bring Me The Horizon

Do I Wanna Know- Arctic Monkeys

What Do You Mean?- Justin Bieber

Man! I Feel Like a Women! - Shania Twain

No Heart - 21 Savage, Metro Boomin

Mr. Brightside-The Killers

My Bad - Teddy Swims

Triggered - Chase Atlantic

Acquainted - The Weeknd

Been Like This - Doja Cat

TOO LATE - Chase Atlantic

Heaven - Julia Michaels

If I Were a Boy - Beyoncé

Too Sweet - Hozier

HEARTLESS (with Goody Grace) - PLVTINUM, Goody
Grace

I Mean It (feat. Remo) - G-Easy, Remo the Hitmaker

Conversations In The Dark - John Legend

Work Out - J. Cole

I Feel Like I'm Drowning - Two Feet

Wicked Games - The Weeknd

High - Whethan & Dua Lipa

Who Do You Love? - YG, Drake

Cry To Me - Marc Broussard

Use Me - PLAZA

Dial Tone - Catch Your Breath

act ii: date @ 8 (feat. Drake) - 4batz, Drake

Beautiful Things - Acoustic - Benson Boone

Never Know - Bad Omen

Sweet Symphony - Joy Oladokun ft. Chris Stapleton

Daydreams - We Three

A Bar Song (Tipsy) - Shaboozey

Say You Won't Let Go - James Arthur
Son of a Sinner - Jelly Roll
THE WITHDRAWLS - Kae
Oh Nah (feat. The Weeknd, Wiz Khalifa, & DJ Mustard) -
Remix - Ty Dolla $ign, The Weeknd, Wiz Khalifa, Mustard
Nonsense - Sabrina Carpenter
Believer - Imagine Dragons
Loveeeeeee Song - Rhianna, Future
Work Song - Hozier

CHAPTER 1
NO PARTNER, NO PLAY

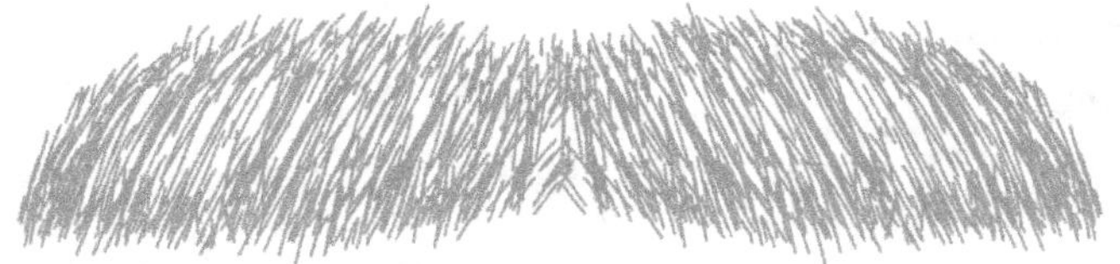

ROCKWELL

"I love these briefs and wear them every ti—" A call cuts off the TikTok I'm filming from… I look closer. The Dean of Palm University. *Great.*

You never want to get a call from a lead privileged white man on a Monday morning; I reluctantly answer the call. "Dean, how can I help you this lovely morning?" I know he can hear the irritation in my voice, but I can't find it in me to care. It's my senior year, after all.

"Rockwell, could you please come to my office as soon as possible." My blood runs cold. I'm on a sports scholarship for sand volleyball and sand volleyball only. No academics, no rich parents to bail me out, and sure as hell no student loans.

"Yes, sir. I'll be there in fifteen." I hang up before he can say anything else. My TikTok is sitting there half filmed, playing on repeat. I save it to drafts, mentally noting to film some more when I get back. The brand deal isn't due to the company for a couple of weeks, but I do not like to rush to complete them.

Social media and brand deals are how I make extra income to survive. Thank whoever is listening that the NIL ruling passed because I would've been royally fucked without it.

I shoot a text off to Sanders, my doubles partner, to make sure he's up and ready for practice in a couple of hours.

ROCKY

Are you up, shit bag?

Three delivered messages from me over the weekend. You better be up.

*Throwing on some joggers and a cropped tee, I grab my protein shake and my keys, lock my apartment door, and jog down the outside steps. I live above the Delectable Desserts. It's a little artisanal baked goods and food store. The bougie people in this godforsaken town love this damn place. The owners, Kevin and Nancy, just so happen to rent out the little apartment they had built above the shop. It's the cheapest rent within a fifty-mile radius of Palm University, and it just so happens to be a five-minute drive to campus.

I park outside the admin building, walk in, and nod to the receptionist, one of the nicest older ladies you'll meet. I guess she was ready for me. "Dr. Andreson is ready for you." The fact that he makes her put the "Doctor" in front

____

* Candy (feat. Trippie Redd) - MGK, Trippie Redd

of his last name makes me want to throw up. It probably wouldn't bother me nearly as bad if he was a nice person.

I knock on his door, and it's immediately pulled open by Coach Taylor.

This can't be good.

Coach grits out, "Sit down, Rocky." I have a deep-rooted respect for Cameron Taylor. He looks out for his players and treats us with the respect we deserve. He truly has our best interests at heart and wants us to succeed in all aspects of life. Something tells me he and I have more in common than he leads on.

"I don't understand what's going on." I try to keep my tone even.

The Dean is looking at me, sadness actually covering his face.

This has to be bad for this prick to be sad.

"Aaron Sanders is being accused of raping a woman at the party this past weekend. Charges were filed, and he was placed in jail, but his parents got him out on bail. From this point forward, he is kicked off the team and expelled from the school indefinitely." That's why this piece of shit was sad. One of his own got caught and made his precious school look bad. It's been no secret that the Dean is best friends with Aaron Sanders' dad. That's why he's had no accountability his entire collegiate career.

Until now.

If that were me, I would still be sitting in jail, but then again, I would never do that to anyone.

You don't take what isn't yours.

Sanders is the epitome of white privilege; daddy of his pays for everything, and if anything goes wrong, a check is thrown at you to act like it never happened. I'm honestly surprised he actually has charges.

"Surprised his parents weren't able to pay the poor girl off. He deserves to rot in jail for that." I can't help myself. They both know how horrific Sanders is. I can usually ignore his shitty behavior, but this is a whole new level even for him. "I won't have him as a doubles partner ever again."

The Dean barks, "We understand, Rockwell." Well fuck, must've hit a nerve. Pissed him off talking about his besties kid. Birds of a feather and whatever the rest of that saying is.

Coach breaks the tension. "At this point in time, you do not have a partner; you will move to the top of the alternate's list. Your scholarship is still safe as long as you continue to show up to practice and help the rest of the team. You'll be in limbo unless another teammate becomes available." Fuck, this is not what I needed my senior year trying to push to make Team USA.

"What are the odds of me getting another partner I can play with by the time the first game comes in February? You know I want to make the US team, Coach." I'm trying so hard not to sound whiny, but fuck, this sucks.

"You never know what could happen, Rocky. Just keep your head up and train like you have been. Stay ready." I give Coach a nod and murmur a quick thank you to both of them, striding out the door of the Dean's office. I guess I'll head to the gym early and work off some of the steam rolling off me.

God bless the soul that is on the other side receiving my hits today.

CHAPTER 2
FEEL INVINCIBLE—I THINK?

CLAYTON

"**S**hit," Jax grunts under his breath as he receives another one of Rocky's hits. "I legitimately think my arms are going to bruise."

*It's the first day back at practice after the holiday break, and we're all warming up with a simple hitting and receiving drill.

Actually, let me rephrase that. *We're* warming up and Rocky is hitting like his main goal is to send the volleyball through the gym floor.

Not that I blame him, really.

By the time we woke up this morning, the news about Aaron Sanders had spread like an STD at a frat party. Everyone knew about it, and no one was surprised. Aaron Sanders is and always has been a grade-A piece of shit. How he made it this far in life is one of life's great myster-

---

* Feel Invincible - Skillet

The only thing he had going for him was his volleyball skills, but even that was only going to get him so far. I don't know when I felt worse for Rocky, honestly; when Sanders had to be his partner or now that he is left without him.

Rocky never wanted Sanders as a partner, but he wanted to win even more. That's about the only thing he and I have in common. Winning the Division I championship for men's doubles beach volleyball and making it to Team USA. I can practically feel that 2028 gold medal between my teeth. I know Rockwell Campos is talented. The man has more intuition for the game than anyone I've ever seen.

Not that I'd ever say that out loud.

His defense rivals Phil Dalhausser's, his sets hit the mark with uncanny precision, and his side-out percentage is the highest on the team. I would have been his doubles partner in a heartbeat… if he wasn't such a sanctimonious prick.

He walks around avoiding anyone and everything, constantly acting like he's better than the rest of us because he grew up with less money, meaning he must have had a "harder" life. He seems to have it permanently ingrained in his brain that just because I grew up with money, I had it easy.

Little does he fucking know.

"Don't be such a pansy-ass," I jab at Jax as I get in my ready position, watching Coach Taylor set another ball to Rocky for an outside hit.

I watch in slow motion as Rocky takes his approach, swings his arms forward, jumps in the air, and twists his torso.

Line hit.

Rockwell Campos may be amazing, but I'm better. I'm Clay fucking Aldrich.

As his hand makes contact with the ball, I move to the line just in time to receive the pass.

God, I love practicing in the gym. It's so much easier to move than on sand.

The ball hits my forearms, but I'm not prepared for the sheer force behind his hit, and it knocks me on my ass.

Rocky's gaze locks with mine, and I don't find a hint of remorse behind those green eyes. All that's there is smug satisfaction and unrelenting anger.

Asshole.

Jax is laughing his ass off as he walks over to me and holds out his hand. "Who's the pansy-ass?"

I grab his hand with more force than necessary. "Shut the hell up."

Jackson Baker is my best friend and genuinely one of the best people I've ever met, but that doesn't mean I won't deck him in the face.

While the rest of the practice was just more drills, Rocky's intensity didn't waver, and by the time we headed to the weight room, we all made sure to give him a wide berth.

Coach Taylor doesn't police when we hit the gym as long as we get it done. Most of us find it easier for muscle recovery to do it after practice, and it gives us time to fuck around and have some fun without Coach breathing down our necks. So, in typical Campos fashion… he avoids it at all costs. He usually lifts weights before practice, I'm assuming it's so he doesn't have to talk to anyone on the team, so I was slightly surprised when he followed us into the weight room. But if I had the day he was having, I'd have some extra aggression to work out too.

I don't know what compels me to do so, but as everyone else shuffles into the weight room, I stop and pull Rocky to the side. I'm not oblivious, I know some of his story and how hard he worked to get here. If something or someone ruined my shot at the Olympics, I couldn't even imagine the range of emotions I'd be feeling.

Already on the defensive, Rocky stands with his fists clenched at his sides and his jaw ticking in frustration as he looks up at me. He's only a couple of inches shorter than my six foot six. "What, Aldrich?"

Take a deep breath, Clay.

"I heard about Sanders, and I just wanted to say I'm sorry. You don't deserve what's happening to you."

"I don't need your sympathy," he bites out as he takes a small step back.

In and out. In and out.

"I didn't say you did. I just wanted you to know I'm on your side."

Rocky snorts out a sarcastic laugh as if my words are the most ridiculous thing he's ever heard in his life. "I don't want or need you on my side. All of you are the same."

I don't have to ask what he means by all of *you*. Rich trust fund kids who make up about eighty percent of this school. But I am *nothing* like Aaron Sanders, and the fact that he's automatically making that assumption sets my teeth on fucking edge. "Aaron Sanders is a piece of shit, and I would never do what he did."

"Maybe not. But that doesn't mean I want anything to do with you. So fuck off and leave me alone."

Do not punch him, Clay. Do not *punch him.*

"You know what, Campos? Despite my better instincts, I was just trying to show you a little compassion, but I see now that was a total waste of my goddamn time. Just because you grew up poor doesn't give you the right to act like an asshole." I take a step forward, closing the space he put between us and stab the center of his chest with my pointer finger. "You want to be a prick and alienate everyone around you? Fine. But you're not better than any of us just because you grew up different than the rest of us."

I can tell I struck a nerve when he inhales a ragged breath. Instead of responding, he simply steps around me, shoving my shoulder with his in the process.

Taking a deep breath of my own, I follow him into the weight room and head toward Jax, who's racking weights onto a barbell for some chest presses. He looks between Rocky and me, who both have equally annoyed and pissed-off looks on our faces. "What was that about?"

"Nothing. You want to go first or me?"

He waves his hand out with a bemused look on his face. "Be my guest."

Thirty minutes go by as the sounds of weights, grunts, and the occasional snide joke fill the room. Just as I'm about to do a set of lateral raises, I see Rocky, who is now doing chest presses, loading more weights onto his barbell.

He was already struggling with his last couple of reps... *don't ask me how I know because I definitely wasn't watching...* so I know he's going to need a spotter this time.

"Jax," I whisper as I nod in Rocky's direction, "go spot him."

"No. I'm in the middle of a superset. You do it," he grunts out from his spot on the bench.

I look between my weights resting on the floor and Rocky—once, twice, three times. "Jesus fucking Christ," I groan under my breath.

I may not like him, but that doesn't mean I want him to die.

I stomp over to him like a petulant child just as he's getting himself situated under the bar. "Here, man, let me spot you."

"I'm fine," he says as he puts his hands on the bar.

I place one hand between his and push down, preventing him from lifting it. "You're not fine. You could barely do three reps of the last weight. You're going to crush yourself."

"Let go, Aldrich."

"No, Campos."

He's off the bench and in front of me in what feels like a split second. His nostrils flare with each infuriated breath, and for a moment, I find myself getting lost in his eyes. The deep pools of green and dark eyelashes pull me in like the tide to the shore. And then he speaks, and the moment is gone almost as fast as it came. "What did you not understand about what I said in the hallway? Fuck off and leave me alone."

"God, no wonder Sanders was the only one who would be your partner. I am not going to let you hurt yourself just because you want to be an asshole."

"Today is not the day to fuck with me, Clayton."

I can't help it. It's like an involuntary reflex. The corner of my mouth turns up as I say, "Oh, I think I'd fuck with you any day, Rockwell."

Or just fuck you.

"Back. Off."

I lower my head so it's just above his. "Make. Me."

I'm not exactly sure what it is, but I watch as he wages some sort of internal war within himself. I'm just about to make another smart remark when, suddenly, he blinks, and his hands are on my chest, shoving me backward.

Okay, now *I'm going to punch him.*

It only takes another second for me to lunge back and knock him on his ass. The two of us roll around on the ground for a few minutes, throwing half-assed punches before Jax grabs me, and a couple of the junior teammates grab Rocky.

"Enough!" Jax shouts between us. Like me, he rarely gets angry or yells, but when he does, you know to listen the fuck up. "If Coach Taylor sees you, you're both fucking done! Get it the hell together." Then he turns and looks directly at me. "Leave him alone, okay? He's had a tough day. Don't make it worse," he says low enough for only me to hear.

Jax… always the mediator.

Rocky storms off without another word, and the rest of the team goes about their business pretending like they didn't see or hear a thing. For the next twenty minutes Jax and I finish our workout, all while he casts me worried glances every few minutes.

I'm a lover, not a fighter. So the fact that I just got in a fistfight with someone is enough to cause my best friend concern. Not just someone… a teammate. Wisely, though, he chooses not to make another comment on it while I spend the rest of our workout replaying the entire interaction over and over again in my head.

I don't know what it is about Rocky Campos, but he gets under my skin like no one ever has.

One thing I do know, though, I sure as fuck am glad I don't have to be partners with someone like him.

CHAPTER 3
NOT SO SWEET SERENDIPITY

ROCKWELL

I'm finishing up one of my papers for the Curriculum and Instructional Design class I'm taking this semester. This is my first assignment and class with this professor, but these upper-level education classes that I thought were going to be grueling, have been so fucking interesting. Doing the coursework has actually been fun. The semester has just started, but with it being volleyball season now, I can't afford to get behind on classwork.

Choosing history as my major is something everyone's on my ass about, but it's the only subject that keeps my interest long enough for me to comprehend it. Not long ago, I decided to go down the education route to become a high school teacher and, hopefully, a coach one day. More things these rich fucks don't understand. Maybe if they shared some of that wealth of theirs with the teachers and schools, or just put it back into the communities, our education system wouldn't be so pathetic. Teachers being heavily underpaid is a major issue in our country, but I have a passion for history and helping kids find the same love I have for it as well.

If I hadn't had the caring and compassionate teachers that I had all throughout my earlier years, I could have easily slipped through the cracks and become just another drop-out statistic. Having two working parents and a younger sister that requires more care and attention than myself, it sometimes felt like I was pushed to the wayside. The teachers helped pick up any of that slack and mold the man I am today. I want to be able to do that for other kids.

Shutting my laptop and setting it on my desk, I start getting ready to head to the gym. I find one of my Nickelback cropped tees, five-inch inseam athletic shorts, and my lifting shoes and head into the bathroom. I have some unruly hair. I re-wet it to get some of the curls to form again and throw a little gel in it as well. Can't forget to stop by my full-length mirror to get a picture. I am the brand rep for the shorts I have on, and I can never pass up an opportunity to throw a rep code out.

On my way out, I grab my volleyball bag that has all the shit I'll need for practice after I get done lifting. Not that I'll be getting a ton of playing time if we're not just running drills. This not having a partner shit is already getting old.

Heading down the front steps after locking my apartment door, I pull my phone out and call my mom. I haven't talked to her in a day or two. I try to call and check in at least every other day, mainly to make sure my younger sister, Liliana, isn't driving my parents completely insane.

My mom, Cassandra, picks up on the second ring. "Hi,

Filho, how are you today?" I love hearing my mom speak Portuguese. I miss it so fucking much. I feel a little guilty; I haven't told her or my dad what happened with Sanders. I'm so in denial it's not even funny at this point.

I grab the door handle to my basic as fuck Toyota Camry—it may be basic but this thing has gotten me anywhere I've needed to go these past three years. "I've been better, Momma." Fuck, I sound so defeated. This isn't me. I need to get my shit together. I'm still on the team and have my scholarship and health. I need to stop the sulking.

"What's happened, Rockwell?"

"My partner got in trouble with the law, so he got kicked out of school and, of course, off the team." I pause for a minute, but she doesn't fill the silence. She just leaves me the room to keep venting. "I still have my scholarship, and I'm at the top of the list for the alternates, but it just sucks. I have goals, and not being able to play because of Sanders being a pig, royally screws with those plans." I shouldn't be talking on the phone and driving, so I quickly throw my Airpod in so I can still talk but have both hands free.

"*Foder*, I'm so sorry, Rocky. When did this happen?" I let out a schoolgirl giggle; it'll never not be funny hearing my mom cuss like a sailor.

"Yesterday. This will be the second practice on the sidelines watching. I'm trying to make the best of it and hit the weights even harder to stay ready if I get the opportunity."

"That's all you can do. You call if you need something, okay?"

"I will, Momma, *amo você*."

"*Amo você*, and always will with everything in me."

I couldn't have asked for better parents. They did

everything they could, and still do, to give my sister and me the best life we could have. We weren't rich by any means, but the love we have as a family is overflowing. At times, their relationship makes me want to vomit, especially when my dad, Joesph, is at my mother's feet at all times. When she moved to the states for him so they could get married, he took her last name so she could "keep some of her ancestry from Brazil." They say it was love at first sight, and to this day, they're still obsessed with each other. They make my standards for relationships pretty much unattainable.

I park in one of the closest spots since I'm the first one here due to lifting before practice instead of after. If I'm pissed off enough, I'll even hit some cardio after to blow off the extra steam.

My entire workout flies by, and before I know it, I've gone through my whole leg day, and I'm making my way toward the gym we're practicing in. Hopefully, Coach wants to run drills today; I don't want to sit on the sidelines and watch them scrimmage. I want in on the action.

I head to the locker room to get my pads on and take out my nose ring and earring—it's my favorite one. An upside-down dangling cross. I find it beyond comical when the ladies at Momma's church glare at me when they realize what it is. Every time I wear it she tells me to stop antagonizing them, and every time, all I do is laugh.

We fly through warm-ups and start to pepper around to loosen up some more. Coach calls out that we are going to be scrimmaging this practice, and I huff out with the most dramatic eye roll I can muster. Coach looks at me but doesn't say anything; he knows how I'm feeling.

Jax and Clayton are on one side, scrimmaging one of

the junior teams. It's been a tight game so far and fairly entertaining, I will give them that.

The juniors serve and send a rocket over the net. Jax passes it to the front of the net beautifully, right into Clayton's waiting hands. Clayton sets it at the perfect height for where Jax is on the court. Jax takes off in his approach, but on that second step he doesn't land right, and he hits the ground, grabbing his knee before he makes it to his third step.

The ball hits the ground right in front of him. The sound resembles a bomb on the quietest of battlefields.

Theo, our athletic trainer, comes barreling out from the staffing offices and lands on his knees beside Jax, who's been inconsolable since he hit the ground. But once those first hushed words are passed between Theo and him, he's instantly calmed.

What the fuck is going on there?

You know what, I don't even want to know. I have enough to worry about already.

I lock eyes with Clayton across the gym, and for the first time since I've met him, I know the two of us are thinking the same thing. "There's no fucking way."

CHAPTER 4
WE'RE ALL IN THIS TOGETHER, UNFORTUNATELY

CLAYTON

We made it twenty whole minutes.

Rocky and I had our first doubles practice on Wednesday afternoon after Coach Taylor was informed by Jax's parents, who called from the hospital, that he has a total ACL and MCL tear and will be out for the rest of the season. We made it twenty minutes before Coach lost his shit on us and kicked us out.

Twenty minutes of Rocky throwing the biggest temper tantrum known to man because, apparently, being forced to partner with me is comparable to being paired up with Lucifer himself. Twenty minutes of the two of us bickering back and forth and arguing about every single thing. Twenty of the longest fucking minutes of my entire life.

It didn't help that instead of taking it easy on us and having a junior team play the other side of the net, Coach had Prescott McDaniels and Chadwick Augustus playing against us. They were the only other senior doubles team left and, besides Aaron Sanders, are the two douchiest assholes I have ever met in my entire life. And that's saying a lot considering the life I grew up in. What's even worse, they're good. Like really fucking good.

The two seemed to take some perverse satisfaction in watching Rocky and I struggle and fall apart. And for twenty minutes, the two of them played against us like it was the championship game of our senior year.

Finally, after Chad drilled a hit between Rocky and me and we stood still as we watched it land on the gym floor directly between us without moving an inch… for the fifth time… Taylor had had enough.

Not that I blamed him. That was some rookie-level shit.

Neither one of us was up on the net blocking, moving to get a pass, or setting each other up for a hit. And we sure as shit were not communicating.

Definitely not championship material, let alone Team USA.

He explicitly told us to take the rest of the day and Thursday to figure out what we wanted.

"How bad do the two of you want this? How badly do you want to make Team USA? Because if there's even the smallest chance of the two of you making it, you need to get it the hell together; I don't care if you like one another off the court or not. On the court, you need to figure out how to work as a team. Because you're each other's only option. If that's something you want, show up to this gym for Friday morning practice ready to work. If not, don't even bother coming back."

I don't have to know Rockwell Campos to know what his answer was going to be. Because it was the exact same as mine. I want this year's championship. I want to be on Team USA. And I want to feel that gold medal in the palm of my hand.

*Regardless of how much my life was planned out for me and how uncertain I am about every single step of that plan, there is one thing I have never questioned. I am meant to be on that sand. It's the one place I feel truly at peace. Where every expectation of who I'm supposed to be falls away, and all that's left is who I am.

Clay Aldrich.

Not Clayton Aldrich, son of the legendary Charles Aldrich.

Just. Clay.

So here I am, sending a text to my best friend and ex-partner about the man who drives me up a fucking wall—who also happens to be my new partner—before driving across town to practice.

ME

Are you sure you can't come back?

JAX

Yeah, let me just hop in my time machine and unfuck my knee.

I snort a laugh.

ME

Okay, okay. Easy killer. Someone's a little grumpy today?

JAX

I had a meeting with my new physical therapist and Theo this morning to outline my recovery program. So yeah, I'm a little fucking grumpy.

---

* pretty toxic revolver - mgk

Feeling slightly bad that I poked fun at him when I know I would hate being in his shoes, I answer:

ME

I really am sorry, man. I would kill to have you back on that court with me.

JAX

I know you are. Just give him a chance, Clay. The guy might surprise you.

Sighing, knowing Jax is right, I pocket my phone as I climb into my Mercedes-AMG CLS, ready to put my differences with Rockwell Campos aside and make the most out of my senior year. I spent the last day and a half anxiously baking in my apartment, trying to make sense of all the thoughts swimming around in my head. I wouldn't be surprised if I gained ten pounds from the amount of cookies I consumed. In the end though, I've decided I'm not going to let his shitty attitude and constant need to see the world half-empty get in my way of achieving my dreams.

I'm just about to pull onto campus when my phone rings through the car. I look at the dash, and as if he knew I thought about him for only a second, my father's name lights up the screen. Letting it ring a couple more times, mentally preparing myself for what I know this conversation is going to be about, I inhale a deep breath and reluctantly hit the answer button on the steering wheel.

"Hey, Dad."

"Why am I just now finding out that Jackson got hurt?" No, "Hi, son. How are you?" Because there never is. He only ever calls me for two things: school and volleyball.

"I'm assuming you talked to Coach Taylor?"

"I called him to see how your first few days back after the break were." Of course, he did. "Imagine my surprise when he told me Rockwell Campos was your new partner." He says Rocky's name as if the words are poison on his tongue.

I should have known he would have talked to Coach Taylor eventually. The two of them used to be doubles partners when my dad won silver in the Olympics. He was twenty-eight when it happened. Cameron Taylor and Charles Aldrich were two of the best players the sport has ever seen. I was only two, so I don't remember any of it. Not that it matters because the old man talks about it like it happened yesterday. Once my dad retired, he started a small real estate company. However, with his and my mother's family connections, that small company quickly grew, and Aldrich Real Estate is now a Fortune 500 company. My dad spent his entire life working, and my mother spent her entire life acting as Miami's leading socialite. If it weren't for Marissa, the household nanny and housekeeper, I would have had no parental figure in my life whatsoever.

It was all a linear equation. The more successful my father became, the more ruthless he grew to be. The more ruthless he became, the more disassociated my mother became. The more dissociated my mother became, the less our house felt like home. The faster our home fell apart, the harder my father pushed me to become a mirror image of him. And the more he pushed, and the less my mother tried to stop him, the ball of resentment that festered inside of me grew until it rivaled the size of Jupiter. Now, all that's left is the occasional phone call where he never fails to remind me that my actions and behavior are a direct reflection of him and his image.

"Yes, Rocky is my partner now." I don't divulge any extra information. I've learned the less I say, the faster he can berate me and the sooner this entire conversation can be over with.

"And what exactly are you going to do about it?"

"What do you mean what am I going to do about it?"

His exaggerated sigh sounds through the interior of the car like the soundtrack to my entire life. "How do you expect to win with a partner like *him?*"

A partner like him? An unfamiliar protective instinct rears its head. "Rocky is a great player. One of the best I've ever seen, actually."

He scoffs on the other end of the line as if I've just uttered the most outlandish sentence he's ever heard in his entire life. "Cameron told me all about him."

I highly doubt that. While my dad and Coach Taylor used to be thick as thieves, their relationship dwindled at the speed at which Dad's company grew. Rapidly. My father wasn't the same man he once was and didn't hesitate to push Coach to the side once he could no longer gain anything from their friendship. Not that Coach seems to mind much. I have a sneaking suspicion he is more than happy with the fact that the two of them are no longer on speaking terms.

"And what exactly is that?" I ask as I pull into the parking lot outside of the gym.

"That he's some low-life kid from the ghetto of San Diego." Considering Cameron Taylor was once some "low-life kid from the ghetto," I find it very unlikely those were the words that came out of his mouth, but I choose not to acknowledge the statement anyway. "And he's at the school on scholarship. Which, considering the footage I've seen of him playing and the fact that he's received no formal training his entire life, comes as a complete surprise to me."

I put the car in park and look out the windshield just as Dad is finishing his rant to find Rocky leaning against the hood of his Toyota Camry, arms crossed and staring at me. And just like that day in the gym, my eyes lock with his, and I can't help the inexplicable pull they have on me.

"I have spent too much time and invested too much money to watch you throw this chance away, Clayton. You're too close." With my stare entangled with Rocky's, this entire conversation feels just… *wrong.*

"What do you expect me to do, Dad?" I snap. "Rocky was the only other senior player available. I cannot just magically conjure up another one."

"Watch your tone, Son." It's rare I ever talk back to him. One, I usually don't give enough of a fuck about his opinion to care. And two, I learned a long time ago that arguing with him is a waste of both time and energy. Charles Aldrich doesn't back down, and he's never wrong.

So he thinks.

But regardless of what I think of Rocky, I am not going to let anyone talk about my new partner that way.

End of discussion.

"Rocky is my new partner, Dad. There's nothing you or I can do that's going to change that. He, Coach Taylor, and I have already weighed all of our options, and this was the only way we could play the rest of the season with any chance at winning. Let alone gain the attention of the Team USA scouts. So leave it alone. I have it handled." I hang up the phone before he can get another word in.

I'm sure I'll pay for that later.

With Rocky's stare still burning a hole into my head, I can't help but break the tension by pulling my eyes from his and raking them over his body. I'm not blind. Rocky Campos is hot. Even though I'm slightly taller than him, all six foot three of him is packed with muscle. His corded arms, thick thighs, and lean waist are covered in a deep walnut skin. The intricate sleeve he has covering his right leg is something I could spend hours looking at. He still has in the nose ring and dangly earring he usually takes out before practice and games. And I haven't even gotten to his face yet. His annoyingly gorgeous fucking face. Even with that goddamn mustache. Never once in my entire life have I found a mustache attractive… I guess there's a first time for everything. His curly black hair is always perfectly messy. The kind of messy you just want to run your fingers through. And he has one of the sharpest jawlines I have ever seen. I love watching it flex in annoyance every time I piss him off.

Speaking of said jaw, I unashamedly watch it clench when my eyes meet his again, not even hiding the fact that I was fully checking him out. And if the look on his face were anything to go by, he knows that's exactly what I was doing too. Rolling his eyes, he drops his arms and shoves off the hood of his Camry. Pushing the phone call with Dad out of my mind, I grab my duffle from the passenger seat and climb out of the car.

With my eyes locked on Rocky's ass and my head in the game, I follow him into the gym for our first real practice as partners.

CHAPTER 5
IT'S GETTIN' HOT IN HERE

CLAYTON

Well, fuck me.

Rocky and I are ten minutes away from finishing our first successful practice as partners. After an hour of grueling drills, Coach had us scrimmage against Prescott and Chad *again*, seeing as they're the only other senior team. I knew the moment they walked onto the other side of the court they thought it was going to be a repeat of last time.

Well, it turns out when Rocky and I aren't at one another's throats, we're actually… good. No. Not just good. We have the potential to be unstoppable.

I'm not sure what kind of voodoo magic the universe is working on us, but I do know that I have never, *and I mean never*, had a doubles partner with whom I clicked this effortlessly with on the court.

Of course, it had to be Rockwell Campos, the one

person who can't seem to stand the sight of me off the court.

Chad's jump serve echoes through the gym as it bolts across the court. In rapid succession, I receive it in the back row while Rocky automatically moves toward the net. My pass finds his hands beautifully, and, like he can read my mind, Rocky quickly sets to the outside just in time for me to hit a perfect line hit.

Prescott barely has time to react as he dives for the ball, but he's nowhere near quick enough.

Side out.

And neither Rocky nor I had to utter a word.

Voodoo magic, I'm telling you. Like, whatever witch has our dolls… keep it up.

The last ten minutes of practice go on like that, and I grow increasingly more amused as Prescott and Chadwick become increasingly more agitated.

Serves them right for getting cocky.

After such an intense practice, all of us forgo the weights for the day and head straight to the locker room once Coach dismisses us. With a pretty satisfied smirk on his face, might I add.

Prescott and Chadwick hightail it out of the locker room like their asses are on fire while Rocky and I take our time showering and getting changed.

I've just thrown my shirt on when I hear my phone ring inside my duffle. Sitting on the bench, I pull my cell out to find a call from Chloé, one of my usual hookups. I groan inwardly, not wanting to accept the call. Every time the two of us hook up, she expects it to become something more than what it is when I have explicitly told her several times that I'm looking for nothing more than casual.

*It's no secret to anyone that I'm a perpetual flirt. I enjoy indulging in both men and women, and I am not ashamed or embarrassed to admit it, much to my father's absolute horror. Everyone I hook up with knows the score… except Chloé.

But I'm a sucker, so I accept the call anyway.

I put it on speakerphone and set it on the bench next to me so I can tie my tennis shoes.

"Clay, baby! What are you doing tonight?" Her bubbly voice pierces through the silent locker room.

Not your, baby. But alright.

"Hey, Chlo. Not much, probably staying in to study." I actually don't have shit to study for this week, but the last thing I want to do is go out and party with her. All I really want is to lay in bed and watch *New Girl* reruns until I pass out.

"Boo! Come out with me! I haven't seen you in weeks, and I miss you."

I'm just about to politely decline again when I look up from tying my shoe to find Rocky glaring daggers at me again. But it's different this time. It's not his usual, "God, Clay. You're so fucking annoying" look. It's something darker. Deeper.

Is he… jealous?

Let's test it, shall we?

"Actually, you're right. I miss you too."

No, I don't.

Rocky clenches his jaw so hard I'm surprised his teeth don't crack.

Holy. Shit.

------

* Lust - Chase Atlantic

I've seen men and women look at me that way enough to know that look like the back of my hand. Rockwell Campos is jealous.

Oh my god… this is amazing.

Focus, Clay.

"Yay!" Chloé squeals through the phone. "Okay, perfect. Pick me up at eight." *I won't. I'm going to call in an hour and tell her I don't feel good.* "We can go to dinner before we hit up the house party over at…" The rest of what she's saying fades into the background as I watch Rocky grip the bench so hard his knuckles turn white.

"Sounds good, Chlo."

No idea what she just said.

"I'll make sure to wear that black lace piece you like." My eyes lock with Rocky's, and I shoot him a wink. I can practically feel the anger radiating off of him in waves so hot they would burn me if I could reach out and touch them.

With a grin a mile wide, I answer, "Perfect. I gotta go, but I'll see you later."

No, you won't.

With my eyes still locked on Rocky's, I slide my phone into my shorts pocket, sling my duffle over my shoulder, and walk toward the door. But not before stopping right in front of him on my way out.

Raising my hand, I run it across his heaving chest, lean in, and whisper, "Jealousy looks good on you, Rockwell."

With an ego the size of the Grand Canyon, I walk away and yell over my shoulder, "See you Monday, partner!"

CHAPTER 6
HARD LIMIT

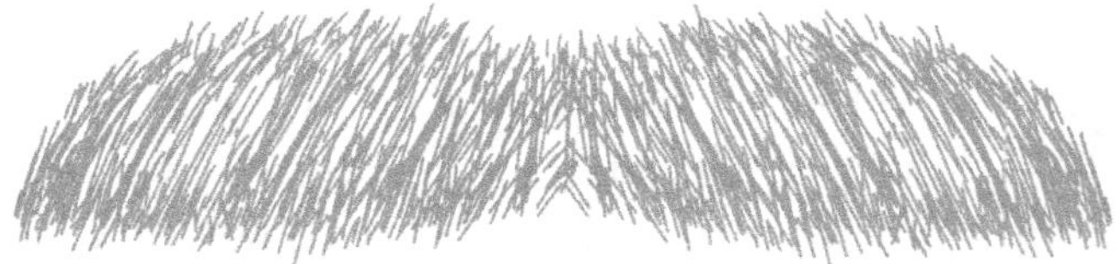

ROCKWELL

"Jealousy looks good on you, Rockwell." I'm going to lay this motherfucker out. I am not jealous of that *plaything* of his.

*"See you Monday, partner!" he throws over his shoulder as he's walking out of the locker room. Clay is a flirt, and I normally don't pay attention to it. I don't know what just came over me, but that feeling is getting put into a box and locked away, never to come out again. I can't be jealous of Clay getting some pussy. Maybe that's what I need too.

---

* Roses - Awaken I Am

I'm walking out of my upper-level history class, which focuses on South America. It's been my favorite history class so far. Having the opportunity to learn the history of where my mom is from and the countries surrounding Brazil has been nothing short of amazing.

I look up from my phone and run right into fucking Aldrich. It's been about three weeks since we became doubles partners, and to my dismay, we're actually good together. On the court, we're becoming more and more in sync. Our relationship off the court, however, is still up for debate.

"Campos! Let's go grab some lunch!" He grabs my arm and starts dragging me toward Relax and Roast, a little cafe on campus that has the best food.

"Did you need something, Aldrich?" I ask in the most annoyed tone I can muster, not wanting him to know that he doesn't annoy me as much as I lead on.

"Just wanted to chat off the court. We never get to do that, and we need to figure out our shit if we want to win the championship this year and have any chance of getting onto Team USA." No matter how annoyed I act with him, he is always so positive and ends up rubbing off on me—*most of the time.*

We get to the register and I order the croissant club sandwich like I always do and add on one of their fire-ass protein smoothies. "I'll take the same, and on one ticket, please." He throws his card down on the counter before I can even blink. He looks at me, smirking. "It was my idea for lunch. The least I can do is pay." Then he winks at me... *again.*

We make our way over to a small two-seat table that feels a little too intimate for two teammates. I set our food down with Clayton right behind me, but I hear his name called out from a feminine voice on the other side of the cafe. "Hang on, I'll be right back."

He sets our drinks down and jogs over to where Chloe is leaning back in a chair surrounded by her crew of cackling sorority friends. The same Chloe that was on the phone with him a few weeks back. I roll my eyes so hard they hit the back of my head. So very Clayton, inviting me out to lunch and then running off to his plaything's table. *Fuck, that was some jealous shit.*

I start to sip my smoothie, trying to kill some time and not look like the needy friend I feel like I'm being right now. I don't know why these pangs of jealousy keep hitting me when I'm around Clayton. He's clearly a man, and as far as I know, I'm straight. Never in my life have I been attracted to a guy, but I keep finding myself peeking at him in the locker room, sweaty after a hard practice, and admiring the heavily corded muscles in his lean six-foot-six body. Or the way his boyish dimples come out anytime he's being a pain in the ass, softening his hard exterior. His deep brown hair matching the shade of his eyes. He's got the perfect sun-kissed skin from playing sand for years, even with it being the end of January. Cocks have never done it for me, but apparently, the one attached to him doesn't totally offend me.

He comes back from talking to the blonde bimbo, sitting down in his chair across from me, pulling me out of my wet daydream. The cherry on top of it all is my semi-hard cock I'm dealing with just from thinking about this fuck sitting across the table from me.

He's got his normal smirk plastered across his face, and

I can only imagine the scowl I'm wearing. "Did you wait for me to eat, Baby?"

I grit out, "I'm not your fucking Baby, Aldrich."

He holds his hands up in defense. "Hard limit. Okay, got it."

We eat in silence for a minute, meeting one another's eyes a couple of times.

Clay finally breaks the silence, asking, "Why do you despise me so much?"

Oh, my time to shine. "One, you've never had to work for a thing in your life." Counting on my hand, I hold up two fingers. "Two, Coach Taylor might as well be sucking your cock, and three, you're constantly saying inappropriate things to me."

Both of his brows are pretty much touching his hair. Here he goes, holding his hand up, mocking what I just did. "One, just because I grew up with money doesn't mean my life wasn't hard, just in different ways. Two, you've seen my dick more than Coach Taylor has. Three, have you seen yourself? You're gorgeous, and I speak three languages; flirting just so happens to be one of them." My face is on fire.

"Okay, cut the shit. What the hell did you really want to talk about? We both know you're obsessed with me."

"Ah-ah, I think we know who's obsessed with who. I saw the mean mugs thrown at me while I was over there talking to Chloe." He leans into me across the table, whispering, "It's okay to explore, Campos."

I'm staring at his lips; he licks the bottom one pulling it between his teeth—fuck his teeth are perfect. When it's clear I'm not going to respond, he sits back and says, "We need to get along so we can win. Shared goal and all, you know."

I shake my head, pulling myself out of whatever trance this fucking man puts me in. "Yeah, yeah, I think we can get along fine. We're going to be stuck together for a while. Might as well make the most of it, right?"

"Now we're on the same page, Rock Man." I pin him with another death glare, and he adds, "We'll work on the nicknames later."

CHAPTER 7
CHOPPY WATERS

CLAYTON

It's been three weeks since our cease-fire that day at the coffee shop, and I'm pleased to admit that it's been relatively smooth sailing. Okay, maybe not *smooth* sailing… more like mildly choppy sailing.

So much so that, despite how bummed I am that I'm not playing with Jax this season, I'm actually pretty excited for today's scrimmage in Destin. As long as the two of us play like we have been in practice, we should breeze through two sets with no problem.

To get in the spirit, I put on my pre-pregame playlist and turn the volume up as loud as it will go. I'm not even ashamed to admit that "Pretty Girl Rock" by Keri Hilson is the first song that comes on. That song slaps, and you *cannot* convince me otherwise.

When I pull into the practice gym parking lot, because Rocky refuses to tell me where he lives—something about already having too much "Clay in his life," whatever that means—I immediately see him leaning against the front of his Toyota Camry. His ever-permanent scowl is already in place and his uniform is on and ready.

Like an itch I have to scratch, I feel the need to fuck with him a little. Rolling down my window, I pull up directly in front of him, point my finger at his broad chest, and belt the song at the top of my lungs.

Shaking his head, he grabs his duffle off the hood of his car and walks around the front of mine to climb into the passenger seat. I don't stop pointing and singing the entire time. Rocky opens the back door to throw his bag in, and he must think I'm not looking because my heart nearly stops in my chest as I watch a smile spread across his face.

Not the closed-lipped smile he gives everyone else when he's trying to engage in conversation.

No. A *real* smile.

A beautiful fucking smile.

A smile so pure that I selfishly want to be the only one that ever gets to see it. And from now until the end of time, I'm going to do everything in my power to see it at least once a day.

Fuck. Me.

But just as fast as it spread across his face, it disappears as he closes the door and climbs in the front. He clicks his seat belt on, reaches for the volume nob, and turns it down so it's barely audible.

"What, and I cannot stress this enough, in the actual fuck was that?"

There he is.

"Okay, rude. Never turn down a man's music," I reply impudently, putting my Mercedes in drive and pulling out of the parking lot.

"You wanted to drive, so that means I'm the DJ. Deal with it."

He disconnects my phone from the Bluetooth and connects his own. Quickly glancing from the road, I look over to find him scrolling through his music. "Rocky, I swear on all that is good and holy, if you just turned off Keri Hilson to turn on some screamo-rock shit, I will pull this car over and—" *The opening chord of The All-American Rejects' "Dirty Little Secret" sounds through the car, effectively cutting off my protests. "I take it back. Song approved."

"That's what I thought," he grumbles.

An hour and a half later, and after Rocky complained several times about my driving, we pull up to the beach we're playing at today. It's one of the few times we get to play on an honest-to-god beach court during the season, and it's one of my favorite games of the year. I don't even care that it doesn't count toward any standings. Coach Taylor isn't even here today. He decided to stay on campus and run an extra practice with Chad and Prescott after saying they could "use some one-on-one time with him."

I don't think douchebag one or two are very happy with the fact that Rocky and I keep whooping their asses in practice.

Oh well.

I shift in my seat to look at Rocky. "You ready?"

"Ready."

"Today will set the tone for the rest of the season. Everyone's heard about us. They're expecting us to fuck up. Let's go out there and prove them wrong."

---

* "Dirty Little Secret" The All-American Rejects

Rocky's eyes flash with a rare moment of admiration before he holds out his fist. "We got this."

After a brief moment of shock that he's willingly initiating contact with me, I bump his fist with mine. "We got this, Campos."

The two of us climb out of the car and I notice my bag slid across the back seat at some point during the drive; I walk around the back of the car to where Rocky is bent inside the back door, retrieving his bag.

Do not look at his ass, Clay. Do not look at his ass.

Fuck. I looked at it.

Feeling impatient and wanting to remove his impeccable ass from my line of site as soon as possible, I sightly bend over and reach around him to grab my bag. Rocky flinches in surprise and stumbles backward half a step.

The moment his ass comes in contact with the half-chub I got from looking at his ass, his entire body freezes.

Fuck.

As much as my dick would like me to stay put, my brain tells me to move. Following its wise advice, I promptly take a step back. Rocky stays still for a moment, and then, like something out of a horror film, he slowly stands and spins to face me. The entire motion feels like it takes five minutes when I know it was nothing longer than two seconds. When his face finally meets mine, I swallow hard. His glare quite literally looks like it would scare the devil himself.

Rocky takes a deep breath through his nose, and just when I think he's about to chew my asshole a new one, he storms off in the direction of the court without so much as a word.

I look down at my dick. "Now look what you did."

Remember when I said Jax and I were similar in the respect that I don't get mad or yell often, but when I do, you better sit down and listen to the fuck up?

Yeah, now I'm fucking pissed.

We're barely ten minutes into the first set, and we're down one to six.

ONE TO FUCKING SIX!

Every ounce of progress we made over the last three weeks has seemingly evaporated into the humid, gulf air. Rocky is too busy acting like I stole his goddamn birthday, all because he accidentally backed his ass up into my minorly hard dick.

Whoopty-fucking-doo! It's a dick. He has one. They get hard.

Get the hell over it.

Now he wants to stand out here and act like our futures aren't on the line because he can't pull his head out of his ass.

Destin serves the ball. Rocky has to dig for it but he manages to pass it to me. He's up and out of the sand just as I'm about to set it back row, knowing he won't have enough time to reach the net. But instead of doing the smart play and waiting for my set, he attacks the right side. I watch in mounting frustration as my set falls flat in the sand.

The ref blows the whistle and signals for us to switch sides now that we're at seven points. And instead of acknowledging that he screwed up, he storms off the court, grabs his water bottle, and moves to the opposite bench.

Yeah, this is not fucking happening today.

Forgoing my much-needed water break, I make my way over to him in a few long strides, trying and failing to calm the rage bubbling inside of me.

By the time Rocky's gaze meets mine I'm in front of him with his jersey fisted in both my hands before he has a chance to side-step me again. "What the fuck is your problem?"

He tries to push off of me, but my hold on his jersey only tightens. I'm more than aware of the ref and the spectators staring at us, but I don't care. "Nothing is my problem, Aldrich. Get the fuck off of me."

We're back to Aldrich now? Cool. Great.

It's like that day in the hallway all those weeks ago. I will not fucking stand for it any longer.

We're supposed to be partners.

"I thought we were good? I thought we put all this bullshit behind us? So, what the fuck is the problem?" Without even knowing it, I realize I've pulled him closer to me. Our bodies are now only an inch apart, my face directly above his. I can see the sweat from the hot Florida sun dripping down his forehead.

A look of resignation crosses his face before he inhales a deep breath and says softly, "Nothing, Clay. I'm fine."

I tip my head ever so slightly. If he moved even a fraction of an inch, our lips would touch. My voice is low now, practically a growl, as I answer, "If you're fine, then fucking act like it. This isn't a one-man show. If you want to be part of a team, then pull your head out of your ass and get it in the goddamn game."

He opens and closes his mouth a couple times as his green eyes wage war with mine, but before he has a chance to respond I shove off of him, retrieve the volley-ball, and head to the back of the court to get ready for my serve.

CHAPTER 8
COLD SHOWER

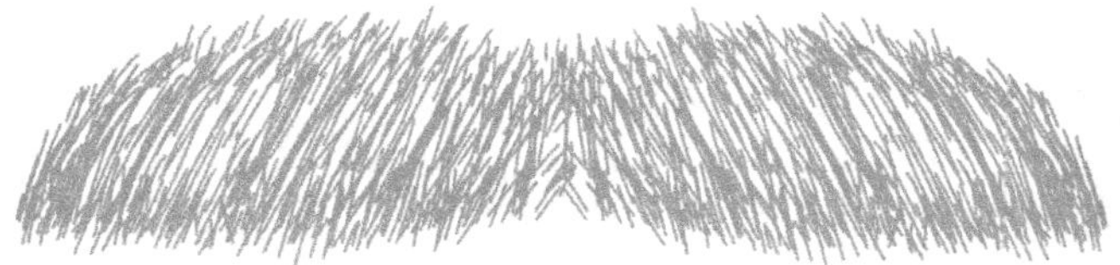

ROCKWELL

We could've had this bagged in two sets, but because of my temper tantrum, we lost the first one. After Clay chewed my ass, we tried to make a comeback but there just wasn't enough time. I won't say I didn't deserve his anger either.

I did.

I was sulking and trying to process how feeling Clay's dick rubbing against my ass affected me earlier. It should *not* have stirred up the feelings it did. My goddamn stomach flipped, and it may as well have fallen out of my ass.

However, as the sets have gone on, both our playing and our attitudes seem to have improved.

Clay has his fingers up behind his back, signaling for me to hit right in between where our opponents are on the other side of the court. But instead of focusing on the hand signal like I should be, what am I doing?

Staring at his fucking juicy ass in those shorts.

He's a man, and my cock is stirring. In the middle of a scrimmage. Is this some kind of crisis?

I toss the ball up with the perfect spin, make my approach, and it hits my hand perfectly. The ball flies through the air and lands with a thud in the sand right in the middle of both the opponents, exactly where Clay wanted it.

Ace.

*He looks over his shoulder, giving me a wink, pretty much saying I told you so. And fuck, if my cock wasn't already hard, it sure as shit is now. I'm sure this could be an ad for the brief brand I'm sponsored by.

Board Briefs: they're great at keeping sand out and boners in.

I do the same thing five more times before the ref blows the whistle to tell us to switch sides for the last time. Clay runs up, slapping me on the ass—nothing sexual, just telling me that was a hell of a job. That many aces in a row in college is unheard of.

When we make it over to the bench, I grab my water bottle and spray some into my mouth, ignoring the water dribbles down my chin. I look up at Clay, but he's too busy staring at what I'm guessing is the water running down my chin and neck. "You okay there, *Garotão*." He's full-on blushing now. "We've almost got the win." I spray a little more water in my mouth. Clay turns away from me, so I slap his ass back, just like he did mine earlier. "Get your head in the game, Clay."

I jog back onto the court with a smirk on my face, because I know that's going to fuck with his head. I

---

* Doomed - Bring Me The Horizon

shouldn't find joy in this, especially in the middle of the game, but I can't help myself.

As I get back behind the line to serve again, all I can think about is pissed-off Clay and the way he looked when he was in my face earlier. I may have been sulking, but my body responded in a way it never has to anyone else besides him. Just that little brush against me... *Cock, rock hard.*

As strange as it made me feel, he did pull me out of the funk I was in, reminding me that we have a goal. We play off of one another; our energy, our communication, it's all in sync. He knew exactly what to say to get my head back in the game. The cherry on top is a pissed-off Clay may just be one of my favorite versions of him. I've never seen him like that before, but I'd be lying if I said I didn't want to see it again.

Making a note to keep pissing him off.

We've rallied back and forth a couple of points, but I've kept serve the whole time. It's fourteen to zero. We're sweeping them like we should've been this whole time, but we had to get that first set out of the way—bickering like a couple of teenage girls.

I'm sure we're going to be the talk of the sand with how we were acting with one another earlier. And we'll probably get an ass chewing from Coach when he hears about it. Clay grabbing my shirt like the fucking caveman he's *not*. Why do I like caveman Clay, though? Someone sedate me.

I'm not into men.

I'm not into men.

I'm not into men.

The ref blows her whistle, and I toss the ball for what

will be my last serve of the game. They get a pass, setting it up, and their big guy goes up for an outside hit. I read his body angled to the center of the court, but Clay's up there like the brick wall he is. The guy swings right into his hands, and his hit doesn't stand a chance. Clay blocks it and it bounces straight down.

"FUCK YES, CLAY!" I'm running to him at the net and wrapping my arms around his chest, picking him up in an all-consuming hug. He's holding around my neck, and I'm spinning us around like we just won the goddamn Olympics. It's nothing more than a scrimmage, but it's our first win as partners.

The longer I hold onto him, the more I think about what this is and what it must look like. I love the way his muscular body feels against mine, the sweat from the game we just played, and the sand in between us.

I'm loving it too much.

Fuck, I can't do this.

I let him go like he's burning me. I can not do this right now. I walk over to the bench, grab my bag, and sprint to the hotel across the street from the beach.

Whatever that was, I need it out of my system… *Now.*

Of course we have a shared hotel room today. Because why wouldn't we? I didn't take the time to use the outdoor showers at the beach because my cock was screaming at me for some relief. I sure as fuck don't need to be staring at Clay while water runs down his body with these confusing-ass thoughts running through my head.

That would be anything but relief.

I toss my bag on the floor beside my bed and practically run into the bathroom.

As I peel my clothes off of me, all kinds of sand hits the

tiles, and my cock hits my stomach with a hard flop. It's been painfully pulsing since that celebration hug on the court that caused my brain to malfunction.

I need to be shocked out of this, so I flip the shower on as cold as it can go and get in, hissing when the water hits me.

I go through my normal routine, washing my hair, then my body, and by the end, my cock is somehow harder than it was when I got in here. It's like my dick is begging for release. So, I take the L, turn the heat up in the shower, drop a little dollop of conditioner into my hand, and grip my pulsing cock.

I try not to think of what has me running my hand up and down my length, but I keep picturing Clay's ass in his shorts, the sweat I'm not repulsed by dripping down his body, and those fucking eyes of his seeing through the lies I'm feeding him.

And maybe what they would look like, looking up at me from his knees.

I brace my hand on the wall, the hot water beating down on my back, and my fist picking up pace. There's no way Clay's back in here yet, so I let the noises flow out of me. The moans and whimpers leaving me should be embarrassing, but I keep fucking my fist shamelessly.

"Ahhh, fuck."

Before I know it, my thighs are tingling and my orgasm is racing up the base of my spine. A couple more whimpers and one word leaves my lips, feeling better than I ever thought it would.

"Clay."

CHAPTER 9
TWO CAN PLAY

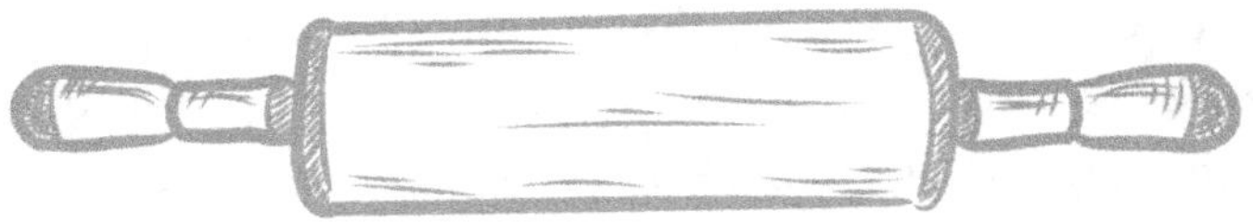

CLAYTON

A hurricane-force wind couldn't knock the smile off my face as I walk across the street to our hotel after rinsing off the sand in the outdoor showers.

For two reasons specifically.

One, we won our first game as partners. Despite everything, we pulled through and showed them that, as a pair, we have the potential to be unstoppable. Regardless of how much I wanted to punch him during the first set.

Two, and most importantly, Rocky hugged me… and ran.

Now, I know, I know, that doesn't sound like something I should be excited about. But it is. Because I felt the way he lingered a moment too long in my arms. I heard the way his breath hitched right before he let go. He liked it. He liked it a lot.

So much so that he freaked out and bolted.

One by one, I'm knocking down the impenetrable bricks that are The Great Wall of Rocky.

After stopping at the front desk and collecting my room key, I step into the elevator and head up to our floor. Rocky has been back for ten minutes now, so hopefully that has given him enough time to sufficiently panic and recover so I won't have to deal with two moody episodes in the span of one day.

A man can only take so much.

The elevator opens, and I walk down the hall, eager to see just how he plans to explain Usain bolting off of the beach. Reaching our room, I slide in the key card and push the door open after it beeps.

"Honey, I'm—" The sound of the shower running cuts off my greeting. Shrugging, I move through the room and set my bag on the floor next to the bed by the window. I take a seat on the desk chair, not wanting to sit on the bed until I can fully shower, and pull out my phone. Immediately, I see a missed call from my dad exactly ten minutes after the scrimmage ended.

Typical.

Choosing not to call him back, I busy myself by scrolling through Instagram, attempting to fight the vise that's trying to tighten around my chest at the thought of my father's unyielding criticism.

I'm about to make a post about today's scrimmage when I hear a noise come from the bathroom. I pause, waiting to hear it again. A few seconds go by, and just as I'm about to go back to what I was doing, I hear it again.

**Was that a fucking moan?*

---

*   Talk Dirty - Daniel Di Angelo

I throw my phone onto the bed and stand up out of the chair like my ass is on fire.

He is not doing what I think he's doing. I could not get that lucky.

"Ahhh, fuck," Rocky moans.

My eyes go wide, and my hand flies over my mouth as I try to muffle my laugh. "Holy fucking shit. He's jacking off in the shower," I whisper to no one but myself. "I can't wait to give him so much shit about this when he—"

"Clay." The sound of my name spilling from the bathroom knocks the air from my lungs for the second time today.

Did he just—did he just say Clay?

He did. Oh my god. Rockwell Campos just moaned my name while jacking off in the shower.

If I've ever said it before, I take it back. This is the best day of my life.

The sound of the shower turning off is the only thing that unfreezes me from my spot in the middle of the room. I frantically spin around in circles before picking up my phone and duffle, and sliding my sandals back on. Quickly, I tip-toe to the door while trying to adjust my hard-on and crack it open.

If he knows I was in here he will literally never speak to me again. No matter how much I want to throw it in his face, I have to act like I heard nothing. Just as I hear him turn the bathroom doorknob, I close the hotel room door.

Stepping out of the bathroom with nothing but a towel around his waist and a pair of flushed cheeks—which I'm doing everything in my power not to stare at too long because if I do, I know my dick will bust out of my shorts —he looks at anything and everything but me, and rubs the back of his neck. "Hey, sorry I dipped out so fast, I uh —really had to shit."

"Far be it from me to hinder your bathroom habits," I answer, rubbing my hand across my mouth, trying to stifle the laugh sitting at the back of my throat.

"Right, well, shower's all yours if you want it." I watch as he walks toward the bed closest to the door.

"Yeah, I rinsed off the sand back at the beach, but I could use a good scrub."

"Mhmm," he answers noncommittally.

I bite the inside of my lip, finding his sudden shyness rather adorable. "Hey, after I'm done showering, do you want to go grab some dinner and celebrate the win?"

Sitting on the end of his bed, still in his towel, he reaches down and rifles through his duffle, grabbing a fresh change of clothes. "I'm actually pretty tired. You cool if we just order in and hang out here?"

He still won't look at me.

"Rockwell?"

"Hmmm?" He pretends to search through his bag some more, even though I know he's already grabbed what he needs.

"You good?"

"Yup. Super good. Just-just trying to find my deodorant."

I look into the bathroom out of the corner of my eye to find his deodorant already sitting next to the sink.

You know what?

Two can play at this game.

"Right. Well"—I shoot my thumb out in the direction of the bathroom— "I'm going to shower, and then we can order some dinner."

"Alright. Cool. Sounds great."
Time to put on a show.

CHAPTER 10
RE-ROCKED UP

ROCKWELL

What in the fuck was that?

I'm staring at the wall in front of my bed, still in my towel, as I hear Clay turn the shower on. I hope to fuck he wasn't in here while I was in the shower jacking off harder than I have in a while; I know for a fact his name came out of my mouth loud enough for him to hear if he was.

Deciding to get out of my head, I stand and throw my thin gray joggers and my old Bulls crop top on. I also put my earring and nose ring back in. I fucking hate having to take them out for games.

Right as I get my nose ring through, I hear the loudest moan I've ever heard in my life echoing off the bathroom walls.

Fuck no, he is not.

"You feel so good, Baby." No, no, no. The one fucking time I don't bring my soundproof headphones. "Slow

52

down, please." My cock starts twitching to life again at the sound of his obnoxious moans.

So much for thinking rubbing one out would get Clay out of my system. I have a bad feeling he's going to fully fill my masturbation fantasies from here on out, and that shouldn't be happening.

I'm straight.

Or at least I thought I was until Clayton FUCKING Aldrich came crashing into my life.

But I'm not above storing this away in the spank bank. I pull my phone out, go to the voice memo app, lean against the wall by the bathroom door, and hit record. This dick bag knows what he's doing, too. Why else would he leave the door wide the fuck open?

He's almost whimpering now. "Rocky, Baby."

The way my name sounds falling from his lips, and that nickname, has the potential to be my undoing. I have to get some relief. With my free hand, I start rubbing my fully erect cock once again through my joggers. This is getting ridiculous, but I can't find it in me to care.

After this, I really am done. I can't do this. Especially with my fucking doubles partner.

"You're going to let me take that tight hole of yours?" I gasp out unexpectedly and cover my mouth with my free hand, but not before I hear Clay snicker. He knows I'm out here listening; he's putting on an erotic audio show just for me.

I don't know why it didn't occur to me that someone's ass is going to be getting used, and I'm not entirely repulsed by it being mine.

Shamelessly, I pull my cock out and palm it in the strong grip I love so much. I've got to make this quick since he's probably almost done, and I sure as shit don't need him getting out and seeing me with my dick in my hand and my phone out recording his filthy sounds.

"Is your hand as tight around your cock as mine is, Baby?" I have to bite my lip to keep him from hearing the moan that's wanting to escape me. "Can you come with me?"

I can hear him pumping his cock. He's getting faster and faster, and I find myself matching his rhythm.

Before I know it, the back of my thighs start to tingle in the all-too-familiar feeling. "Fuck, Rocky, Baby. I'm co-coming." That sends the lightning shock I was waiting for right to my lower back and down my balls. I throw my head back, trying to stay as quiet as I can, but it gets past my lips again. "Fuck, Clay."

I've barely finished when I hear the shower shutting off, pulling me out of my blissed-out space for the second time tonight. I hurry to hit the stop button on the recording and wipe my hand and dick on my joggers to clean my orgasm off. Practically sprinting to my duffle, I dig through it for another pair of pants. I throw my soiled ones onto the floor and step into the new pair right as Clay walks out of the bathroom with a sick look of joy covering his stupidly perfect face.

CHAPTER 11
ANYONE WANT A SAUSAGE?

CLAYTON

The rest of our evening was filled with tension—both awkward and sexual—so thick you could cut it with a knife. No matter how hard I tried to get the same smile I saw earlier that day I just couldn't do it. Not after I ordered his favorite pizza for dinner, not when I said we could watch *Love Island*—which I've never seen a straight man watch that show, but that's neither here nor there—and not even when I offered to cuddle when we went to bed. That one was a major loss for him there because I am a top-tier big spoon.

*It was all worth it, though. What may have started as a game to show Rocky that he's not the only one who's having those thoughts, very quickly turned into quite possibly the hottest five minutes of my entire life. And all I was doing was touching myself.

---

* What Do You Mean - Justin Bieber

Just knowing he was on the other side of that door, listening to my every moan and whimper, got me more and more turned on until I wasn't even acting anymore. The entire show was all for him, and I'd gladly let him listen in any time.

Fuck, if only I could get someone else to listen in while *he* was the one touching *me*.

The thought has me tightening my grip on the steering wheel while trying to keep my rapidly growing dick at bay. If I get hard in this car, Rocky will one hundred percent open the passenger door and jump out of it.

"Down, boy," I whisper softly while looking down at the crotch of my jeans.

"What did you say?"

The sound of Rocky's voice is enough to startle all thoughts of fucking him in public away because that's the first time he's spoken a word since we got in the car to drive back to Pensacola. He hasn't mentioned last night, and I sure as shit am not going to be the one to bring it up. The fact that he didn't check into another hotel room last night was a miracle in and of itself.

"I said, 'Oh boy.'" He pinches his brow in confusion. "I'm starving. Do you want to stop and grab some breakfast? We never ate before we left, and this big boy's got to eat." I dramatically rub my stomach.

Rocky's eyes darken slightly at the nickname, but I wisely choose not to comment on it. "Can't you just wait until we get back? I gotta hurry up and get home. I have to uh—study."

He doesn't have to study shit.

"Awe, come on, Rocky. I could go for a good sausage."

He snaps his head back toward me, eyes wide. "What? You don't like sausage? I loooove sausage?"

I can tell he's doing everything in his power to not laugh. "Clayton…" he warns.

"If you aren't sure, you could always try mine first to see if you like it."

Rocky tips his head back against the seat and lets out a loud laugh. Not even caring if we crash and die, I pull my eyes from the road and watch the entire thing, letting the sounds falling from his lips seep into the very fiber of my bones. Hoping that if I focus hard enough, the beautiful and rare sound can somehow become a part of me. When he gets his breathing under control, he looks at me out of the corner of his eyes and is still grinning from ear to ear. "Would you shut the fuck up and drive the car."

"The first part is highly unlikely; the second part should be no problem."

Still leaning against the headrest, he rolls his head to the side so he's facing me. "Really? Because that would mean you need to look at the road."

"I know." I let my stare linger a second longer, taking in everything that is this moment before turning to look back at the road.

A few more minutes go by when my phone rings through the car. I groan when I see my dad's name on the screen on the dash. I already avoided him all day yesterday; there's no way I'm getting out of it today. "You can answer it if you need to. I'd hate to miss a call from my old man."

"Trust me. I wouldn't hate it in the slightest." Rocky looks at me quizzically before I accept the call.

"It's about time you picked up the phone that I paid

for," he bites out before I even have the chance to say hello. Instead of sinking back into his seat like everyone else does at the sound of my father's voice, Rocky sits up straighter. "I tried to call Coach Taylor when you didn't answer, but he said he wasn't even at the scrimmage. What is that about?"

"He didn't need to be there. It was just a simple scrimmage. Rocky and I had it handled."

"You and Rocky?" The disdain in his voice is crystal clear.

"Yes. Me and Rocky."

"What did I tell you about that Campos kid? He's not going to help you get to the top, Clayton."

If Rocky is hurt by my dad's words, he doesn't show it. His entire body remains still and steady. "And what did I tell you? There was no one else to partner with. He and I were each other's only choice. We're good, Dad. We're great actually. We lost the first set but that's just because we were getting our feet under us. We absolutely dominated the second and third, and—"

"You lost the first set?" he booms. "Jax would have never let you lose against Destin. And what's going on in your economics class? I checked your grades this morning, and it says you're getting an eighty-five percent. You're better than that, Clayton."

I can feel the tightness in my chest start to set in, my hands are growing sweaty as they grip the steering wheel harder and harder, and I can feel the water stinging at my eyes. Before I can open my mouth to respond, Rocky's deep voice wraps around me like a blanket. "Yeah, uh, Mr. Aldrich, this is Rockwell Campos. Clay will have to call you back later. We're about to stop for some sausage. Have a good day!"

Rocky hits the end-call button, and I immediately feel like I can breathe. "Well, your dad is just… *lovely.*"

"If he didn't like you before, he definitely doesn't now."

"Somehow, I don't think I'm going to lose any sleep over it."

Not knowing how to respond, and my mind to busy swimming with thoughts of my father, we sit for a few moments in silence. Much to my surprise though, Rocky's the first to cave.

I know it's because he's feeling sorry for me, but I can't really find it in me to care.

"What sign are you?" he asks. The totally random question causes a small smile to tug at the corners of my lips.

"A Leo. Why?"

"Oh my god." His light chuckle causes the frost that was forming over my heart due to my dad's call to thaw. "Of course you are."

"What's that supposed to mean?" I ask, feigning ignorance.

"Clay." He stares at me deadpan. "You are the leoist leo that ever leoed."

He's not wrong, but I'm not telling him that.

"Alright then, smartass. What are you?"

"I'm an Aquarius." He crosses his arms and puffs his chest out with pride.

The scoff that leaves my lips could be heard a mile away. "Oh, I'm Rocky. I'm quiet and hard to read, and I never speak my feelings because god forbid people know what I'm thinking," I mock.

He glares at me before relenting. "Okay, that's fair."

"That's what I thought. Wait. If your an Aquarius when is your birthday?"

Rocky rubs the back of his neck. "Uh, next Saturday. The seventeenth."

It just so happens I have exactly zero things planned next weekend. Not even a game or practice. How... serendipitous.

As if he can see the gears turning in my brain, he points his finger right at me. "Clay. Don't you do anything or I swear—"

"Oh don't get your panties in a twist. I'm not going to do anything."

I'm totally throwing him a party.

CHAPTER 12
LET'S GO, BOYS!

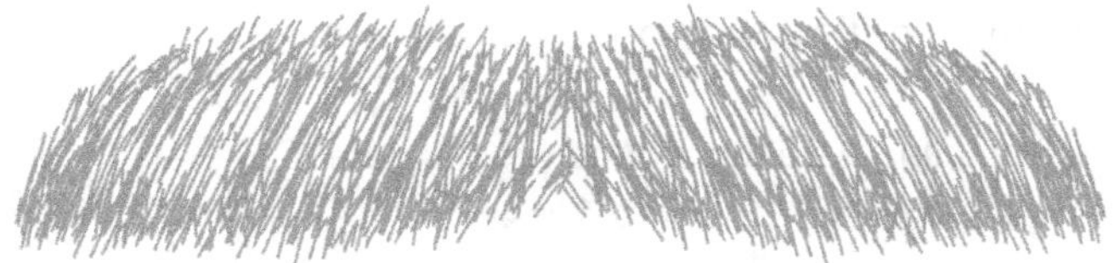

ROCKWELL

He's throwing me a party. I just know it.

If he is, the least I can do is show up looking good as fuck. I just got out of the shower after spending all day catching up on schoolwork and filming a couple of brand deals, then sending them off to the companies for approval. This is the most nerve-wracking part for me—what if they hate it?

The worst thing that could happen is that you'll have to re-do it, dumbass.

I have the perfect outfit in mind for tonight, pairing my favorite Nirvana crop with some low-rise, baggy, old-school, skater jeans, and my Nike Air Force 1's. To finish off the look I'm changing out my normal black hoop nose ring for gold to match my three thin gold chains and my signature earring.

Styling my hair like normal—having to use gel because of the Florida humidity—I stop in front of my full-length mirror, and if I do say so myself... I look fucking hot. I take a picture to upload to Instagram for my birthday with the caption:

> I'm feeling a lot older than 22, but here's to another trip around the sun.

Not even two minutes after posting, Clay's profile pops up with a notification. I open it and groan.

> You can take a trip around your favorite Leo since we're ruled by the sun, Baby.

I don't fight the smile that forms as I stare down at my phone. I can't explain the rage I felt when Clay's dad talked to him on the phone the way he was. I didn't give a flying fuck about what he had to say about me. It's the normal "Oh, he's poor, a bad influence, hasn't played volleyball since he could walk" story. Clay was shutting down, and I wasn't about to see the light that shines in that boy fade because of his piece of shit father.

He really is my sun. Or at least he feels like he is.

I don't care who you are to a child or what you've done for them; if there's no love in the household, you're poor in the only area that matters.

My parents made sure we knew we could come to them no matter what. We may not have had the fanciest shit, but we never went without, either. I went to public schools with some of the best teachers I could've asked for. Our house was overflowing with love, and I know for a fact that's not the environment that Clay grew up in.

Hanging up on his fuck of a dad was the most exhilarating thing I had done in a while, and the visible relief it gave Clay made it a hundred times better.

I get to my car and pull my phone out to text Jax, but I quickly see he's now added me to a group chat, and these two idiots have been texting back and forth for the last twenty minutes. Clicking into it, I realize it's only Jax, Clay, and me. I don't know why Clay roped Jax into this, but he's the one that I've had to go to to get any sort of information since Clay's still playing like he doesn't have anything to do with this.

The first thing I notice is that Jax has named the group chat: *The Office*

I can only attest to the fact that the other day Clay mentioned that him and Jax were Jim and Pam, and I was their new Dwight. To which I took total offense to because I am nothing if not a Stanley.

Not bothering to go back and reread all of their bromance-worthy messages, I quickly shoot a quick one of my own:

The Office

ME

I'm on my way

JAX

See you when you get here, Birthday Boy!
Be safe!

CLAY

Better get ready to blow!

Candles, of course. Not me. Actually…

JAX

If you don't stop he's not going to
show up.

Jax's driveway comes into view, and I murmur a "shit" under my breath. There's got to be at least thirty cars lining the road and covering his driveway. How mad will they be if I just turn around and go back to my apartment?

Before I can even think about turning around, Jax, Clay, and a few of the other players are waving me down from their spot on the porch, so I find the next parking spot I see on the road and pull in. I'm walking up the driveway when I find Clay with a shit-eating grin covering his face and Jax behind him, looking like a cowering puppy that just pissed on the floor.

"What the actual fuckery are you two wearing?" Clay and Jax have on matching Shania Twain shirts that are cut into crop tops. And now that I'm looking around, everyone is wearing crop tops with shorts or jeans. "What the fuck is going on?" I'm still looking around, thinking this is some kind of alternate universe. Usually, they're all making fun of me for my many cropped shirt choices.

Clay takes me out of my misery. "We're doing a 'dress

like the birthday slut' theme. Found the trend on TikTok! And guess who's the slut?" He's pointing at me, biting his bottom lip, trying to hold back a laugh. All I'm wondering is how he set this up in less than a week and why he cared enough to actually make it a themed party.

Clay gets me out of my thoughts by throwing his hand up in the air, making a circle like he's riding a horse about to rope some cattle, and yells out, "LET'S GO, BOYS!" Then he decides to kick in Jax's front fucking door.

I grab Jax by the back of his shirt, being careful with his knee, and ask lowly, "How much alcohol have you all fed him?"

"To everyone's surprise, not a fucking drop." He's smirking now, and if that knee weren't in a brace from surgery, I would be meaner to him. Jax is one of the sweetest souls I've met; no matter how much he can piss me off, at times, I can't stay mad at him.

Running my hand down my face, I murmur under my breath, "Dear fucking god. Somebody get me a drink."

A drink is what they get me—and another and another —until I have thoroughly lost count of how many I've consumed. I can't tell you the last time I've let loose like this, but it's much needed. The music is loud and I can feel the bass in my bones. The living room is looking very dance floor-ish right about now, and I'm ready to shake some ass.

*The intro to my favorite rap song plays over the speaker, and before I can stop myself, my feet are moving on their own. I'm in the middle of the living room in Jax's house dancing alone, putting on a show, but that doesn't

____

* No Heart - 21 Savage, Metro Boomin

last long once I see Chloe approaching out of the corner of my eye.

Oh, this is going to be fun.

I lean down to whisper in her ear, "You look great tonight, Chloe." I look up and lock eyes with Clay. He does not look happy.

But I don't back away from the blonde in front of me.

I want to kick him off that ledge that he's often teetering on. Pissed off, jealous Clay is my favorite.

Still at her neck and keeping full eye contact with him from across the room, I rub my nose up to her hair, inhaling as I go. She does smell good, I'll give her that, but it's not doing it for me. I want a certain scent and that happens to be whatever the fuck Clay wears.

I put my hand on the back of her neck, debating whether to kiss her, but before I can, I'm pushed away from dear ol' Chloe. I fake gasp, grabbing my chest as if he hurt me.

"It's my birthday, Clayton." Putting on a show, I stick my lower lip out, trying to ignore the fact that the room is still spinning from the copious amounts of alcohol I've had. "You're going to cock block your partner on his birthday? That's an all-time low for you, *Garotão*."

I see something cross his face, but it's gone before my alcoholic brain can figure out what it was.

I lean into him, and he willingly holds me up. "Clayton?"

"Yeah, Rocky?"

"You're so fucking hot in your Shania Twain crop top."

CHAPTER 13
HAPPY BIRTHDAY, BABY

CLAYTON

"Oh, I am, huh?" I clench my molars in irritation while simultaneously trying to fight the smile that's trying to form from his drunk admission.

"Yeah, you are. I mean, you're hot in pretty much anything, but this… " He fiddles with the hem of my new favorite shirt. "This is like, super hot."

I slowly start stepping forward, backing Rocky up until he bumps into the wall in Jax's living room. He doesn't so much as flinch when his back hits the wall, his eyes gazing up at me in a euphoric alcohol-induced haze.

"Rockwell."

"Yeah, Clay?"

The dominating, possessive beast inside of me, the one very few have gotten the chance to see, roars to life the moment my name leaves his lips. The same lips that were about to touch Chloé's skin. I grip his jaw in my hand, forcing him to look up at me when I know all his eyes want to do is spin in circles. I want to make sure I'm about to make my point crystal fucking clear. "Don't let me see you touch Chloé again."

"Why? It's not like the two of you are exclusive. I know how you are, Clay." His voice is soft, barely audible over the roar of the music, but there's an underlying note of apprehensiveness.

Leaning down, I brush my lips against the shell of his ear, my hand still tightly gripping his sharp jaw. His body shivers in my hold as he feels my breath skate across my skin. "Chloé isn't the one I give a fuck about, Rockwell. She can touch whoever she wants."

Slowly, I stand upright so I can stare back down at him. I watch as his eyes dance back and forth between mine. And for a moment, it's as if he's stone-cold sober. He swallows roughly, and I watch his Adam's apple bob in his throat. I force myself not to bend down and run my tongue over it.

Then, as if the thought were plastered on a flashing marquee sign on my forehead, Rocky's eyes flash with panic before he reaches up and gently wraps his hand around my wrist, prompting me to let his face go. We both drop our hands at our sides, but I don't move another inch. "I-I need another drink."

The corners of my mouth turn up in a coy smile. If I've learned anything about Rockwell Campos, it's not to push him when faced with uncomfortable emotional situations. When he's backed into a corner and faced with a truth he isn't ready to deal with, he runs. And now is no exception. "Anything for the birthday boy."

Despite my words, I still don't move. If he wants out of

this situation, he's going to have to do it himself. Slowly, he pushes himself off of the wall, brushing the fronts of our bodies against one another. His breath hitches when he feels how turned on I am brushing against his stomach. My only response is a raise of my brows and a shrug of my shoulders.

He quickly sidesteps around me without another word. "Meet me on the dance floor later, partner!" I half yell, half laugh, as he bolts across the makeshift dance floor toward the kitchen where all the alcohol is.

If he wasn't drunk already, he sure as shit is about to be.

It's been two hours since our *conversation,* and Rocky is officially on a different planet. My cheeks literally hurt from smiling as I watch him from my spot on the couch next to Jax.

It's been a little over six weeks since his surgery, and he's healing faster and better than any of us expected.

Like freakishly well, actually.

He's allowed to bear full weight on his leg, which is wrapped up in a top-of-the-line brace, and only uses a single crutch when necessary. But he spent all afternoon helping me set up for this party at his house—which I begged him to let me have here since my condo is so far from campus—and has been buzzing around like the social butterfly he is since it started. Like the best friend I am, I could tell his body was starting to get tired, so I forced him to rest.

Which conveniently happened to be the perfect vantage point for me to watch Rocky shake his ass on the dance floor.

"Emerson!" he yells to his little brother on the other side of the room. Emerson is a sophomore at Palm University and the right defenseman on the third line for the hockey team. Unfortunately for him, he also lives with his big brother, Jackson, in the house their parents bought for them and has been stuck doing his bidding for the last six weeks. In the most dramatic fashion possible, Emerson rolls his eyes and pulls his stare away from the brunette he is talking to. Actually, scratch that. He pulls his eyes away from the *breasts* of the brunette he was talking to and sulks over to where we're sitting.

"Yes, Jackson?" he drawls. "What can I do for you now?"

"I like the enthusiasm, Em. Go check the ice around the keg."

"Fine." Emerson spins on his heel without so much as an argument.

The two of us laugh and tip back our beers. I had every intention of getting drunk tonight, it isn't often I have a free and clear weekend, but after seeing how heavily Rocky is leaning into one, I decided against it.

"Since when does he listen to you so well?" I ask my best friend.

Jax's grin is practically sinister. "Since three weeks ago when I called Mom to tattle that he wasn't helping me, and she then proceeded to chew him a new asshole."

I bark out a laugh. "Jesus fucking Christ. I don't know who's more childish. You or the twins."

Jackson is the oldest of four. He also has a set of

sixteen-year-old twin brothers, Bryson and Grayson. The four of their names sound like they're members of a country western band. And considering they're all from Billings, Montana, they very well could be.

Jax takes another swig of beer and puffs out his chest in pride. "Oh me, definitely."

Emerson comes stomping back over. "Ice is good. Anything else?"

My eyes stray to Rocky just in time to watch him put his hands on his knees and twerk. Swear on my life… he's literally twerking.

"Why can't Clay do it?" I don't know what Jax asked for, and I don't care; my eyes don't leave Rocky's ass as he continues to shake it for the entire party to see. But I do hear Jax answer, voice full of amusement, "Because he's… *busy.*"

I know my best friend well enough to know I've totally been busted, but I also know he won't call me out on it. Jax is a true ride or die.

*The music changes to Teddy Swim's "My Bad," and the entire house starts cheering. Twenty seconds into the song, the entire party is singing along word for word, including Rocky.

I watch in awe as he tips his head back, finger pointed in the air, eyes closed, as if there are no burdens in the world holding him back. A radiant glow covers his rich walnut skin. His cheeks are flushed, and his movements are fluid. Unlike the carefully crafted mask he usually wears.

Drunk or not, he looks… beautiful.

———————————

* My Bad - Teddy Swims

Standing up, I slide the lightweight flannel I'm wearing down my arms and drape it over the couch next to Jax, leaving me in the most epic shirt known to man and a pair of light-wash jeans. "Are you going somewhere?" he asks as he looks from me to Rocky and then back to me.

"Yup, gonna go dance."

"Figured as much."

I point down at him and glare, although we both know there's no real heat behind it. "Not a word, Jackson."

He zips his mouth closed, locks the key, and throws it behind his shoulder.

Fucking smartass.

The song is on its second chorus by the time I reach Rocky, and like he can immediately feel my presence, he opens his eyes and looks at me. The two of us sway to the beat of the music, shouting the lyrics at the top of our lungs, all the while not daring to look away from one another.

It's like we're in our own little bubble, and I never want to pop it.

Someone knocks into Rocky as they walk past him, causing him to stumble forward and into me. My hands grip his waist, stopping us both from falling on our asses. My hands feel like they're on fire as they rest against his skin underneath the hem of his cropped T-shirt.

"You good?" I ask him.

Just like they did a couple of hours ago, his eyes clear, and it's as if I can see his every thought running through his eyes in rapid succession. It takes him a minute to respond, but when he does, the roughness in his voice almost sends me to my knees. "So good."

The song ends, and the dance floor clears as people

leave to get their next drink, yet Rocky and I remain still. I can feel everyone's eyes on us, but as far as I'm concerned, they can all fuck off.

"I'm—I'm, uh, feeling a bit tired. You wanna—You wanna go to bed?" he asks me nervously.

"Yeah, I was planning on staying here tonight anyway. My stuff is upstairs in their extra room. You sure you don't want to stay down here and ride out the rest of the party, though?" Right on cue, he hiccups and sways in my hold.

"Yeahhhhh. I think I've had enough."

I huff out a laugh. "Yeah, you're probably right. Come on. Jax should have an extra toothbrush somewhere. If he doesn't, you can just steal Emerson's."

Reluctantly, I let go of him, grab my flannel from the back of the couch—ignoring Jax's know-it-all smile—and head toward the stairs. I let Rocky go first so I can catch him just in case he falls.

After rifling through the bathroom drawers, I find a spare toothbrush and watch in amusement as Rocky brushes his teeth, all while trying not to throw up. I brush my own, shove two aspirin down his throat, along with a glass of water, and practically shove him down the hall and into the guest bedroom.

Thankfully, I had enough wherewithal to pack an extra T-shirt and basketball shorts. Grabbing them out of my duffle, I help Rocky get undressed, letting my hands graze over his bare skin slightly longer than necessary, and put on the clean clothes.

Once I slide his arms through the shirt, he reaches up and brushes a wayward curl off of my forehead. "You really are so pretty," he says.

I don't know how many times I've heard that from

both men and women since I started at this school four years ago, but something about the way he says it has a blush spreading across my face. "So are you. Now let's get you to bed before you pass out."

I shuffle him backward until his calves hit the bed, and he plops down like a sack of potatoes. I lay him back and cover him with the comforter before he looks up at me and pouts. "You're not coming in with me?"

God, do I fucking want to.

"No, I'm not coming in with you. You're drunk, and I'm sleeping on the floor." I grab the extra pillow and blanket and set up shop on the floor next to him. "But I'll be right here if you need me, okay?"

I can already see him nuzzling further into the pillow as his eyes start to drift closed. His mouth opens into the largest yawn known to mankind. "Thank you for the party, Clayton."

"You're welcome, Rockwell."

It takes all of point-two seconds for a snore to fall from his pouty lips, and I stare there, absolutely bewildered by everything that is him for a moment before stepping up to the side of the bed. Going against every one of my instincts, I bend down, caress the side of his face, softly press my lips to his forehead, and whisper, "Happy Birthday, Baby."

I'm so fucked.

CHAPTER 14
WHAT HAPPENS IN NEW ORLEANS...

ROCKWELL

The New Orleans Renegades put up a fight, but we pulled the season opener out of our asses in two sets. The two of us are locked in. When I say we're in our groove, we're in the goddamn groove.

We are *the groove.*

The Renegades' campus is cool as fuck and in the heart of downtown New Orleans. In previous seasons I never did anything after away games because Sanders wasn't someone I wanted to be around if I could help it. Everything in me told me that's exactly how Clay and I were going to be, but fuck… he's grown on me.

The shops, bars, and restaurants littering Bourbon Street are almost too much to take in at once, but I don't have a chance to look for long anyway when I hear Clay shriek at the top of his lungs, literally sounding like a toddler who has found their long-lost toy.

Whipping my head around, I grit out, "What in the flying fuck are you screeching about, Clayton?"

"Don't you dare start the Clayton shit, *Rockwell*. And this!" He shoots his arms out toward a little cafe on the corner. It is cute I'll give him that, but was all that really necessary?

Is anything ever necessary with Clay?

He keeps going, of course. "This is the home of the best pastries you'll ever taste! The Beignets in New Orleans aren't like anything you've ever tasted. Come on, we have to get some!"

I'm looking at him in awe. Never have I ever seen this man light up like this. Is it psychotic that I want to be a Beignet so I can bring him this much happiness?

Probably.

I'm a few steps behind, but I manage to jog to the door and hold it open for him before he's practically sprinting up to the register. Their menu reads that they don't pre-make anything, so you need to allow time for them to be made. Clay puts the order in for lord knows how many damn pastries and has his black card out before I can even pull my wallet out. I roll my eyes and head toward the tables in the back lining the huge floor-to-ceiling window.

I sit down in the ornate black metal chair, which is as cool-looking as it is uncomfortable. This thing looks like it may break, but it'll be fine, right? That's how I know the food is about to be fire, because it looks very questionable in here. It can go two ways: we may walk out of here with food poisoning or it will be the best food to ever make it in our mouths.

"They said like ten minutes," Clay says, walking up and setting down the two coffees he also got for us.

"Why do you look like a kid in a candy shop?"

"You're going to make fun of me if I tell you, and you need no more ammo."

"I'm going to make fun of you regardless, so you might as well tell me."

Like he really is embarrassed about this, his words come out in a rush, "I bake when my anxiety is getting the best of me. It empties my head enough to not feel the pressure I do from every other part of my life." Fuck I wasn't expecting that.

Taking a note out of Clay's book, I try to lighten the mood with humor for once. "You going to bake for me, *Garotão?*" I don't want to brush off his struggle with anxiety, but I can tell he really doesn't want to talk about it right now.

I'll store this in the back of my head for later.

He leans back and scoots his hips up to get comfortable, and all I can do is stare at his fucking crotch.

He clears his throat and says, "You like what you see, Baby?" That fucking smirk and those goddamn perfect teeth are going to be the death of me.

I shake my head, stuttering out, "Y-yeah, fuck off, Clay." He knows the pull he has on me, and the shithead keeps playing.

The morning after my birthday, I could feel myself falling face first for this man, and I haven't stopped since.

Of course, I'm not saying a word about it; I'm just trying to remain blissfully ignorant, living in my delusions. I woke up in Jax's spare room, with Clay beside the bed, curled up in the fetal position. I laid there with my pounding head for way too long, just watching him sleep. Now that I think about it, my head should've been hurting a lot worse than it was; I really dove off the deep end when Clay rubbed his cock up against mine. He woke up not long after I did and immediately started talking a mile a minute. I should've known he was a goddamn morning person… but I found myself smiling anyways.

*The hotel room tonight will be the real test of my willpower.

I pull myself out of my daydream, thanking whoever the hell people pray to nowadays that we're in the back of the cafe, in the middle of the day on Bourbon Street because my cock has other plans right now. My body must be having some sort of visceral reaction because anytime I'm near him, my dick is at half-mast… *minimum*.

The lady behind the counter brings our order out and sets the bag down in front of us, along with a pair of plates so we can eat a few here. The moment the bag hits the table, the delicious aroma floods my senses.

Clay pulls one out, sets it on my plate, and then grabs one for himself. "I gave you a plain one. I snatched the jelly, but we can share if you want to try some of mine." He shoots me a wink, picking his up and taking a bite.

He lets out a feral moan, and when I say feral, I mean it. I feel my cheeks blushing as I feel all the blood in my body rush straight to my cock.

"Oh. My. Fucking. God. Rocky, this is so good. You have to try it." Before I can even argue, he's thrusting the damn pastry into my mouth, ensuring I touch the part that his lips have as well.

That shouldn't be that hot.

———————————

* Triggered - Chase Atlantic

I can't lie and say the moaning wasn't deserved. I groan out, "Fuck, that is good."

He takes another bite, getting to the filling. Some of the jelly gets onto the side of his mouth. I reach out and swipe it off of his lip, making sure I run the pad of my thumb over his pouty bottom lip. He lets out another moan, all while looking me right in the eye while I suck the jelly clean from my thumb.

An impulsive urge takes over me as I let go of my thumb and tell him, "You moan so pretty, *Garotão*. You know… I have a recording to prove it." I'm smirking, but not for long. His eyes go dark, and he grabs the bagged pastries and my arm, dragging me out of the cafe.

CHAPTER 15
EROTIC AUDIO

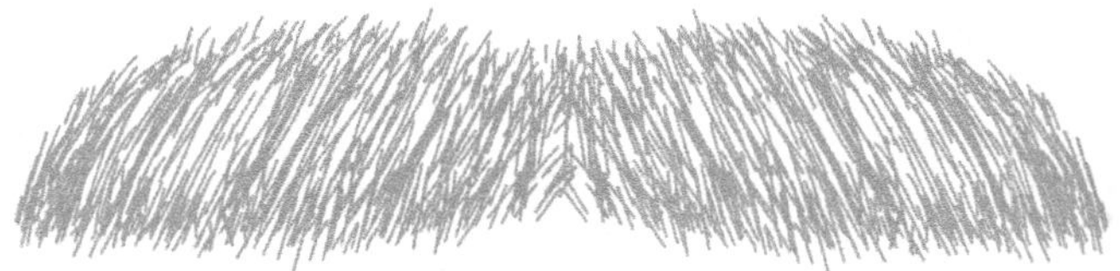

ROCKWELL

He's been dragging me down Bourbon Street a couple of blocks when I finally ask, "Clay, what's wrong?" Ignoring my question entirely, he continues stomping down the street.

*I'm not entirely sure what's happening, but I'm also not sure I want to stop it. I knew bringing up the recording was a gamble, but I did it anyway. Why? I guess it could be to answer all of the unanswered questions floating between him and I. To explore a part of my sexuality I never dreamed of until I became close to him. I feel like a teenage boy again with all of these random sexual fantasies rolling around in my head.

They're not random jackass: it's only when you're around Clay.

Once we arrive at the hotel, we're up the elevator and

---

* Been Like This - Doja Cat

at our door before I can even blink—my wrist still in Clay's tight grip.

I like the feeling of his hand forcefully gripping my wrist.

Once he unlocks it, he throws the door open, shoves me into the room, sets his bag down, and looks at me with so much lust it makes my stomach flip.

"Play it for me," he grits out.

Oh fuck, I've done it now. I'm about to get sued or something, all because I couldn't control myself.

I don't regret it though.

The amount of times I've had my cock in my hand listening to that damn audio is sickening.

"I can delete it if y—" I can't even finish the sentence. He has his hands on my shoulders, pushing me back toward the door. My back hits it, and my mouth goes dry.

"Don't you fucking dare delete it." The front of his body is covering mine, and *fuck* if I don't feel his rock-hard erection rubbing against mine. We both look down to see where we're touching, and I hesitantly rock my hips. Slowly, so fucking slowly, I'm testing the waters to see if this is something I'm really going to like or not.

I tilt my head back, looking at the ceiling as I ask in confusion, "Why does this feel so good?" A moment of hesitation hangs in the air before he grabs the back of my neck, pulls my head up, and smashes his lips to mine. I let his tongue in to dance with mine, still tasting the sweet jelly on him. The heat in the kiss alone has my whole body burning with desire, but I need more.

Our lips part, and he says, "Stop doubting yourself, Rocky. It's okay to want this."

I look away, not out of embarrassment, but from the look of pure want covering his face. I grab my phone and pull up the audio. It's in my favorites, and I don't even find any shame in that. He drags me further into the hotel room, and I sit on the edge of the bed. My eyes follow Clay as he paces the room.

I question, "Are you okay?" He doesn't respond again, which is starting to worry me. Usually, I can't get him to shut the fuck up.

"I know you feel this too, Rocky. I've been taking this at your pace, but I don't know how much longer I can do that."

"I don't know how to feel about any of this, Clay. I feel like we're just now starting to get along, and I don't want to jeopardize that."

He wears a devious grin as he looks down at me on the the bed. "Let's do what we do best. Let's play, Rocky, Baby."

He grabs his wallet out of his pants, opens it up, and pulls out two black packets. "Really, Clay? Didn't think you'd need a little blue pill to get it up"

He rolls his eyes but answers me, "No, it's lube, Rocky." I don't want to be Rocky anymore.

I want to be his Baby.

I look at him sideways, wondering why he would need lube, and it hits me. I grab my chest and question him, "Are you trying to fuck me?"

"Not tonight, but I sure as hell plan to." I feel my cock twitch in my shorts. Clearly, I'm not opposed to it.

He stands again, pulling his shirt off and then his shorts and boxers. A flash of metal catches my eyes, and my jaw practically hits the floor.

Clayton fucking Aldrich has his goddamn cock pierced.

I shout, almost as loud as he did earlier, "No, you do not!"

He's smiling down at me. "You like it? Hurt like a bitch, but I promise, you'll be thanking me... eventually." The switch in him flips again from his playful self to this dominant man that I need to see more of. I watch as he clenches his jaw and grits out, "I'm not going to ask again. Play the recording, Rocky."

I pause a beat as a shiver rushes through me before hitting play on the recording, and his eyes narrow from the first couple of seconds of hearing the audio. "Is this from the shower?"

I nod my head, too embarrassed to admit that I did this. He just sounded so good. I couldn't miss out on being able to hear it whenever I wanted to.

Quickly, I stand and strip out of all my clothes, trying not to think too hard about the fact that he's going to be seeing me completely bare, and lay back on the bed. Clay crawls up my body, growling into my ear, "How did you know I like putting on a show?"

"I di—I didn't know."

The audio is playing on my phone on a loop—exactly how it does when I'm on my own. It never takes long, though.

"And what have you been doing with this audio for the past couple weeks, Baby?" The whimper that comes out of me should be embarrassing, but I can't find it in me to care.

Okay, turned-on Clayton is definitely hotter than pissed-off Clayton.

"Using it for my... me time." Groaning, he slides back down my body hovering right above my jutted-out dick.

He slides his stubble-lined chin across the head of my cock, and I gasp.

"Fuck, Clay." I've never been so close to begging in my life.

"Are you ready for the best head of your life, Baby?" In a split second, I decide I'm completely done fighting this. Nothing that's wrong should feel this good, and we've barely even started. I give him a nod. "No, Rocky. I need your words."

"Yes, Clayton." I roll my eyes, but they never make it back to their resting position as he sucks the head of my cock like a goddamn leech; I feel my back arching off the bed already. Fuck, I'm not going to last.

My hands fly to his dark brown waves, holding him in place. "Hold on. Fuck, Clay, hold the fuck on." I cannot come this fast; he'll never let me live it down.

He pops off my dick and looks up at me as he whispers seductively, "You're so responsive for me, Baby." I'm going to melt into this mattress. If his mouth is stuffed full of cock, at least I won't come from his words alone.

I think that would be even more embarrassing.

I need the attention off of me. I lean up on my elbows and rush out, "Can—can I suck your cock?" He just smirks at me again. I'm used to being so confident in the bedroom, but this is uncharted territory for me.

"We can both have what we want," he answers before flipping around so his legs are toward my head. I'm wide-eyed, looking at him, wondering what in the fuck he has in mind. "Suck my cock, Baby. I'll go easy on you… this time." With that, he mounts my face, but his hips are high enough off the bed that I have to lift my head a little to reach the tip of him.

I feel him spread my legs apart and pull them up so they're encasing his head. My ass is on full display for him, and I've never felt more exposed while equally as eager. He lets out a feral groan, and I feel his finger brush against my virgin hole. "This tight hole is so stunning."

Goosebumps cover my body; I don't know if it's from his filthy words or his mere touch. His cock is still right above my mouth. Reaching up, I grab him at the base, stroking him a few times just like I do on my own. I hear the lube packet opening, and I immediately tense. We're conditioned as men to think we can never enjoy anything anally. However, I'd be lying if I said I wasn't curious to see what it would feel like.

I take his leaking cock into my mouth, his flavor dancing on my tongue, and I surprisingly don't hate it. I feel the lube dribble onto me. Clay starts to massage it in, circling his fingers around my hole. I tense again. "I need you to relax for me, Baby. Focus on what you're doing up there. You're doing so well."

Involuntarily, a whimper escapes me, and I know it's from his praise. Doing as he says, I start bobbing up and down on Clay's cock as I feel him simultaneously breach the ring of muscle. I'm already a panting mess. Clay adjusts, putting one knee up, bringing his dick further into my throat. His balls are practically sitting on my nose. Knowing it's something I usually like, I grab them and give them a nice tug, all while feeling him take my dick back into his mouth.

He starts pumping his finger in and out of me slowly before adding another, causing my eyes to roll back into my head. Humming around him, Clay curls them just so, and my hips buck off the bed, pushing me to the back of

Clay's throat. I can feel the sheen of sweat covering my body as his fingers rub just the right spot.

He pulls his mouth off and, with a clenched jaw, says, "Look at you with your mouth stuffed full of my cock." His thrusts pick up speed, making me gag every time he bottoms out. I reach my hands up, grab both of his ass cheeks and moan again.

God, his ass is phenomenal.

I focus back on breathing and the spit running down my cheeks. He keeps lazily pumping his fingers in and out of me, and in a lust-filled voice, he says, "I can't wait to wreck this pretty hole."

I whimper again, which quickly turns into more gagging. He's full on face fucking me now, and I can't move an inch with my head pressed against the mattress. My dick is lying on my stomach, but even without it being touched, I can still feel the build of an orgasm. "Yes, Baby. You like being my little cock whore."

Fuck.

Clay rubs his fingers back and forth a few more times before he groans out, "I'm coming, Baby, just for you."

His taste hitting the back of my tongue has me following right behind him, coming all over my own stomach, with his fingers still deep in my ass. I just came without him even touching my dick.

I didn't even know that was possible.

Slowly, he pulls out of my mouth; I lay my head back on the bed. But not more than a second later, I feel his tongue cleaning up my mess, and then he's spinning around on all fours, so his face is hovering over mine. As he grips my face and pulls my jaw open, I look wide-eyed up at him as he lets my own cum fall from his mouth into mine.

I swallow, and he gently pats my cheek. The lust is thick in his voice. "My whore gets all the cum."

CHAPTER 16
INDIFFERENCE IS BULLSHIT

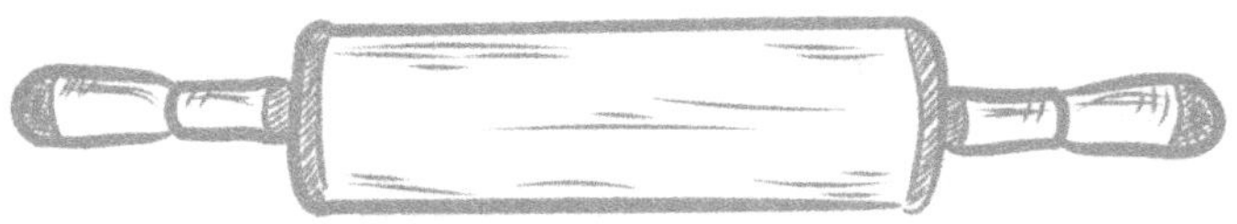

CLAYTON

"Hey, girl, hey." I wink at Nancy at her usual spot behind the checkout counter as I enter my favorite artisanal baking supply shop.

Her face blushes the way it always does when I greet her. "Hi, sweetheart."

And like he always does, her husband grumbles from his spot next to her, "You ever going to stop hitting on my wife, boy?"

"Only when she stops looking so beautiful, old man."

Nancy tucks a strand of silver hair behind her ear before winking back at me. "Oh, hush, Kevin. Let the poor boy be." Kevin huffs out a sigh and continues flipping through the pile of paperwork on the counter in front of him.

"Got anything good for me today, Nanc?"

"Sure do. Got some more of that double zero flour you

88

like, and there may or may not be an apron around here somewhere that says, 'Kiss me if I look hot in this apron.'"

Tipping my head back dramatically, I clutch my chest. "Nancy, you really do know the way to my heart."

She laughs as I make a beeline to where I know the apron is hanging, making sure that's the first thing I throw in my basket; not because I need it, but because I know she ordered it especially for me. And it's also clever as hell. I also stock up on my favorite double zero flour, which I use for most of my breads and doughs. Mindlessly, I move about the rest of the store, stocking up on all the things I know I'm short on. Which, considering the excessive amount of sourdough, cookies, and muffins littering my kitchen counters, is almost everything.

Besides business school, volleyball, and fucking… there's one other thing I can confidently say I'm really good at. Baking. I'm not even ashamed of it, either. Women love a man in the kitchen, and men love to eat. It's a win-win all around.

*From the moment I learned how to use a stove, Marissa taught me everything she knew about baking. And before I turned twelve, I knew how to make her world-famous double chocolate cake from scratch. I loved it. And soon, it became my escape when I was feeling anxious about everything in life. Whenever my dad harps on me relentlessly about how I'm never enough, I bake. Whenever my mom insists on being anywhere but around her only child, I bake. Whenever the pressure of becoming the next volleyball star feels like too much, I bake. And whenever I start panicking about the fact that I can feel

---

* TOO LATE - Chase Atlantic

myself falling deeper and deeper for a certain bull-headed man, even though I've never wanted a serious relationship in my life, I bake.

So it's safe to say I spend a lot of time baking. Especially the past few days.

It's been three days since our night in the hotel room. Three days since Rocky trusted me with his body. Three days since I felt his shivers of pleasure beneath my hands. Three days since I tasted him on my tongue. Three days since my entire world shifted on it's axis.

And now I'm standing in front of a shelf full of chocolate chips, shifting my basket in front of my rapidly growing dick. If Kevin finds out I have a boner in front of his wife, not only will he kill me, but he will never let me shop here again.

Which would be a great travesty. Because how will I ever continue my astounding apron collection?

I try to force the thoughts of that night from my mind but the only thing that's ready to take their place is Rocky's face the following morning. It was the same one he wore on the way home from our game and the same one he had yesterday at our Monday morning practice.

It wasn't one of panic—no, I think I'd almost have that. Instead, it was one of indifference, like what we did together was neither here nor there; like it wasn't as life-altering for him as it was for me.

What's more, I know that's a heaping pile of dog shit.

I know he feels something for me. And if what he's feeling is a fraction of the emotions coursing through my body like a tsunami crashing into the Florida shoreline, there's no way he would be *indifferent*.

Which means he's hiding it.

Like he always does.

I'm about sick and fucking tired of his aloofness. I have enough people in my life who are only in it when it's convenient for them. I don't want Rocky to be one of them. He *can't* be one of them. Neither my waistline nor my mind can handle his indecisiveness any longer. Either he's in this, or he's out.

I've wanted nothing more than to confront him about it, but it's nearly impossible to do when he's been the epitome of cordial since we woke up Sunday morning. He smiles and gives me one-word answers, but it's like pulling teeth to get him to do anything else. Every time I text him to ask if we can talk he says he's busy studying, and he dipped out of practice so fast the last two days there was practically a cloud of smoke behind him.

I think I'd literally kill for an eye roll or a "What the fuck, Clay?"

Forcing myself out of my existential crisis in the middle of Delectable Desserts, I grab the chocolate I need for the raspberry chocolate mousse and head toward the checkout counter. I'm rounding the corner of the aisle when a familiar deep voice stops me in my tracks.

"Here's the rent check, Mrs. Wilkins."

"Thank you. But for the hundredth time, Rockwell, I really wish you'd just call me Nancy."

"I know. I'll remember one of these days," he answers while shooting her one of his rare authentic smiles. The same one I've been dying to see for the last two days.

Nancy spots me over Rocky's shoulder. "Find everything you need, sweetheart?"

He does a double-take before turning to face me. It's then that I see it, though; for a split second, his entire body relaxes, and he inhales a deep breath like his entire being is relieved to see me.

And those five seconds are enough to quiet the anxious thoughts running through my mind… at least for a few moments. It's enough to give me hope.

Hope that he truly wants me as much as I want him.

"Clay?" he asks, brows pinching in confusion.

Walking up next to him, I put my overflowing basket on the counter. He looks down at it and chuckles lightly before looking back at me. "What are you doing flirting with my girl?" I ask him.

"She's not *your* girl, Clayton," Kevin grumbles, not even sparing me a glance. "See, Nancy. This is why I like this one better." He points up at Rocky while simultaneously flipping through his papers.

Gasping, I answer dramatically, "I'm hurt, Kev, really. I thought we were friends."

Kevin doesn't dignify me with a response. Instead, he starts scanning my groceries as Nancy and I laugh among ourselves.

"Organizing a bake sale?" Rocky asks with a mischievous twinkle in his eye. I didn't realize how much I missed that in the span of three days until just now.

"No bake sale. Just trying out a new raspberry chocolate mousse recipe."

Rocky's face morphs from mischievous to genuinely perplexed in the span of two seconds. "Did you just say the words 'raspberry chocolate mousse'?"

"Sure did." I puff my chest out proudly.

"Clay here is an amazing baker," Nancy interjects, equally as proud. "His cannolis are literally heaven on earth. I don't know what he puts in that cream, but it is the most delectable thing I've ever tasted. You should try it, Rockwell!"

I can't fucking help it. "Oh, he has, Nanc. Rocky was a big fan of my cream."

Rocky's face snaps toward mine so fast I wouldn't be surprised if he gave himself whiplash. Curling my lips in, using every ounce of my self-control not to burst out in uncontrollable laughter, I stare into his mortified eyes, all while pulling out my card and handing it to Kevin.

"Oh, that's wonderful." Nancy claps in excitement. The sweet lady has no idea she just set up the world's most perfect double entendre. "I didn't know the two of you knew one another."

I clap Rocky on his muscular shoulder, savoring the way he inhales a ragged breath at my touch. "Rockwell and I have gotten to know one another *very* well."

"Alright, well, I gotta go shower. You have a good day, Mr. and Mrs. Wilkins," Rocky quickly blurts out, clearly wanting to remove himself as fast as possible.

I watch in amusement as Rocky's perky ass bolts out the front door, all while Nancy calls after him. "It's Nancy!"

Snatching my card out of Kevin's outstretched hand, grabbing my bags off the counter, and kissing Nancy on the cheek, I race after Rocky. I laugh as I hear Kevin's grumbling in the background.

By the time I catch up to him, Rocky is rounding the corner of the building. "Rock! Wait!"

For a moment, I think he's going to bolt up the metal staircase, but I am grateful when he turns around to face me with a wide-eyed smile plastered across his face. Before I can get a word out, he's stomping toward me, and in the next second, he has my face in his hand. Squeezing it so hard, he purses my lips. He brings his face close enough to mine that I can feel the hair from that goddamn mustache ghost against my lips.

"Embarass me like that again, *Garotão*, and I'll chop your balls off, grind them to dust, and mix them into your precious cream. Understand?"

I'd take his threat more seriously if he wasn't still grinning at me like the Kool-Aid Man. "Sorry. She set up the shot. I had to take it."

Leaning forward a fraction of an inch, his lips graze mine. *"Essa maldita boca."*

Much to my disappointment, Rocky takes a step back. Remembering what I heard him say to Nancy, I ask, "So, rent check, huh?"

Scrubbing a hand down his face, he answers, "Yeah. I rent out the apartment upstairs. But, had I known you were the Pillsbury Doughboy, I would have braved the dilapidated apartment above the pizzeria down the street."

I bark out a laugh. "First of all, nothing about my impeccable physique says 'Pillsbury Doughboy.' Second of all, now that I know you live above one of my favorite places on earth, all the more reason to show up more often." I didn't think it was possible, but Rockwell Campos fucking blushes. "So you gonna invite me up, or what?"

I don't know when I'm going to get another opportunity like this with him, but I'm sure as hell not going to waste it.

Rocky's eyes search my face for a moment before he chuckles lowly and shakes his head. Turning on his heels, he starts walking up the stairs. "Come on, Betty Crocker."

Indifferent, my ass.

CHAPTER 17

TELL ME SOMETHING REAL

CLAYTON

When I say I could not have pictured a more Rockyesque apartment if I tried, I'm not lying.

Rocky's apartment is entirely open concept, save for what I'm assuming is his bedroom and bathroom in the far corner. All the walls are made entirely of dark brick, with one of them containing large windows above Delectable Dessert's sign out front. There's a large gray rug in the living room, and on top of it sits a dark brown leather sectional and a natural wood coffee table. A large flat-screen TV sits opposite the sectional, and next to it is a shelf with dozens of books. There are several potted plants throughout the space along with a plethora of framed pictures of what I'm assuming is his family.

And his kitchen… The *things* I could cook in this kitchen.

The black kitchen cabinets match the matte black vent

hood that climbs up the wall. There are several natural wood open shelves on either side of the vent hood and matching counter tops. The large kitchen island has three wood and iron stools and a matte black three-light pendant fixture hanging above it.

I can feel myself practically drooling just looking at it.

However, upon closer inspection, I notice that not a single kitchen appliance is sitting on the counters beside a coffee pot, and the open shelves are practically bare besides some basic crockery.

He doesn't even use the damn thing.

What a fucking travesty.

Rocky steps into my line of sight and leans against the kitchen counter, crossing his arms across his chest and tipping his head to the side as he stares at me.

The sight of him in this kitchen is enough to make my dick twitch in my jeans.

"Any of that need to go in a fridge?" He nods to the several brown paper bags in my hands.

"Just a few things."

"Go ahead and put them in the fridge, and you can just set the rest of it on the counter. I'm gonna go grab a quick shower," he says as he throws his thumb over his shoulder in the direction of the room in the corner. "Feel free to grab something to drink while you're in there and turn on the TV. The remote's on the coffee table."

Rocky grabs his duffle from the floor and walks into his room, leaving the door open a crack behind him. Doing as he says I set the grocery bags on the kitchen island and put the necessary items in the fridge. Just as I close it I hear the chime of a text ring through the room. I spot Rocky's phone face down on the island next to my grocery bags, and in two long strides, I'm at the edge of the counter staring down at it.

I reach out to grab the phone but my hand stops mid-air. What if it's someone else he's hooking up with? There's no way I could handle that without flying off the handle. But... *what if it's someone else he's hooking up with?* Reaching out further, I grip the phone between my fingertips, only to pause once more before lifting it off the counter.

"Don't do it, Clayton," my subconscious screams at me. *"It's an invasion of privacy."*

Yeah... well... he lost his chance at privacy when he let me hear the sounds he makes when he comes.

Flipping the phone over, an incoming text from someone named *Irmã* fills the screen. Just as I'm mentally preparing myself for a metaphorical kick to the balls, I'm quickly met with the absolute best possible scenario.

IRMÃ

> Did you guys fuck yet or are you still being a little bitch about it? We both know how much you want him. Grow a pair and get after it.

> I promised I wouldn't tell anyone, and I'll keep that promise. But just know that whenever you're ready, no matter what you decide you are... we will all always love you, Irmão. You just have to let yourself be loved back.

The first thought that races through my mind is, "Holy fucking shit. He told someone about the way he feels about me."

But before I have a chance to jump up and down in

excitement, the same thought races through my head. Yet this time, it's in a different tone. Jealous. Darker.

He told someone about the way he feels about me.

He told someone about the way he feels about me... and it wasn't me.

It only takes a split second for me to decide my next move. He might not be ready to own up to his feelings, but I am sure as fuck not going to make it easier for him to ignore it.

I toe off my white trainers and start walking across the apartment. I whip my gray hoodie over my head and toss it on his sectional. My shirt is next, finding a spot on the floor, followed by my jeans and socks. By the time I make it to his cracked bedroom door, I'm in nothing but a pair of briefs. I don't pause when I reach his door, though. No. I shove it open and storm through his room—not even stopping to admire the fact that I'm in Rocky Campos' room—toward the bathroom door, which is also cracked.

Either he's royally enjoying fucking with me, or he's a psychopath that like's to let a draft into his bathroom while he's showering.

Both are equally likely.

I open his bathroom door to find him leaning against his shower wall, just like he was against the counter in the kitchen, staring at me through the glass door with a wicked grin plastered across his face. "About fucking time."

This mother—

In the span of two seconds, I slide my briefs off, climb in the shower, and have him pinned to the shower wall with my hand around his throat.

A shiver rolls through my body when I see his smile

fall from his face, his eyes widen a fraction, and I feel him swallow roughly under my palm. He's nervous.

Good.

"You may think I'm all fun and games, Rockwell." My voice is nothing but a low growl. "But I think it's about time you learned that I am not one to be fucked with."

"Oh, I think I'd fuck with you any day—" I tighten my grip around his neck, effectively cutting off the rebuttal I threw in his face all those weeks ago.

* "Shut. The. Fuck. Up."

I'd be worried I was being too aggressive if I didn't feel his dick throbbing against my hip.

"Get on your knees," I demand. When he doesn't move, I tighten my grip to the point I know he can't breathe. "Do not make me tell you again, Rockwell. Get on your fucking knees."

When I can feel him starting to lower, I release my hold on his throat and take a small step back to give him room, savoring the sound of his sharp inhale, and watch with bated breath as he drops to his knees on the wet tile.

And when he places his palms flat on my thighs and looks up at me with those fucking deep green eyes, I know it right then and there.

He's mine.

"Open your mouth, Baby." He hesitates for just a split second before following my instructions. "Stick your tongue out." He does as I say. Fisting my painfully hard dick, I set the head of it on his outstretched tongue.

Slowly, I slide my cock into his mouth, using every ounce of my restraint not to blow my load the moment his

____

* Wicked Games - The Weeknd

lips close around me. I take a few more languid strokes before pushing further until I hit the back of his throat, holding still until he gags slightly. Giving him a reprieve, I pull back slightly and grip the sides of his face, letting the tips of my fingers thread through his onyx curls.

"Tap my thigh if it's too much, understand?"

He mumbles around me, and the vibrations send a shock wave down to my fucking toes. Not giving either of us another moment to back out, I thrust into his mouth with full force, tipping my head back in a moan when I feel myself slide down his throat. My thrusts rapidly pick up speed as I fuck his mouth without abandon. Relishing in the pain of his fingers digging into my tensed quads.

"Fuck, your throat feels so fucking good."

Rocky lets out a wanton moan, and I feel him release my right leg. Looking down as he fists his dick in his hand, I watch as a bead of cum drips onto the tile floor. "That's it, Baby. Make yourself come while I fuck your face."

I don't know whether the next sound is a whimper, a cry, or a moan, but whatever it is going to play on repeat in my head until the end of time. My hold on his face tightens as I continue to thrust in and out of his mouth, and when I feel his teeth lightly graze the underside of my dick, a shout of pleasure roars through the air. "You have ten seconds to come, or you don't come at all."

Rocky looks up at me, his eyes now dark and filled with lust. I watch as his arm flexes once, twice more, all while never breaking eye contact with me as I'm still moving in and out of him. The sounds he makes when he comes are enough to send me over the cliff I've been standing on since I pinned him to the wall.

"Swallow. Every. Single. Drop," I bite out between

thrusts as I come down his throat, and only when I'm sure he's done as I said do I slowly slide out of his mouth. Rocky doesn't move from his kneeling position, surprisingly waiting for me to give him his next direction.

"Stand up, Baby."

Rocky stands toe to toe with me, and since we're not under the shower's spray, I grip his wrist with my hand and bring the hand he had wrapped around himself to my face. Sticking my tongue out, I run it up the center of his palm, closing my eyes as I savor the taste of him.

"Fuck, Clay," he groans in a pained whisper, and my eyes snap open to meet his. "What are you doing to me?"

"Same thing you're doing to me." I plant a soft kiss on his palm and drop his hand. "Come on, let's get washed up."

The two of us take turns washing up, and I can see every thought running through his mind playing out on his face.

He's not as aloof and mysterious as he thinks he is.

Once we're both clean, Rocky steps out first and wraps a towel around his waist before grabbing an extra one from underneath the sink for me.

He stands at the vanity, hands gripping the counter, as he stares at himself in the mirror. And I know if I let his train of thought run too wild, we'll be back to the way we were the last two days the moment the steam evaporates from his reflection.

I just need one moment.

Stepping up behind him, I wrap my arms around his lean waist and set my chin on his shoulder so I can stare at him in the mirror. "You may not be ready, and that's fine. But just know that this is real for me, Rocky. So, if you can't tell me that yet, then tell me anything. Anything at all. Tell me something real."

He closes his eyes for a moment and takes a deep breath. When he opens them, I can tell that everything he wants to say is right on the tip of his tongue, but he doesn't. Instead, he says softly, "I miss my family. I haven't seen them since we all drove out here before the school year started. Plane tickets are expensive and none of us have been able to swing it this year. I just... I just really miss them."

I don't tell him that I miss mine for an entirely different reason, and instead, I softly smile and say, "Thank you for telling me."

CHAPTER 18
MIXERS ARE OVERRATED

ROCKWELL

I vaguely remember dosing off last night in Clay's arms, but I don't feel them surrounding me when I finally peel my eyes open. The sun is beaming right in my face, and I know it's way later than what my alarm is usually set for.

Then I hear the bass of music from outside my room. Getting up, I head into the bathroom to take care of business, brush my teeth real quick, and throw on a pair of shorts. I open my bedroom door and am immediately hit with the smell of sweet pancakes and savory bacon. *Then I hear Clay belting at the top of his lungs, "If I Were a Boy" by Beyoncé. I stand in my bedroom doorway, staring into my kitchen, as I lean against the frame just taking him in.

For somebody who fights with anxiety like I know he does, he sure does find happiness in the smallest things.

---

* If I Were a Boy - Beyoncé

As he stands at the counter mixing up the pancake batter, I'm busy appreciating a shirtless Clay and the muscles lining his powerful back as he moves the whisk around the bowl.

Thank fuck I don't have a mixer.

His shorts are slung so low I can see the two little dimples on his lower back right above that juicy fucking ass of his. My eyes roam over the rest of him. He's in a pair of my five-inch inseam shorts, and they hug his thighs perfectly, making a groan spill past my lips. He turns around to face me, smiling from ear to ear, and I find myself wearing a matching one as I read his apron.

"Good morning, Baby."

"Kiss me if I look hot in this apron," I read it out loud and stalk up to him. I pin his back against the back wall, forcing him to put his bowl of batter down as I lean in to kiss him.

It doesn't feel like the other ones have.

Those were just us being caught up in one another… in the heat of the moment.

This one is everything.

Everything I've been keeping locked up tight, battling with him and myself, denying the feelings I never thought I would have for a man.

I grab the back of his head, deepening the kiss. He parts his lips, surprisingly letting me in, and I take the lead for once.

He pulls away, smacking at my chest. "Quit distracting me. I'm going to burn the bacon."

"I was just following the instructions on the apron." I shrug, stealing a piece of bacon off the plate. I look over at

Clay's laptop sitting on the counter beside the pancake batter.

"I have a surprise for you." He's not looking at me, but I can see the smile still covering his lips. "Look at the screen."

I lean in and look closer, rolling my eyes. It's plane tickets. "Okay… What about it? You going on some fancy rich kid vacation for spring break that Daddy is paying for?" I see the hurt pass over his face, but he just shakes his head.

"No, Rocky. Look at the city and the date."

"San Diego, and sometime next week?" Then it clicks. I feel the tears already, but I don't want to say anything in case this is some kind of sick joke he's playing on me.

"I talked to Coach Taylor this morning, and he said we could miss the one practice after we play San Diego as long as we win. I bought our tickets back." He flips another piece of bacon before setting the fork down to look at me and grabs my face. "We're going to see your parents, Baby."

My nose is burning, and I know the dam of tears is about to open, but I don't even care.

"Thank you, Clay. Seriously, you don't know how much this means to me." My voice cracks, and I hate showing this weakness, but my mom always yells at me for holding my emotions in. "And I'm sorry for what I said earlier. I have to stop with that shit."

He drags his thumb over my cheek, collecting my tears. "Don't apologize. I am a rich kid. And *Daddy* does pay for anything I've ever wanted. But we can use his money for good this time." He shoots me a wink, and I chuckle. Thankful as always that he breaks up the heavy with some jokes.

I don't know what the fuck Clay Aldrich has done to me, but I'm officially done fighting it.

CHAPTER 19
PRAISE KING

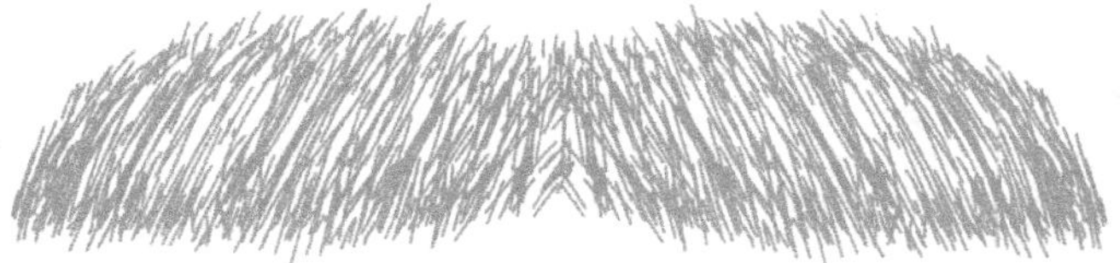

ROCKWELL

This last week has dragged on worse than ever, knowing what's waiting for me this weekend… my family. I'm oddly excited for Clay to meet them, too.

We have about thirty minutes before our game against San Diego starts, and I'm getting warmed up, stretching, and getting my blood pumping when I hear the voice I know all too well scream out, "Filho!"

I'm running over to the stands before Coach can say anything. We landed, ate, and were dropped off here, not having any time to see my parents beforehand. I get to her, wrapping her in the biggest hug and whispering into her hair, "Momma, I've missed you all so much."

I refuse to cry, but goddamn, it feels like it's been a year since I've seen them. I pull away from my mom, wrap my dad in the same hug, and see tears streaming down my mom's face.

Don't cry, Rocky. Don't cry.

"Okay, okay, give me a hug, Lil, so I can get back out there."

If they don't get kicked out from yelling at the refs then that'll be the shock of the trip. I'm jogging back onto the sand, and Clay's just smiling at me. "Fuck, Clay, stop looking at me like that, or I'll really start crying." He throws his hands up in defense, and I continue, "Come on, let's kick some ass."

* Clay is at the net while the refs flip the coin for serve and side. He walks back over to our sideline and informs me, "We have serve, but we're switching sides."

"Good job getting serve."

"It was just luck of the flip, nothing I did."

We grab our stuff, switch to the other side, and go get set up. I always serve first if we win serve. I look at Clay's hands behind his back for the zone. Four. Ref blows the whistle, and I start my serve routine. It's not a long one, but I have to spin my ball in my tossing hand two times, then throw, approach, and jump. It's the perfect serve with just the right amount of topspin on it. The ball lands right in the front right corner of the court.

Ace.

I do that four more times, taking Clay's call before they actually get arms under my serve. My mom is screaming louder than I've ever heard the entire time. Finally, they side out on a block that neither of us was quick enough to get to.

We immediately get the ball back next point, though. I dig up the pass, Clay and his perfect hands set me up on

---

* Too Sweet - Hozier

the right side, and I'm slamming right down the line, a good foot clear of the block. Either they've gotten worse since last year or Clay and I are absolute monsters together.

I'm going with the latter.

Clay goes back to serve, and my mom goes berserk, screaming, "Let's go, Clay!!! That assist was amazing!" I'm surprised she left the damn air horn at home.

I have my hands behind my back, giving him my call: zone six. He does his routine, throws, and approaches, and when I hear his hand hit the ball, I am glad I'm on this side of his serve. Honestly, the man is a freak of nature when it comes to volleyball. I've never seen anything like it.

The ball goes barreling across the net and lands at the top of zone six, right in the middle of them. I run up to Clay, grabbing his shoulders, screaming, "Fuck yeah, Clay! You're doing so good today!"

He shrugs nonchalantly. "Let's see if I can keep going." He's clearly not great at taking compliments, but that's not going to stop me from handing them out whenever I see fit.

We obliterated the first set, twenty-one to five. We're on our sideline resting between side switches. It's currently fourteen to two. "Let's see if you can serve us out of the game, Clay. I bet you can." I give him a wink, and this man blushes. He hates the praise, but the challenge… he can't turn down.

"I'll try," he says on a huff.

The ref blows the whistle, and he turns quickly, but I give him a slap on the ass before he can get too far. "You're looking good back behind that line, *Garotão*."

He looks at me over his shoulder, blushing. After giving him another smirk, I follow him back onto the court, getting into position.

He does his normal serve routine, hits the ball twice to knock the sand off, two spins, but when he throws it up, his toss looks off to me, and I know it is when it slams into the net.

He never misses his serve…

I walk up to him, slap his hand, and say, "It's okay! Keep your head up!"

He hangs his head, whispering, "I'm sorry."

"Clay, it's okay. We're up eleven points; we're doing just fine."

The taller one on the other team is serving again, and it goes straight to Clay. I'm already moving toward the net to grab the set. He passes it beautifully to me before he's running up to take a middle hit. He yells out a two, so I jump and set it low; we're basically jumping at the same time, and he's practically hitting it out of my hands. Their smaller guy isn't even jumping to block him yet. It hits in the wide open back corner.

I pick him up, spinning us around while screaming, "LET'S FUCKING GO!"

"Shit, that was a good set, Baby!" My eyes widen at the public slip of the pet name, but neither of us comment on it further. It really was a good set, though. Now that we're on the same wavelength, we're such a good pair. It pisses me off that we haven't played together for the past three years.

I ended up serving the game out after that. Every fiber in me knows that that one word, that one little slip-up, that one "Baby" was the match that lit the fire deep inside of me. And every time Clay cheered for me, it was like adding gasoline to the flames. I want to be able to do that for him, too… if he'd let me.

We shake hands with the other team, and I pat the refs on the back, always trying to be respectful of them. Dragging Clay by the hand, I pull across the court to finally meet my parents, who are still patiently waiting in the stands. I hear him talking to me through clenched teeth, "Rocky, what are you doing?"

We're in front of my parents and Liliana, my sister, before I excitedly introduce him to my family. "This is my partner, Clayton. But he goes by, Clay." I feel him stiffen under the arm I've slung over his shoulder, but I keep going. "This is my mom, Cassandra; my dad, Joseph; and my baby sister, Liliana."

"It's so nice to meet you all." He reaches his hand toward my mom.

She shoos his hand away. "We're a hugging family, *Amor*. Come here." She pulls him into one of the big hugs she's known for. My heart swells at her already giving him a nickname. My family have always been the most accepting people, and it's something my mother ingrained in me too. I know that's exactly how they'll treat Clay… no matter what he is to me.

Both of my parents preached "you never know what someone is going through behind closed doors." Some peoples lives can look so put together, and they can have anything they've ever wanted, but they are surrounded by people who only see them as that—not for who they really are. A person lacking love and true connections with others. Or it could be the opposite… the person you're not accepting or bullying could have nothing. No food, clothes, or even a roof over their heads, but no one wants to take time out of their day to actually help them.

I'm so thankful for growing up around parents that never treated anyone different. Until you know the true feelings and intentions behind someone's actions, you have no clue what they go through day in and day out. It still makes me feel like a piece of shit for judging Clay before really knowing what he fought with and how his father treats him. All I saw was him flaunting around his shit, but now I know that he's so much more than a guy that grew up with rich parents.

I hear him mumbling and apologizing for being sweaty and sandy, but my mom couldn't care less. She pushes him away by his shoulders but holds him at a distance, looking him over. With the most motherly tone, she tells him, "You did so good out there, Clayton. I can't get over how well you two play together." I chuckle to myself. The sand's not the only place we play well together. But I decide that's best to keep to myself.

"Okay, Momma, we've gotta go shower. Did you all drive separately so I can have a car to drive home?"

"Yeah, here you go." My Dad tosses the keys to his car to me.

"Clay, I hope you didn't think you were getting out of coming over for dinner?" my mom asks him.

"I would love a home-cooked meal, Mrs. Campos."

"Now, Clay, none of that 'Mrs. Campos' stuff! Call me Cassandra, Cass, or even Momma."

I start to head to the outdoor showers, pulling Clay with me and yelling over my shoulder, "We'll see you at home."

I'm starting to worry that my family's excessive love and affection might be a little bit too much for him to handle. Nothing like diving into the deep end, I suppose.

CHAPTER 20
FRIENDS? PARTNERS? TEAMMATES?

CLAYTON

Rocky and I are in his parent's car as he drives us the thirty minutes to Imperial Beach where we'll be spending spring break. *"HEART-LESS" by PLVTINUM and Goody Grace rings through the speakers of the Chevy Cruze as Rocky sings along, and I can't help but stare at the wide smile on his face.

It's as if just being in California, being near his family, has unlocked the side of him that he keeps buried. The one he lets no one else see. The one I've only been privy to a handful of times. The one I'd sell my soul to see every morning when I wake up and every evening when I go to bed.

Whoa. That thought was a new one.

His aviators cover his eyes as he drives, but I can see the smile lines peeking out the sides as he sings, not even

---

* HEARTLESS (with Goody Grace) - PLVTINUM, Goody Grace

ashamed that his pitch isn't remotely in tune. His hands tap the top of the steering wheel to the beat, and I have to force myself to look away, fully aware I've had my eyes locked on him for the last two minutes.

But I can't help it. He's just so fucking pretty.

Nevertheless, I look out the passenger window and admire San Diego Bay as we drive down Highway Five toward Rocky's childhood home. My phone vibrates in my lap, and I open it already knowing it's a message from Jax.

JAX

Good game today! The two of you were dialed the fuck in. Looked like a hot one, though; make sure you replenish your electrolytes for… later.

ME

What exactly is "later"?

Jackson totally knows there's something going on between Rocky and I. My best friend is quite literally the smartest person I know and not a whole hell of a lot gets past him. So, even though I haven't told him *much,* he definitely knows we're more than just partners at this point.

JAX

Some team bonding if I had to take a guess.

I curl my lips in and try not to bust out in laughter.

ME

Here's what's going to happen, Jackson. We're both going to pretend I have no idea what you're talking about and I'm going to pretend that I didn't see you coming out of Theo's office two days ago when you had no reason to be in there. Deal?

Three gray dots appear and disappear a couple of times before his message finally comes through.

JAX

Okay, well played.

Have fun bonding.

I roll my eyes and smile as I lock my phone and set it back in my lap, forcing myself to think about all of the ways Rocky and I could possibly "bond" this week.

I booked a hotel suite for the two of us at a resort right on the beach, hoping we would have *hours* of uninterrupted time over the week for *activities*, but one look at Rocky with his family and I knew he'd prefer to spend the week at their home.

I'll still keep the hotel just in case though. With any luck, I'll get to steal him away… at least for a night.

I'm not sure what happened today, but something about being around Rocky's family… being around Rocky the way he was today… seems to have set me on edge. And I'm not entirely sure if it's in a good or bad way.

Rocky's words of praise had me digging deep through the whole game. My passes were perfection, my hits were lethal, and my serves hit the mark almost every single time. I was on fire. But, beneath it all, I felt a wave of anxiousness rolling through me.

Between hearing Rocky's family cheer me on from the stands—people I had literally known for five minutes—and Rocky's upbeat enthusiasm, it almost felt like too much to handle.

They were all just so… so… *supportive.*

And as grateful as I am for it, to have people behind me who want the best for me—who *see* the best in me—I don't know how to handle it.

I've never had that in my life. Never. Not once.

My dad only cares when my actions directly affect his image. If I do something "right" not a single word, but if I do something that doesn't meet his impossibly high and unattainable standards, which is almost always, he's on the phone faster than I can blink. And god forbid he actually *shows up* for something.

And my mom… she's more checked out than she ever was. My dad's constant berating has slowly chipped away at the loving and attentive mother I once had when I was a small child. Now, she's just a socialite who floats in the air of Miami's humid breeze, flaunting her money up and down Ocean Drive and only speaking to me on my birthday and holidays.

Suffice it to say, the Campos' warm welcome is something I wasn't prepared for.

I wonder if Cassandra has ingredients for chocolate chip cookies?

Noticing me anxiously bouncing my leg up and down, Rocky takes me by surprise and wraps his large hand around my thigh, just below the hem of my athletic shorts, halting my movements. The feel of his warm hand on my skin slightly calms the anxiety that's buzzing inside of me.

"You okay?" he asks, taking his eyes off the road for a moment to look over at me. One look at my face and his smile falls and is replaced with a look of concern.

Giving him a half-hearted smile, I answer, "Fine."

"Clay…" He drags my name out, knowing damn well that I'm feeling more than just *fine*.

Since when is he so in tune with emotions?

"Talk to me."

A heavy sigh escapes me, and I absentmindedly fidget with his fingers on my thigh. "Seeing how your family, how your parents, acted today just got me thinking."

"About your parents?"

"I couldn't tell you the last time I experienced how your family made me feel today. They made me feel seen. They made me feel wanted. And they don't even know me. My own parents haven't done that for me since I was a child. And it all just made me feel a little—"

"Overwhelmed?"

Of course he gets me. I don't know when it happened, but Rocky can read almost my every thought. Sometimes he knows how to articulate what I'm feeling better than I do.

I didn't know how much I needed that in my life until he came along. Someone who can help me figure out exactly what I'm feeling when my own thoughts just feel too *big*.

"I know my family is a lot." He gives me a sympathetic smile. "But they have always wanted what was best for me. And because you're in my life, they're going to want the best for you too." His hand gives my leg a firm squeeze, and he begins stroking his thumb along my skin. Goosebumps skate up my leg. I'm not entirely used to him being this affectionate, but I'm certainly not opposed. "That means you are going to be treated as one of their own. The hugs will be neverending, the conversations will always be loud, and Lil will give you endless shit. It may be a lot but I wouldn't change it for the world. But if at any point it feels like too much, you just tell me and we will take a break. We'll go on a walk or hide in my room until you feel like you can breathe. You just need to tell me. Okay?"

"Thank you for understanding. For not judging."

"I would never judge you, *Garotão*." I snort a laugh and raise my brow. "Okay, I would never judge you about something like this. Your terrible taste in music, yes. You're feelings, never."

As much as I want to fucking swoon over the sentimental part of that statement, instead, I reach out and pull at his curls on the nape of his neck. "I do not have terrible taste in music."

"You wore a Shania Twain shirt to my birthday party, Clayton."

I pull harder. "Shania Twain is an icon. Disrespect her, and I'm not sure we can be friends."

Rocky's hand moves up my thigh slightly as he looks over at me again. I may not be able to see his eyes behind his shades, but I know he narrowed his gaze at me. "That's what we are, huh? Friends?"

No, no it's not. I want to be so much more than that. But I'm not entirely sure he's ready to hear it. "Partners?" I ask, feigning ignorance.

His hand moves higher under my shorts. His breath

hitches when he realizes I'm not wearing any briefs. "Partners?"

"Teammates?" I swallow hard as I feel the tip of his finger brush against the head of my dick as it twitches in my shorts. His grip on the steering wheel tightens to the point of his knuckles turning white.

I don't miss the tent forming beneath his shorts as he shifts in his seat.

"Rocky…"

"Hmm?" he asks, as he runs his finger along the length of my matching erection.

"If you don't stop right now, I will make you pull this car over so I can fuck you on the side of the highway where everyone can see. So unless you want to show up to your parents freshly fucked, I suggest you remove your hand."

I stare at his profile and watch as his eyes widen. He slowly removes his hand from my shorts and uses it to adjust his straining cock. My *teammate's* ragged breaths fill the car, and my wishful thinking leads me to believe that he's excited at the idea. But we can't. As much as I am dying to sink into him, I'm not going to let the first time he's with a man, or the first time he's with me, be over the trunk of a car.

Ten tension-filled minutes later, Rocky's pulling off the highway and driving through a residential neighborhood before slowly coming to a stop in front of a small craftsman style home. It has a dark gray stucco exterior, and black shutters and windows, causing the bright yellow door to stand out.

Rocky removes his aviators and sets them on top of his head, finally letting me see those green eyes. I can see the nervousness in his gaze. "It's—it's not much but this is where I grew up. They were able to redo the exterior a few years ago, but the inside is still the same as it was when I was a kid."

Now it's me who grips his thigh, silently reassuring him before I say, "It looks like the perfect place to grow up."

He pulls his eyes from me and smiles as he looks back at his childhood home. "It really was. We didn't have much, but that house is filled with love. So much so it's nauseating sometimes."

I tip my head back in laughter.

"You ready for this?" he asks, not forgetting how overwhelming this all is for me.

Taking stock of my feelings, I realize I'm no longer on the brink of crippling anxiety. Now it's something much more manageable. Don't get me wrong, this all is still making me incredibly nervous and I know I'm going to feel wildly uncomfortable, but I also know that Rocky is responsible for quieting all of the noise, allowing me to be as present as possible.

Giving him my most reassuring smile, I answer, "Let's go. I'm about to be Momma Campos' favorite."

"I don't doubt that for a second." Rocky winks before throwing open the driver's side door and climbing out.

All it takes is a little fucking wink, and now I feel like I can't breathe for an entirely different reason. "So incredibly fucked," I mumble to myself before grabbing our bags and following him up to the bright yellow door.

CHAPTER 21
HOME (SUPER) SWEET HOME

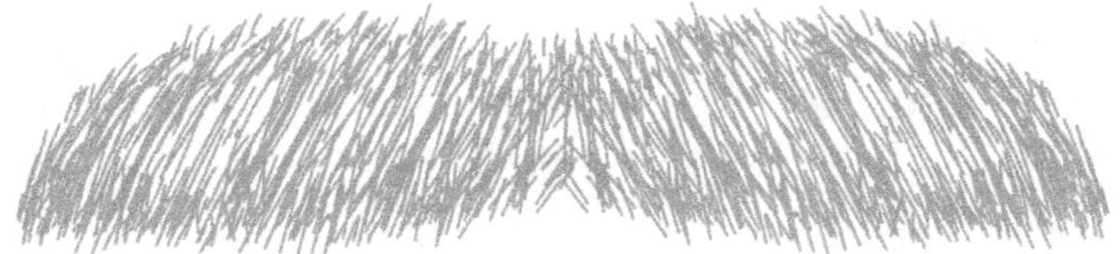

ROCKWELL

Clay's right behind me as we walk through the front door of my childhood home. I've always been self-conscious about the size of our home and how outdated it is inside… but I always remind myself that it's the love and memories that fill these walls that really matters.

I'm not surprised at all when Clay's dad was radio silent because we fucking swept today. He only calls when he feels like he has something to bitch about, and today there wasn't one thing that he could've found wrong with our game today.

*I can feel Clay's body heat with how close he is to my back, so I turn around and throw my arms out. "Well… this is the living room." It's big enough to fit a couch and

---

*   I Mean It (feat. Remo) - G-Easy, Remo the Hitmaker

loveseat, a couple of end tables, and an entertainment center with the TV mounted above it.

The thing I love the most about our house, though, is the original hardwood floors my dad has restored over the years. The deep oak color ties everything together, and they cover the whole house besides the bathroom. Just a little three-bedroom, single-bath home in SoCal, but what else do you need?

I walk him into the eat-in kitchen, and his face lights up when he sees my mom by the oven with her apron on. Hers is a lot more worn out than the one Clay had on at my place, but you can tell it's been well-loved.

"*Amor*, I hope you brought your appetite with you."

"It smells delicious, Momma." Fuck, have I missed her cooking. That was honestly the hardest part about leaving for school freshman year. Obviously, I miss my family, but missing out on the home-cooked meals was enough to send me over the edge.

I grab Clay by the forearm, dragging him behind me to show him the rest of the house before dinner is ready. All that's left of the tour is the bathroom and bedrooms. Quickly, I show him those before heading to my bedroom to breathe for a minute.

I flop down on my childhood bed, staring at the wall my bed is pushed against. It's covered in old posters of athletes I've always looked up to and, of course, half-naked women. I've never been embarrassed about my room, but there's a first time for everything.

Clay breaks the silence after spinning around, taking in my full room. "If this room doesn't scream high school boy I don't know what does. It's about time I get to bring my high school fantasies to life."

"Fantasies, huh?"

"I wasn't out about my sexuality until freshman year at Palm. My hot as fuck friends from high school did have rooms just like this though." Sporting a mischievous grin, he starts to run his hands up my thighs as he continues, "Let me suck you under these posters."

I throw my head back, basking in the feel of his hands on me, but then I remember we're in my house with my parents and sister, and the damn door is still open.

Hissing, I grab his hands to stop him. "Not right now, Clay." I can't be sporting a goddamn boner when we head back into the kitchen.

We're all sitting at the table, Clay beside me, enjoying my Momma's favorite Brazilian dinner she makes, *escondidinho*—pretty much a better version of a Sheppard's Pie. I turn to my right, looking at Clay, and then down at his plate... He's already finished what he had, and right when I see the clean plate so does Momma. "Rocky, go get that boy some more. He's starving." We meet eyes, and I can tell he's still nervous.

I chuckle, trying to ease the tension in his shoulders. "You don't have to eat more if you're full, but if you do want more, there's plenty, I promise. Momma doesn't know how to cook in small portions."

Actually, that's a lie. I think she does, but she just loves to feed people. Food is my momma's love language, and it was always a huge way for her to teach us about Brazil.

One of my favorite memories was listening to her tell us stories of her childhood while we helped her out with dinner.

He finally answers, "I would love more, but I can get it."

"No, no, I'll get it. You're a guest in this house, relax." I grab his plate and make my way to the attached kitchen. I can see my sister across the table eyeballing Clay before looking up at me. I know she knows there's something more between us, but she's keeping it to herself... for now. She's most likely stock-pilling evidence to call me out later.

I hear my mom ask Clay, "They must come to all of your games while living so close to the school. What I would give to be so close to my, *Filho*..." She trails off, lost in thought, and I'm practically running back to my seat, throwing the plate down in front of a now stiff Clay. I completely forgot to warn my parents about the sensitive topic.

Quickly, I change the subject, announcing, "Did I tell you guys that Clay threw me a birthday party this year?"

Luckily Lil catches on and asks, "Oh! Let me see the pictures! I know your vain ass took some." She loves giving me endless shit about the fact that social media is my job, but she can't deny that it pays well and works perfectly with my hectic schedule.

I'm convinced Lil is just jealous of the fact that my socials have blown up over the last few years in comparison to the ones for her business. My sister is an incredibly talented esthetician, but the market here is beyond over-saturated, and she's not getting the clientele base she deserves. I told her to move to Florida by me so I can refer everyone I know to her, but she's always been iffy about leaving home. I know it's because she's scared to leave our parents without any children nearby, but, just like I do, they would only want what's best for her.

Grabbing my phone from my pocket, I pull up the pictures from my party. My sister immediately starts laughing her ass off while scrolling through them. "Why the hell is everyone in crop tops? Is that Shania Twain?" She zooms in like a fifty-year-old on one of the pictures. "Let's go, boys? All of you are dumb as hell." She's now howling with laughter and that's what finally pulls Clay back to the present and out of that head of his.

"We did the 'dress like the birthday… boy' theme," Clay stutters, realizing that is definitely not the word they used the day of the party.

Before I know it, he and Lil are chatting it up, and they quickly form a plan to go see Shania in concert by the end of dinner. I roll my eyes dramatically, but my heart is on the verge of bursting. I love being able to show Clay what a caring home looks like.

I throw the suggestion out there, "How about we have a cookout tomorrow? We all can run to the store in the morning to get what we'll need."

My mom's looking at me like I've hung the moon, as Dad excitidly shouts, "I call grill duty!"

I catch myself staring at Clay as he slides his shorts down his muscular thighs, but stop that train of thought and instead ask him, "How are you feeling, *Garotão*? My parents overwhelmed you enough for a lifetime today. And don't even get me started on Lil."

"I love your sister. We're besties now," he states matter-of-factly, crossing his arms over his chest while still only in his briefs. My eyes shamelessly rake over his corded arms before roaming down his stomach and each knot of muscle covering it, right to the patch of hair leading down into his briefs. And don't get me started on his V-cut. I suddenly have the ravenous urge to feel it under my tongue.

I pry my eyes off his gorgeous body and force them back to meet his gaze, only to realize he just watched me eye fuck him as I realized just how delicious he looks in my childhood bedroom.

His full-beam smile is out, and he raises a brow at me. "Are you done?"

"To be determined," I answer with a shrug and a sly smile.

Clay booked a resort for the week, but my Mom was not about to let him stay in a hotel by himself. I offered him the couch but, in that same breath, told him he was more than welcome to sleep in my bed with me, fully aware that my parents wouldn't care or question it. I'm not going to lie—when he decided on my bed, I was relieved, but I quickly remembered that we'd need to behave. I don't know if anyone could stop us once we get going again.

The deep-rooted desire I have to hear his moans of pleasure again is visceral; the sounds that come out of him when he's turned on need to be studied because no one has the right to sound that sexy.

Actually, better yet, somebody can study why they do what they do to me.

This is the first night we've actually planned to sleep together, and it almost feels like it's going to elevate whatever this is between us. But I think we're both ignoring that… for now.

CHAPTER 22
MOMMA KNOWS BEST

CLAYTON

Rocky and I spent the night together in his bed, and I'd be lying if I said I didn't love every single second of it.

*The two of us have spent the night together a couple of times, but this felt different. I'm not sure if it's because it was in the home where he grew up, a place filled with so much love and laughter, or if it was because there wasn't anything inherently sexual about it. Sure, we fell asleep wrapped around one another—which don't even get me started on how completely right that felt—but there was nothing nefarious happening. We just held one another as we slept… all night. And when I woke up shortly before he did, with his head on my chest, I laid perfectly still so as not to wake him any sooner than necessary, trying to soak up as much of the moment as possible.

---

* Conversations In The Dark - John Legend

If this is what the next four nights are going to feel like, it's seriously not going to help that I'm so deep down the Rocky Campos rabbit hole that it's not even funny.

The five of us spent the morning sleeping in, followed by shoveling our faces with an all-you-can-eat buffet of waffles, bacon, and fruit, courtesy of Momma Campos. After some quick power naps, thanks to the food comas we were all sporting, we are now on at the store to get more, you guessed it, food.

Rocky was right, cooking is definitely Cassandra's love language. At this rate, I'm going to leave spring break ten pounds heavier.

Cassandra and Joseph are at the other end of the store, grabbing some meat from the deli counter for the barbecue, I can hear Rocky and Lil two aisles over arguing over which kinds of chips to buy, and I'm mindlessly wandering the baked goods aisle contemplating what kind of chocolate I want to buy for the cookies I'm going to bake.

Finally spotting one of my favorite brands, I reach down to grab a couple bars of semi-sweet chocolate when I see the hellions round the corner, their arms filled with bags of chips. They dump at least eight different kinds into the cart, and I cover my mouth as I snort out a laugh.

"Ummm, what is all of this?" I ask the two siblings in front of me. Rocky looks beyond perturbed, and Liliana looks like she's two seconds away from punching him in the dick. It's actually pretty fucking funny. I hadn't realized how much the two of them look alike until now. While she's shorter than Rocky, Liliana stands pretty tall for a woman; I'm guessing around five ten. She has jet black hair that cascades down her back in soft waves, framing her face which is covered in the same deep walnut skin, and her eyes shine green just like her brothers. However, hers look to be a couple of shades lighter. More like a sage green rather than Rocky's deep emeralds. My eyes also find the small beauty mark she has just above her lip. She really is quite beautiful.

So is her brother.

"Dickhole over here wouldn't let me pick the chips even though it's my turn."

"And I told her that I haven't been home since school started, so I should get to pick regardless. You can choose dessert."

Fucking siblings. I've heard plenty of these ridiculous arguments between Jax and his brothers, but watching Lil get Rocky so flustered is a sight to behold. I haven't seen anybody be able to get under his skin this easily. Well, besides me, of course. "Oh my god. Just get all of the chips. I got stuff to make chocolate chip cookies anyway."

Both of their heads snap toward me, and they have different expressions. Lil's is one of surprise, while Rocky's is now full of concern.

"You bake?" Liliana raises a brow in suspicion.

"Sure do. Pretty good at it to if I do say so myself. I didn't bring my 'Kiss the Cook' apron, but the rules still apply." I shoot her a mischievous wink and she doesn't so much as blush. Instead, she just scoffs and rolls her eyes.

"You good?" Rocky asks, worry lacing his voice.

"Yeah…" I drawl. "I'm fine. Why?"

Lil's stare bounces between us. Clearly, completely confused.

"You're baking."

"Yes. I wanted to make something for dessert."

"So I ask again… you good?"

Suddenly it dawns on me, and I soften. "I'm okay, Rocky. I just wanted to do something nice for your family."

His lips curl up at the sides. "If you're sure?"

"I am."

The two of us stare at one another until Liliana's voice cuts through the silence. "Okaaaaay. I don't know what that was all about, but let's go find Mom and Dad, shall we?"

She walks past me without waiting for our response, clearly uncomfortable and confused. As Rocky moves to follow her, he quickly grabs the side of my face and gently grazes his thumb along my cheekbone. "Really, I'm okay. I promise."

Taking my word for what it is, he nods and removes his hand. "Come on. We better follow her before she finds a small child she can make cry."

I bark out a laugh and follow him until we find his parents. They drop what they have in their hands into the cart, and we head to the checkout counter. Once the cashier is done scanning our ridiculous amount of groceries, I quickly hand him my Amex before Cassandra and Joe have a chance to grab their wallets. Her mouth drops open in protest, but before she can speak a word, I bend over and pop a quick kiss on her cheek, and whisper, "Please. It's the least I can do."

Reaching up she gently cups my face, much like her son did only minutes ago. "*Garoto doce.*"

Smiling, I stand up straight and nod at Joe, who doesn't argue with his wife's approval.

Once we all get back to the house Rocky and his dad

get started on the grill while I busy myself getting out everything I need for the cookies.

I'm just about to start sifting flour into the bowl when Cassandra stands next to me, tying her apron around her waist. "Want some help?"

"Love some."

Following the recipe I have memorized, she starts creaming butter and brown sugar in the stand mixer. "I'm glad my *Filho* found you this year."

Warmth blooms in my chest, and I smile. "Me too. It definitely wasn't the game plan, but I'm starting to think everything is working out the way it was supposed to."

"Rockwell has always been such a serious boy. He seems… different. Happier. Lighter. I think I can thank you for that." Her hip bumps into mine.

"You raised a great son. Truly. Rocky is…" Rocky is so many things. Amazing. Talented. Beautiful. Smart. Intuitive. But the one word I can think that summarizes it all is —"He's really special. He means a lot to me."

She rests her hand on top of mine just as I'm about to grab the baking soda. "*O amor não tem lei.*"

My eyes start to sting as I look down at her. She doesn't delve deeper into the subject. Instead, she just smiles and goes about her tasks as I do mine. We busy ourselves with light conversation. Her asking me about my childhood, and me asking about hers in Brazil. I'm fully aware that I could ask her about Rocky when he was a child, and with any luck there will be time for that down the road, but right now I want to learn more about the woman who raised Rocky. What better chance than to ask her myself?

I try to pay as close attention as possible to her words

as we scoop balls of dough onto cookie sheets, but her words continue to ring through my mind.

"*O amor não tem lei.*"

And as I watch Rocky walk through the deck door with his dad, plate of steaks in hand, and a smile a mile wide, I realize I couldn't agree more.

CHAPTER 23
LIEUTENANT LIL

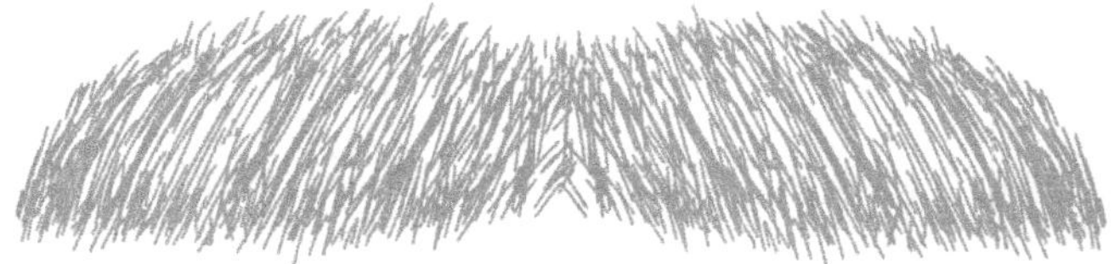

ROCKWELL

We've spent the last couple of days with my parents, enjoying spring break, showing Clay the city I grew up in, and eating our hearts out with all the home-cooked meals we could want. Clay has been so peaceful compared to how wound up he usually is at school. It makes me tear up thinking about how much stress his family causes him… especially his dick head of a father. I think he needed this time with my family more than I did.

It makes me even more thankful for the parents my soul was brought to; then Clay's soul aligned with my path, no matter how hard I fought it in the beginning… so I could show him what the true meaning of family and unconditional love is.

Clay's dad, Charles, constantly reminds Clay that the only reason Clay is as talented as he is, is because of him, saying Clay would have never gotten anywhere if it weren't for his genes or money. Like all of that makes up for acting like an arrogant, egotistical asshole and being an absent father. What a fucking joke. It's no wonder Clay has such a hard time hearing how incredible he is, he's never even heard it from the two people that should shower him with love and praise unconditionally. I couldn't imagine bringing a child into this world, looking at them, and only thinking about what that child could do to make me look better. For his entire life, Clay's every feeling, thought, and desire has been shoved to the side in order to accomplish the goal of being Charles Aldrich's son. Not just *Clay*.

Both of us are cuddled up in my bed, still not fully awake, watching *Emily in Paris*, per his orders. He about stroked out when I said I hadn't seen it… Like, I would've ever watched this shit on my own. It is funny as fuck, even though I would never admit that to him. His head is lying on my shoulder, his leg slung over the top of mine, and I'm skating my fingers over his back.

*I push off getting up for as long as possible. I'm way too content with Clay beside me in my bed.

As if she knows I feel at peace, Lil comes barreling into my room, yelling, "Up! Let's go run some drills, ladies!"

"Can you fucking knock, Lil? Goddamn." Clay's instantly sitting up with his back up against the wall.

"Language!" I hear Mom yell from the living room. "Goddamn" is her least favorite cuss word but one of my favorites.

With the most exhausted voice, I tell my annoying little sister, "Out. We'll be ready in a minute."

We agreed to go to the beach today to run some drills

---

* Work Out - J. Cole

with my dad and Lil, knowing I'd also be able to shoot content for a couple of brand contracts I have while we're there, but I figured it would be later on… I should've known better with her. She's always been a morning person.

Climbing out of bed, I slide on one my favorite pairs of black shorts that make my ass look out of this world and my American Dad crop that I cut up myself with Rodgers on the front dressed in one of his many get-ups. Clay throws on some matching shorts, and fuck, I can't keep my eyes off his thighs and that lean waist of his. He chooses a normal T-shirt, clearly deciding to be boring today.

We walk into the living room, and my dad and Lil are standing at the door, ready to go, but not before we're forced to put on sunscreen. Having a sister who's obsessed with skin and skincare can be annoying sometimes, but I guess we won't croak over from skin cancer, so that's something. After ten minutes of lathering ourselves in sunscreen we all pile into the car for the short drive over to the beach.

I catch myself staring at Clay way too often, especially while we're both stretching out on the sand court. The beach is only a short ten minutes away from the house, but that didn't stop Clay from snuggling up to me in the back seat while my dad drove and Lil rode shotgun. Still fully checking him out, I bend at the hip, making sure my hamstrings are nice and loose, ensuring I'm warmed up since it's been a minute since we played last. We're used to practicing daily, but since we haven't been moving these past couple of days like we normally do, not stretching properly is asking for a torn muscle, and we sure as fuck don't need that.

"Come on, ladies! Let's get a move on! I'm trying to get some hits in." Lord, she's on one today.

Lil played volleyball throughout school. Although she could easily have gone to a D1 college, her true passion was pursuing being an esthetician. Volleyball was her one love for so long, I know she misses it more than she'll admit. I hate that we're a whole country apart, and playing together isn't an option—even if that does look like us just playing pick-up on the beach.

My dad and Lil are on the other side of the net, and Clay looks at me like he's asking, "should we take it easy on them"? He clearly hasn't picked up on the competitive nature of my whole family.

My dad's a big man and scares the shit out of most people, but then he opens his mouth and that's when you find out he's just a softy deep down. He's six-three and bulky, pretty much a spitting image of me without the dark complexion that I got from my momma.

My dad chuckles. "Go ahead and start deflating those egos." He's up at the net, holding the ball, and my sister is on the left side, looking ready to murder us.

Clay mumbles under his breath, "Why am I kind of scared?"

"You honestly should be," I answer him truthfully.

"BALL!" my dad yells out, tossing the volleyball to Lil, who in turn, passes him the perfect ball. He sets her up beautifully, and she approaches, attacking the ball. It's heading for Clay, but it's shorter than he expected. Normally, shorter people can't jump high enough to get on top of the ball, even more so in sand, forcing their hits to go long. I know that's what he was thinking as he readied himself further back because I would've done the same if I didn't know how good my sister was.

Lil has fucking hops, though.

Clay's diving into the sand, reaching out for the ball, but comes up a couple of inches short. It hits the ground right in front of his hands, throwing sand up in his face.

"Oh, this is going to be fun," Lil says while turning around to get back, ready to hit again.

They go through the same routine, but this time she's gunning for me. I'm ready, though, digging the ball up perfectly, right into Clay's waiting hands. He sets me up beautifully. I make my approach, but my dad is there, ready to block as I hit into his hands with all my might, but there's no going around him. The old man stuffs me, causing the ball to ricochet so hard off his hands that Clay is able to pass it back up to me. I send it up in a set, and Clay's approaching it at full speed. Lil tries to block him, but he's got too much height on her and pure fucking power behind him. He slams the ball down the line, and all I hear is slow clapping from my dad.

"Boy, you're fucking good! And you two together..." he says, on a huff. "Untouchable. You each pick up each other's weak spots and build off of them." He's looking at us in amazement, and honestly, I don't know why... That wasn't all that crazy of a play, but what he said rings true. We have each other's backs and always know what the other is going to do before we do it, and it's never been this easy with any other partner I've had.

And what do we do?

Start fucking around with each other like a bunch of dumbasses, risking the championship and the sure track to the Olympics were riding on.

But it's worth it, and if it does work out, we're going to be unstoppable. I can hear the announcers now: *"Clay and Rocky, the power partners on the sand, and the power couple off."*

Speaking of being a couple, he hasn't called me Baby at all since that one slip-up at the last game, and that's way too long for my liking. I didn't realize how much I'd miss something so small until I didn't have it anymore.

Clay's voice pulls me out of my spiral. "You're not so bad yourself, Joe. Did you play?"

"Nope, I just picked up what I could from these two troublemakers—enough to be able to keep up with them and train the best I could with what we had." I really do try not to take for granted what I grew up with and what my parents selflessly offered up. It may not have been money, but my dad willingly learned a new sport—as an adult—regardless of how hard that is... But he did it, and he did it perfectly.

We keep running through drills and talking all kinds of smack, but the same thought won't quiet down in my head...

Why has Clay suddenly stopped calling me Baby? The more I think about it, the more I realize he must be doing it on purpose, and I'm about to be fed the fuck up.

CHAPTER 24
SAY. MY. NAME.

CLAYTON

It's our last night in California before we have to go back to Florida, and we're spending the evening hunkered down at the Campos's kitchen table playing the most intense game of Clue I've ever seen. It's not exactly the typical way I'd spend spring break, but I'm absolutely loving every single second of it.

The way Joe says something smart to Cassandra every time she guesses a clue and makes a mark on her sheet of paper. The way she pinches him in the side every time he makes said smart comment just for him to wink back at her. The way Rocky and Lil quite literally have not stopped arguing since we started this damn game. And the way Rocky looks my way every so often, softly smiling at me as he catches me softly smiling at all of them. But most of all, the way he occasionally squeezes my thigh under the table, silently asking if I'm overwhelmed.

I love it all.

Rocky rolls and his character enters the billiard room on the game board. After he thinks for a few moments, he looks at his sister, who is directly to his left, and asks, "Was it Miss Scarlet, in the billiard room, with the wrench?"

Liliana sighs dramatically as she shows him a card in her hand, and I hear her mutter something about hitting Rocky with a wrench under her breath as Rocky makes another mark on his paper, grinning confidently.

Reaching to my left, I rub my hand along his spine. "Good job, B-buddy." Just like I've tried to do since we arrived a week ago, I stop myself from using the nickname that so easily falls from my lips. But this time I almost let it slide, and judging by the way his smile immediately falls, Rocky noticed.

Curling her lips in, clearly trying not to burst out laughing, Lil claps Rocky on the back and mocks, "Yeah, good job, b-b-buddy."

"*Eu vou matar você*," he snarls at his sister.

As the game continues, every time I say something to Rocky, he grows more and more tense. On his last turn, he hardly even tries to make the correct guesses. I already know what he has marked off on his sheet because I've been sneaking peeks at it the entire time. And when Liliana finally guesses correctly, the game ends, and Rocky abruptly stands from his seat. *Grabbing me by the wrist he pulls me from mine and drags me behind him into the hallway leading toward the bedrooms.

Pulling me into the bathroom, he slams the door closed and pins me against it. With his hands on the door on either side of my head, caging me in, he bites out, "Say it."

---

* I Feel Like I'm Drowning - Two Feet

"Say what?" I ask, clearly beyond confused.

"My name. Say it."

"Rocky… what are—"

"No," he practically growls. "You haven't said it once since we got here. Say my name, *Clayton*."

"I-I didn't know." I'm usually such a confident person, and I'm certainly the last person you'll see stuttering and fumbling over their words when it comes to talking to someone I'm attracted to. But seeing Rocky be so passionate about *me* almost has me at a loss for words. *Almost.* "I know until me, you were one hundred percent straight, and I didn't want to out you in front of your parents if you weren't ready and calling you Baby would basically do that and not to mention I have no idea what you and I actually are, and I'm trying to be respectful when all I really want to do is hold your hand and kiss you and call you Baby, and also not to mention the fact that I haven't gotten off in over a week and every time you so much as look at me, I feel myself getting hard and I'm worried that if I clench my jaw any harder to prevent that from happening at your parents kitchen table I'm going to crack a molar, and you'll have to take me to the emergency dentist and then I'll have to get put under laughing gas and the last thing I want for you is to see me high when—"

Rocky cuts off my incessant rambling by putting his hand over my mouth. His furious scowl now replaced by a small upturn of his lips. "I'm going to remove my hand, and you're going to take a breath." I nod against his palm and do as he says when his hand lowers. "I don't think I've ever heard someone say that many words in a single breath. Not even Lil, and she never shuts the hell up."

I shrug my shoulders innocently, still pressed up against the bathroom door, his arms still caging me in. "Call it a special skill."

"I appreciate the fact that you were worried about my feelings, but don't worry about me. I'm ninety-nine-point-nine-percent positive Lil already knows something is up, and my parents are two of the most supportive people you'll ever meet in your entire life. It's not something that needs to be made a big deal of, nor do I want it made a big deal of. It's not who I am. I'm fine with just being me, being *us*, and everyone else jumping on board. You okay with that?"

Relaxing, I rest my hands on his hips and nod. "If that's what you want, then yeah, I'm okay with that."

"Good." He brings his head closer so his lips dust against mine. "Now… Say. It."

"Baby…" I whisper in the most sultry voice I can manage.

Rocky tips his head back, his Adam's apple bobbing as he lets out a deep moan. Immediately, I feel his erection growing between us. Taking full advantage of the fact that we finally have privacy—not counting sleeping together and the quick moments we have before we go to bed and when we wake up over the last week—I lean forward and take the lobe of his ear between my teeth before repeating, "Baby."

My lips skate lower, gently nipping at the skin of his neck just below his ear. "Baby."

His hips thrust against me.

Trailing my tongue along the column of his neck until I get to the nape where I gently bite again. "My Baby."

"Fuck," he groans out. Threading his fingers through the back of my hair, he pulls so I'm forced to look at him. "You still have the hotel?"

My smile beams from ear to ear. "I never thought I'd hear you ask me that. Yeah, I still have it."

"Get your shit. We're leaving in twenty."

CHAPTER 25
GOODBYES STINK

ROCKWELL

Done is the understatement of the year of what I was after Clay called me "buddy" at the kitchen table while we were all playing Clue.

I'll show him who his goddamn Buddy is.

*In the most seething tone I can muster, I tell him, "Get your shit. We're leaving in twenty." Clay's eyes widen. "And we're not leaving the hotel room until we need to be at the airport."

I know my hard tone shocks him slightly since he's used to being in control in the bedroom, but we're not in the bedroom, and I need him more than I ever thought possible. I'm tired of us not knowing what we are or where we stand with each other.

My parents are the least of my worries.

---

* Wicked Games - The Weeknd

They were sure to teach us growing up that love is love and to always treat people with respect.

I can hear my dad now. *"Treat others the way you want to be treated."* The older I get, the more I realize how important it is to live by that saying. You never know what someone is going through when they walk into their home… if they're lucky enough to have somewhere to call home. In the same breath, walking through those doors could be their living hell.

Mindlessly walking back into the kitchen, my mind wanders off to what I'm hoping happens in the hotel room tonight. The table is cleared and I hear everyone's voices floating in from the living room. Heading to the fridge, I grab some drinks and late-night snacks to take with us, unsure of what the hotel will have and knowing we'll need the energy boost, considering all of the filthy thoughts that are bouncing around in my head that are about to be brought to life.

Tonight is the night.

I've decided.

I'm giving myself fully to Clay. I know he'll protect this soul of mine, and I'll do the same for his.

Stepping into the living room, my hands still full of snacks and drinks, I fill everyone in on the plan. "Hey, Momma, we're going to spend the night at the hotel tonight." No one even looks over at me, too busy watching whatever the hell is on the TV. Lil lets out a low chuckle like she knows exactly what we'll be doing there, and I'm sure she does, especially after walking in on us in my room one too many times.

Clay comes out with both of our bags slung over each of his shoulders and the luggage rolling behind him. "I can't thank you all enough for welcoming me into your home and your family this past week, but I'm going to steal him away for our last night," he says with the biggest smile on his lips. Clay drops the bags he's holding when my mom gets up to wrap him in one of her hugs. The kind that will bring tears to your eyes if you hold it too long.

She really knows how to make you forget everything else going wrong in your life when she wraps her arms around you.

Then he's getting wrapped up in my dad's arms, and dammit if that doesn't pull on my heartstrings even more. Especially knowing his relationship with his own father is so strained. Lil follows suit, giving her goodbyes, but whispers something into his ear, causing Clay to gasp before they're both cackling like a bunch of school girls.

I'm following behind Clay, doing my round of good-byes as well. This is always the worst part. My family is truly some of the best pieces of me and leaving them, not knowing when I'll see them again, causes my body to physically ache. But heading back to school knowing I have Clay by my side is making me feel better.

Wrapping my hands around my mom, and laying my chin on the top of her head, I whisper, "I love you, Momma."

With the softest voice, my Mom replies, "I love you too, Rockwell."

I feel her turn her head towards Clay, but I still have her wrapped up in my arms. "Clay, thank you for planning all of this and letting us see our *Filho*. It means the world to us, and so do you. You will always have a spot in this family, *Amor*. Do you hear me?" Clay's eyes fill with tears, and he nods his head.

"I'll see you all soon," he finally manages, his voice strained with emotion.

"Okay, *Filho,* you two be safe," my mom says, throwing us a wink. It's then that I know that she can clearly see that Clay and I are a lot more than we've been leading on, but she keeps her observations to herself.

Unlike my sister who yells as we're walking out the door, "See you two lovebirds bright and early! Oh! And don't forget to use plenty of lube!"

The last thing I hear is Momma smacking her on the arm as she scolds her in Portuguese. "Ready?" I ask looking at Clay, who's practically buzzing with excitement.

"Oh, you have no idea how ready I am."

CHAPTER 26
SHOW ME WHAT YOU GOT, GAROTÃO.

CLAYTON

Once Rocky pulls up to our resort, located right on the coastal shoreline, the two of us jump out at lightning speed, grabbing our bags and letting the valet park the car.

Neither of us takes more than five seconds to take in our surroundings; we're too worried about getting checked in and up to our suite. It looks like a beautiful hotel; from what I've seen in passing. The lights illuminate the evening sky, a plethora of tropical plants are scattered around the front of the building, and you can hear the Pacific crashing into the shoreline at the back of the hotel. But I couldn't give two flying fucks about any of that right now. The only thing I'm focused on is the man in front of me as we power walk through the coastal-themed lobby, decorated in soft grays, blues, and yellows, toward the check-in counter.

Rocky gets to the counter before me, but I peek over his

shoulder to speak to the small woman behind it, knowing the reservation is under my name. "Checking in for Clayton Aldrich."

The woman tucks a strand of brown hair behind her ear and peers over her thick-framed glasses as she begins to type at her computer. A few moments later her eyes widen as she reads the notes attached to my reservation. I smile inwardly, knowing in reality that I checked in the day we got here not wanting to lose my reservation, just in case things went my way, and have paid for it every day since. I also had the front desk staff leave a note to pretend that I was checking in for the first time if and whenever Rocky and I showed up.

The last thing he needs is to feel guilty that I paid for a hotel we haven't even been staying at.

"Here you are, Mr. Aldrich," she says as she hands me a small envelope with two key cards. "Your suite is on the top floor. The snacks and mini-bar should be fully stocked and on the house." No, they're not. I had them say that, too. I paid for every single one of those items. "The number for room service is posted in your room. Is there anything else you will need?"

"No, thank you."

She smiles softly before nodding at both of us. "Have a good night, gentlemen."

The two of us climb into the elevator, and as the door closes, I can't help but realize we have barely said a word to one another since we climbed into the car to drive over here. Me, because I'm so fucking excited. I know that if I so much as speak one word, I'm just going to word vomit all over the place like I did in the bathroom at his parent's house. And Rocky, likely because he's nervous... and excited… and overwhelmed. But as I peer over at him as he stands in the elevator, shifting back and forth on the balls of his feet, hand gripping the handle of his bag so tight his knuckles are white, I'm not entirely sure which emotion is winning out.

Fuck this.[*]

Dropping my bag to the floor, I shove him against the side of the elevator. Cupping his face, I kiss him fiercely. His bag falls from his hands, and he grips me at my waist, pulling me as close to him as possible. My teeth nip at his bottom lip, and he moans into my mouth. The sound shoots straight to my groin.

The two of us fight for dominance as we push our tongues in and out of each other's mouths, the hairs of his mustache creating the most delicious burn of friction against my lips. There's something to be said about feeling another man against you. Don't get me wrong, women are beautiful and perfect in their own ways, but where their bodies are made of soft and smooth planes, men's bodies are rough and rigid. It's a deliciously stark contrast and one I can't get enough of. Especially when it comes in the form of Rockwell Campos. But as my hips push him against the wall and with his face between my hands, I'm not letting him have the upper hand on this one.

Not tonight.

Tonight, I'm taking care of him. Tonight, I'm going to show him what it feels like to be so wrapped up in pleasure that you know nothing will compare ever again. Nothing will even come close.

And what's more… he's going to let me.

----

[*] High - Ethane & Dua Lipa

I hold one hand steady on the side of his face as the other one skates past his jaw and wraps around his neck. The second I squeeze, I feel his Adam's apple move beneath my hand as he lets out a satisfied groan. One I swallow every second of.

Finally, he relents and lets me take control of his mouth, and I take full advantage of the opportunity. Tasting every inch of him.

His hands slide down past my hips and underneath the hem of my shirt. Rocky runs them along my lower back, and I can feel my entire body shiver.

"Clay." My name sounds like a prayer on his lips as he gasps for air.

Using the hand cupping his face, I tilt his head upward, forcing him to look me in the eye. "Tell me to stop. Tell me to stop right now, and we won't do this. Tell me to stop right now, or the moment this elevator opens, you're mine."

His green eyes dance between mine for a moment before he says two words that are about to change my life as I know it. "Don't stop."

There's no going back after this. I'm a goner. Fucking done.

"Fuck, Baby."

My mouth crashes into his again, and not more than ten seconds later, the elevator doors open on our floor. Pushing off the wall, Rocky guides me into the hallway, his mouth still fused to mine. I laugh against his lips. "Rocky. Baby, our bags."

"Fuck our bags," he mumbles against mine, still trying to push me down the hallway.

Regrettably, I tear my mouth from his. "As much as I

appreciate the enthusiasm, if we lose our uniforms, Coach will literally murder us. Not even being over dramatic."

Rolling his eyes, he agrees. "Shit. You're probably right."

The two of us separate and grab our bags off the elevator floor. When the goods are secured, I grab him by the hand and drag him down the hall until we find the door to our suite.

Swiping the keycard in front of the sensor, it unlocks the door, and I shove it open. As soon as Rocky's body clears the door, I slam it closed and pin him against it. "You sure you're ready for this?"

It isn't lost on me how big of a deal this is. This will be Rocky's first time having sex with a man, and regardless of what I said in the elevator, I want to give him one more chance. I would never push him into doing something he wasn't ready for.

I brace myself for rejection, but instead, I'm pleasantly surprised when he runs his fingers through my brown curls. Smiling, he says, "Show me what you got, *Garotão*."

CHAPTER 27
BRATTY BABY

ROCKWELL

"Show me what you got, *Garotão*." As the words leave my lips, I watch the switch in Clay flip.

His voice drops to a menacing tone. "Shower. Now."

Turning around to head to the bathroom door, I mock salute Clay. "Sir, yes, Sir."

*At lightning-fast speed, he's behind me, pushing his whole body against mine, plastering my front into the wall beside the bathroom door. His hand, gripping my hair on the back of my head, slowly turns my face to the side.

He growls into my ear, grinding his hard cock against my ass, "You better watch that smart mouth, *Baby*. I'm not afraid to stuff it full of your favorite cock."

I teasingly rub my ass across his groin, and he lets out a groan. I can feel the pre-cum lining the tip of my dick. I

---

* Who Do You Love? - YG, Drake

want this man viscerally. "You sound so fucking hot, *Garotão*. Keep going and I'll end up coming in my pants."

Having enough of my smart mouth, he grabs the back of my neck, finally walking us into the bathroom. "Strip," he commands, and I swear I've never taken clothes off so fast in my life. I'm fully bare to him when I finally look up, he's still fully clothed. "Take my shirt off for me."

His tone is suddenly soft, and a part of me wants to keep grating his nerves to keep feral Clay in this moment, but I also know the gravity of the situation we're in. It's not lost on me how big of a deal this is for both of us. For me. And I know he's going to want to take care of me, to be gentle, and what's more… I want him to.

Only this first time, though.

I step forward and reach for the bottom hem of his shirt, pulling it over his head. I take a minute to soak in and appreciate his toned body. Raking my eyes over him, meeting his deep brown eyes, he smirks at me, causing that dimple to pop out that makes me want to fall to my knees. "Now my pants, Baby."

I run my hands around the waistband of his athletic shorts, teasing him before pulling them down slightly to reveal the top of his cock. Fuck, his waist is so narrow compared to his broad shoulders. I grab his hips and run my hands up his side, humming in appreciation. Then, I do as he says, freeing his cock fully from his shorts. I pull them all the way down, letting his shorts pool at his feet, leaving his pulsing pierced cock bobbing between us.

I can't wait to feel that piercing inside of me.

"Clayton Aldrich, you truly are beautiful. Fucking perfect."

He blushes, grabbing my face as he replies, "No, Baby,

you're perfect, but whats more is we're perfect for each other."

Clay places the gentlest kiss on my lips before turning the shower on—if you can even call this thing a shower. It looks big enough to fit ten people with built-in shelves, seats, and six different shower heads. He just might have to pry me out of this thing. Suddenly, I can't help but wonder how much a suite in this place is even running him.

He puts his hand out for me, and I set mine in his grip, letting him pull me into the shower and under the water. I look between us and watch the water cascade over our bodies. Everything with Clay feels so right now. It's hard for me to believe that just a few short months ago, I couldn't get out of my own way. Too busy "hating" this man just because of where he came from, letting that cloud my judgment of who I *thought* he was. But now I know that there is almost nowhere I'd rather be than here. Being wrapped up in Clayton Aldrich feels so good. All I can hope is that I do the same for him.

Clay grabs a few pumps of soap and starts to run his hands all over my body, massaging the soap into my skin. Goosebumps follow his hands wherever they go. He gets my upper half soaped up, before his hand wraps around my dick. The other goes to my balls, but not long enough to enjoy. Before I have a chance to protest, he's down on his knees, cleaning my legs and feet. Once he's satisfied with his work, Clay stands and whispers, "Turn around, Baby. Bend over on the ledge. I'm going to clean this pretty hole of mine."

A wanton whimper leaves my mouth. Only Clay would have the ability to keep his tone soft and gentle while simultaneously saying the dirtiest things, leaving me more turned on than I thought possible.

It's so nice being able to turn my brain off when I'm with him. As a man, I usually take on the more dominant role in the bedroom, but being with another man who clearly loves to be in charge, I let my brain turn off. Focusing only on the pleasure coursing through my body.

I feel his soapy fingers reach my back entrance as he cleans around my hole with gentle pressure. Clay's pulling me up and under the water, running his hand up and down my crack, being sure to get the soap out, before he's pushing me right back into the same position. Bent over on the ledge, I'm holding myself up with my arms. I look back, and he's down on his knees, both of his hands spreading my ass apart.

"Fucking immaculate," Clay moans. Him calling any part of me *his* sends my stomach doing flips every time. I never knew possessiveness was a turn-on of mine… *but it sure as fuck is.*

With a flat tongue, he licks from my balls all the way up to the top of my crack.

"Oh, fuck, Clay." I try to clench my cheeks together, but that only has him spreading me open further.

"Don't try to hide from me, Baby. I want all of you." I relax at his words. Right as I melt into my arms, leaning over further on the ledge, he shoves his tongue into my ass. The stubble lining his chin and cheeks adds to the sensation causing me to shamelessly grind my ass up and down his face. "Use me, Baby. Use my face like the good boy you are."

Another whimper leaves my lips. "More, Clay. I need more."

I don't think about how new this all is or about how nervous I should be. All I can think about is how I need *more*.

More of Clay.

More of whatever he can give me.

The water abruptly turns off, and I'm being drug out of the shower. "Get on your back on the bed, knees to chest."

I listen to Clay's commands, not even bothering to dry off. Laying on the bed, I sprawl out and bring my knees up to my chest. I watch as Clay begins rummaging through his bag before pulling out a bottle of lube.

"Are you sure about this, Rocky?"

"Yes, Clay. I wouldn't be laying here with my asshole out on your hotel bed if I weren't... Now, will you please get at least your fingers inside me? I've been thinking about how hard it had me coming the last time..." I trail off, not sure how far I want to dive into my feelings or how much time I spend thinking about the man in front of me.

"You've been all I can think about for weeks now, Rock —" I throw my hand up in front of his face, cutting him off.

"Baby," I correct him. "We're not going back to Rocky again."

He flings his hands up in truce while striding over to me with the lube bottle in his hand and tossing it onto the bed. He runs his hands up the back of my thighs, humming in appreciation as they graze over my tattoos.

"I want to worship every inch of you, Baby." Clay pulls his lips between his teeth before he continues, "I've been waiting for this moment for way too long, and it's going to take every ounce of my willpower not to sink into you before you're ready." His feral behavior sends a shot of ecstasy straight to my cock.

He runs his hands up and down my thighs one more time before pushing me further backward, putting my ass up in the air for the perfect view from his end. Goosebumps line my skin from his eyes, looking at my most intimate area. I hear the click of the lube cap and feel the cold gel as it drops onto my skin. He's running two fingers around my hole, seemingly mesmerized. My body immediately relaxes and I sink further into the bed.

"Please, *Garotão*. I want to feel your fingers stretch me for that pierced cock of yours."

His eyebrows shoot up, and he questions, "The whore wants to be stretched?"

I'm smiling and nodding while looking into those deep brown eyes that seem to have gotten impossibly darker since we walked into this room. "You're going to use your words for me, Baby. I need to know what you like, and at any point, if it gets to be too much, tell me to stop."

"Yes, Sir." His eyes flare with hunger as he breaches my hole with the first lubed finger, and the neediest whimper escapes me. "More, *Garotão*. I need more. I'll be your good boy."

We lock eyes again, and he asks, "Are you sure you can be my good boy, Baby? You love being a brat ninety-nine percent of the time." He's rubbing that spot inside of me that has my eyes crossing in pleasure, but I still manage a response.

"I think you enjoy me being a br—" I hear the smack before the sting on my ass cheek registers, and at the same time he's finally adding the second finger, causing my back to bow off the bed. He lands one more smack on my ass in the same spot. The tender skin stings as I wait for the pain to turn into pleasure, and it finally does when his calloused hand, from years of weight-lifting and playing in the sand, runs over the tender flesh.

Dominant and firm, yet so so gentle.

A groan rumbles out of Clay, and he mutters, "Look at this hole stretching so nicely for me."

He's climbing on top of me with those fingers buried deep, rubbing along that spot that never fails to have my toes curling.

The lights from outside catch on the two dainty silver chains around his neck that are hanging over me. Never did I think that what would have my dick pulsing between me and another man would be his chains dangling over my face while he was finger fucking my ass... *but here I am.*

CHAPTER 28
NOT EVEN A LITTLE

CLAYTON

Reaching up, Rocky threads one finger through my two silver chains and twists them around it, pulling my face down until his lips brush against mine. I flex my two fingers, still buried deep inside of him, and his mouth opens on a deep groan.

"That's it, Baby. Let me hear you." I move my fingers back and forth until he's practically shaking beneath me, so close to the edge I'm desperate to push him over.

But not yet.

* "Clayton…"

"Hmmmm," I moan in appreciation as my dick drags along the mattress between his legs. "There it is."

His green eyes meet mine. "There what is?"

"My name. The way you say my name. It doesn't

---

* Cry to me- Marc Broussard

matter if you're pissed off, annoyed, or ready to come beneath me. Every time you say my name, it turns me on."

Leaning forward, I bite the side of his neck as I apply pressure to his prostate. "Clayton," he groans again.

"Yeah, Baby. Just like that." I can feel the pre-cum that's pooling on his stomach rub against my skin, so just as his entire body tightens, I slide my fingers from his ass, and the whimper that falls from his mouth has me nearly blowing on the spot. I bite and nip my way down his torso, feeling a perverse sense of satisfaction at watching the purple marks bloom as I go, until my mouth reaches the pre-cum pooled at his naval.

With the head of his dick brushing against the bottom of my chin, I look up at him, his pupils blown with lust and his breath heaving in anticipation, and stick my tongue out. The moment it touches his stomach he fists the sheets at his side. I take my time licking up the cum, careful not to miss a single drop, savoring the way it tastes on my tongue.

"Clay… *please…*"

"I want to come. Please make me come."

I run my tongue down the length of his shaft and he sucks in a deep breath. "You want to come for me?"

"Fuck yes."

Knowing he's ready, I quickly reach for the lube and squirt a generous amount on my dick, hissing the moment I wrap my hand around myself. Grabbing myself at the base I notch the head of it at his entrance. Rocky's entire body tenses. Leaning forward, I balance myself with my forearm on the bed while simultaneously cupping the side of his face. "You ready for me, Baby? You ready to take my dick like the good boy I know you can be?"

His eyes search mine before they narrow, and a hint of mischievousness takes over his face. He can never make anything easy, can he?

My hold on his face tightens. "Answer me."

"I hate you." He says it, but the smile on his face says otherwise.

Leaning forward, opposite my hand, I take the lobe of his ear between my teeth and pull; the hiss of pain that leaves his mouth is like music to my ears. "Hmmm, I hate you too, Rocky Baby."

I gently push my hips forward until only the head of my cock is nestled in his ass.

"Oh, shit. Holy fuck." His voice is strained as his body fights against the intrusion.

Helping him along, I gently bite his neck right below his ear before speaking against his skin. "I hate that you always have to fight me."

I push my hips forward a little more. "Bear down for me, Baby." He follows my instructions and I breath a sigh of relief as he lets me in. "Just like that," I praise and move my lips around to the front of his neck. Biting again.

"I hate that you're so smart, but you don't let anyone see it."

My hips move deeper, and my mouth bites down harder.

"I hate that you can see right through me."

Deeper. Harder.

Rocky's fingers dig into my delts as I fully seat myself inside of him. "I hate that nothing or no one has ever felt this fucking good."

"But you know what I hate the most?" I pull my hips

back until the head of my cock is the only thing that's inside of him.

"What?" he asks, his voice nothing more than a trembling whisper.

I slam my hips forward, and he cries out. I answer with my mouth against his, "I hate that I don't hate you. Not even a little bit. Not even at all."

"Clay…" The room is dark, but if I didn't know any better I'd swear I watch his eyes glass over. Whether it's from the intense feeling of me being buried inside of him or what I just said, I don't know. But I'm going to go with both.

My hips begin pistoning in and out of him at a steady pace. Reaching back, I grab his hands from behind me, one at a time, and pin them to the mattress above his head. With one hand firmly gripping both his wrists and one squeezing his hip, I say, "You feel so fucking good, Baby. So warm. So tight. So. Fucking. Perfect." I enunciate each word with a thrust. Rocky can't even speak anymore. The burn that once resided has now morphed into undeniable pleasure. "You were made for me, Rocky, Baby. Such a good fucking boy for me."

His hands flex against my hold, but I don't let him move an inch. I crash my mouth into him as it opens in a cry of pleasure, and with one more thrust of my hips, without even touching his dick, Rocky spills his cum between us, and I swallow every single pleasure-filled moan.

Only when I know he's coming down from his high do I let myself get lost in the moment. Knowing the second I do, I won't be able to last. I tear my mouth from his and bury my face in the crook of his neck, finally letting go of his hands, letting them fall to my back. As soon as his strong arms wrap around me, I know I'm done. With one more deep thrust, I hold myself deep inside his ass and spill inside of him, coming so hard I swear the feeling tears my soul apart and puts it back together with Rocky woven between every cracked and broken piece.

From this moment, I know that nothing will ever be the same. Who I am from here on out is wrapped up in Rockwell Campos.

With an overwhelming feeling of rightness settling inside of me, I tilt my head slightly, using my hand to force him to face me. And with my head resting next to his and our chests still heaving for air, I whisper, "I love you."

CHAPTER 29
REFRACTORY PERIOD

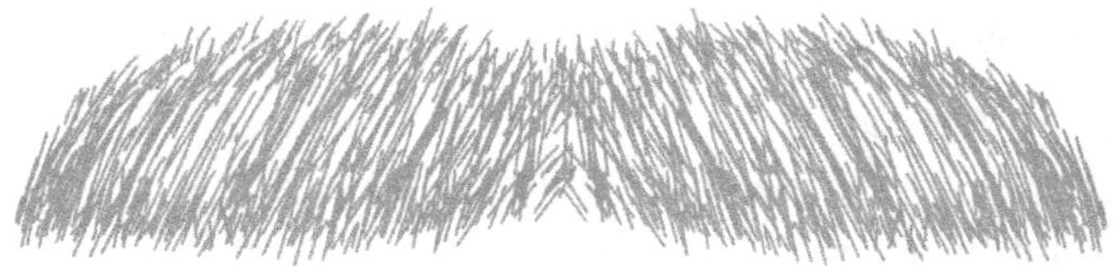

ROCKWELL

Clay's still holding my face, cock buried deep in me, and continues talking like nothing just happened, "I know I just blurted that out, but that doesn't mean I don't mean it. I *feel* deep, Baby, and what I feel for you is love. I feel it in the depths of my soul. So deep that you've embedded yourself into my very being. I know it. If you aren't ready to say it back, I totally understand; I'm not expecting you to, but I don't want to hold it in, and I refuse to take it back."

* Looking him in the eyes, I tell him, "You know how much you mean to me, Clay, but I'm just… I can't…" I don't miss the slight hurt on his face, but he recovers quickly. He pulls out of me slowly, and I feel his seed leaking out of me.

---

* Use Me - PLAZA

Why does that visual of him leaking out of me have my dick twitching?

Clay lays beside me as he holds my face and, with the gentlest smile, whispers, "I know. It's okay. My love for you isn't dependent on you saying it back."

His light shines so fucking bright, and I never want to be the reason it dims. So, I tell myself that I need to be open and honest with him from here on out when it comes to my emotions. This is my first relationship since being in college, and I know Clay has had nothing but short flings. I had a couple of girlfriends throughout high school but tried to stay away from anything that could've turned too serious. Mainly focusing on school and volleyball. Now my first real relationship will be with a man, and I need to wrap my head around that before I go spilling my feelings to him. No matter how deep they may be.

Trying to give him some reassurance I say, "If that was hate… then fuck me like you love me. Give me *everything.*"

Clay's smile grows practically wicked. "Oh, you have no idea what you just asked for."

I look down at his dick, and it's laying there hard as a rock on his stomach, ready to go again. I don't even know if it ever went down. "Do you have a thirty-second refractory period or something?"

I have never come and then ended up hard again that quick, but I just saw him do it with my own eyes.

"Or something…" he trails off with a mischievous grin, but then I watch as his entire demeanor changes and dominant Clay is out to play again. "Now flip over. I need my cum staying in you."

Fuck, that's hot.

I flip over onto my stomach and, just to pester him, say, "Yes, Sir."

A slap echos out, and the sting on the globe of my ass has me biting my bottom lip, trying to contain the moan that wants to come out.

"Now, what did I tell you about being a brat, Baby?"

Slap.

The quietest moan manages to escape me. The pain of the sting has me rutting my pulsing cock into the mattress. I don't answer him, fully aware of what my silence is going to earn me.

Slap.

Same spot as the last one, and I know my ass is turning a beautiful shade of red for him.

"I didn't say you could rub that cock of yours into the mattress, did I? Your pleasure's mine, from here on out. I want to milk the cum out of you until you're begging me to stop." An unexpected whimper leaves my lips as I bask in the mental image of what that would look and sound like.

He keeps going, and I know for a fact Clay's words are going to be the end of me. "I'm going to fuck this tight little hole of *mine*. Use you as a personal fucktoy made just for me."

"Please, *Garotão*. I need you inside of me." I don't know if I'm begging for him to fill me with cock or cum… At this point, probably both.

"What's your safe word? I don't want to hurt you, but I want to push you. I want to fuck you until you think you can't take anymore. I want my cock to be the only one you think about for the rest of your life." I smile over my shoulder at him, because I already know what it's going to be.

Chuckling because I know this will catch his attention, and I can't help myself, I say, "Shania."

His smile beams and my eyes focus in on those fucking dimples on his cheeks. With one hand, he pushes my face into the mattress. I hear him spit, feeling it land on my already soaking back hole a moment later. Clay lines himself back up and groans. "I don't think I've ever seen anything as sexy as my cum leaking out of you."

My body is shaking in anticipation to have him back inside me. The desire to feel his piercing rub across my prostate and the pure ecstasy of feeling him fill me up is indescribable.

Clay rubs the head of his cock up and down my crack. "You kept my cum nice and warm for me, didn't you, Baby? Does the whore want more?" I'm nodding my head up and down as much as I can while he has it pressed into the bed, then another slap lands on my already sensitive ass cheek. "Words, Rocky, or you won't get this cock again."

I shamelessly push my ass further up, trying to get him where I need him so desperately. "Please, Clay. Please, I want you to use me, fuck me, ruin m—" I'm cut off by him shoving his dick in me, breaching the ring of muscle, which he does a lot easier this time.

I feel him lean back, and then he's pulling me up to my knees. "Keep your chest on the bed. I need this perfect ass where I can see it." He's running his hands over the globes, and I hiss out in pain. That only pushes him further. He grabs my hips and starts pistoning into me. He has one leg up, getting an unimaginable angle, the perfect one to hit my prostate just right. "Wrap your hand around that fat cock of yours, Baby. I want to come together."

I start feverishly pumping my cock, whimpering, moaning, and begging, "Please fill me up, *Garotão*."

Clay practically growls, "I love to hear my toy beg." He hammers into me, and I'm matching my strokes to his. Before I know it, the tingling in my thighs has made its way up to the base of my spine, and I'm screaming, "I'm going to come. I-I'm-I'm coming."

I spill inside of my hand, and with a few more grunts from Clay, his cock is jerking inside me.

With his front plastered to my back, still buried deep inside me, he hums in satisfaction. "Fuck, that was good, Baby. I love you."

And as he presses a soft kiss against my shoulder blade, I know the words Clay said ring true. Just as I am in him, Clay is now a part of who I am. Embedded in me so deeply, I don't think I ever want to be without him.

CHAPTER 30
VACUUM-1 ROCKY-0

ROCKWELL

Lil's driving us to the airport today, and to say I wish I brought a goddamn turtle neck with me to California, regardless of it being the start of Summer, is an understatement. I turn to look at Clay, giving him a seething look that doesn't last more than a moment when he smiles at me. How can I even be mad at him when he looks so fucking happy?

*Plus, anytime I think about the hickeys covering me, I can practically feel the blush creep up my neck at the memory of the filthy shit he said and did to me all night long.

I spot Lil getting dropped off by an Uber in front of the hotel. If we were smart, we could've had her drop us off here last night, but we were in a little bit of a rush. She

---

* Dial Tone - Catch Your Breath

comes strutting up to us, and I see her eyes bug out of her head. I know I'm in for the ass-riding of a lifetime.

And not the good kind of ass-riding either.

Like she can't contain herself any longer, she blurts out, "You get into a fight with a vacuum, Rock man?" She snorts a laugh as she reaches for my neck, but the closer she looks, the less capable she is of holding it together. In the next breath, she's bent over wheezing, acting like this is the funniest shit she's ever seen. I peek over at Clay, seeing the little smirk lining his lips. I've never wanted to choke him out as much as I do right in this very moment.

A vacuum could never... and it's not even just my neck. He's marked my entire body. The feral caveman Clay turns into when fucking is a wild thing to experience, but I won't lie and say part of me doesn't love carrying his marks around on me.

Lil is up, finally done with the dramatics, reaching for me, but I pull away before she gets to me. I whisper-yell like I did when we were younger when I was trying to save her from getting in trouble with our parents. But now I'm just trying not to draw even more attention to us than we already are. "Lil! Stop. Let's get in the car so we're not late for our flight."

"Okay, okay. Don't get your panties in a twist." For my sanity, I pretend not to hear the high five she gives Clay behind my back as I storm toward the car.

Clay and I are in the back seat, sitting closer to each other than any teammates should ever be, and I can *almost* see the airport when Lil finally asks, "So... you two?"

Using her government name I warn, "Liliana."

"What? You really don't think I'm so oblivious not to notice you two staring at each other lustfully when you think no one's paying attention, practically drooling. I mean if the sneaking around shit is the kink you're playing, more power to you…" And like she remembers she left something out, continues with her questions, "Or when I would walk into your room, and you're cuddled up together? Or wh—"

Stopping her mid-sentence, with a clenched jaw, I rub my temples. "Enough. We're dating… I guess?" I turn my head slowly to get a read on Clay after those words fall out of my mouth. I just called him my goddamn boyfriend.

Boyfriend… That has a nice ring to it.

The most tender eyes are looking back at me, then that feral smile is back when he says, "Oh, Baby. You're sure as fuck, my boyfriend." He grabs my face with both of his hands and smashes his lips to mine. I close my eyes and melt into the back seat while Clay pushes against me, swallowing up my little whimpers. Then I hear Lil clear her throat, jarring me enough to push on Clay's shoulders, telling him, "Probably shouldn't do that in front of my sister."

He pouts like I just took away his birthday and mumbles, "Not like she doesn't know."

Before I know it, we are outside the airport at the drop off and all out of the car. I hug my sister, not knowing when the next time I'm going to be able to see her and whisper, "Thank you, Lil, for always being there for me."

Even being thousands of miles apart, I know she's always just a phone call away. We fought like cats and dogs growing up, but now I'd commit murder in broad daylight if anyone tried hurting her. She gives me shit about pretty much everything but is always there for me to lean on when I need her.

I pull back from the hug, and she has matching tears lining her eyes; her voice cracks when she finally responds, "Always, Rocky. You were made for each other. I can already tell. Protect him and his light." I've called her one too many times to bitch about his piece of shit dad, and I know that's what she's referring to. I just nod in response, knowing I'll fully burst out in tears if I try to speak. She knows I'll protect him with everything I have.

She spins to face Clay now, holding her arms out wide, ready to grab him up in a hug. When they're hugging, I watch as they speak in whispered tones, and when they pull away, Clay's eyes are brimming with tears too.

She breaks the silence with humor like always, laughing, "Clay, bud, you should have told me to bring my concealer for Rocky's neck. I could've thrown it in your bag before you two love birds left the house or brought it here." She's snickering into her fist. Now, her attention is on me, and she shrugs as I pin her with a glare. "Don't look at me like that. You're the one that's 0-1 with a vacuum."

CHAPTER 31

MILE HIGH CLUB

CLAYTON

Do not ask me why, but airports are one of my favorite places on earth.

They're like my Disney World.

Some people hate it, but I swear, if I could sit at an airport whenever I felt like it, I would. You want a drink at 7:30 a.m.? Go for it. Want to sit at a window and watch planes land and take off? Check. Do you like to spend hours people-watching? You've got it. Want to eat at a five-star steak house for lunch, then walk five steps to get a McFlurry at McDonald's? It's all yours.

It's like there are no rules.

Except the ones strictly enforced by the federal government and the FAA of course. But besides that... the world is your oyster!

Clearly, Rocky doesn't share the same sentiment because the longer we sit at our gate, the more agitated he looks. You'd think a night of being fucked senseless would loosen him up, but clearly not.

I should know better, really. Sometimes I feel like I'm in love with Carl Fredrickson from *Up!* Warm and soft on the inside, cold and hard on the outside.

Maybe I should find him a talking dog... help loosen him up a little bit. Worked for Carl.

Rocky's leg continues to tap furiously in the seat next to me, his elbow propped on the armrest as he rests his scowling face against his hand. "You know for someone who flies several times a year, you're not a very relaxed traveler," I say, leaning down to whisper in his ear.

He shoots me a clearly perturbed look out of the corner of his eye. "I actually don't mind traveling, Clayton. But our flight has already been delayed twice; everyone keeps staring at me because I look like a fucking leopard, and"— he winces as he shifts in his seat, and I have to bite my lip to keep from laughing because I know exactly what he's about to say next—"my ass feels like—"

"You got fucked six ways to Sunday?"

His head snaps in my direction, and his eyes widen. For a moment, I really think he's going to hit me, but then I notice the deep shade of blush covering his almond skin, which is now a few shades darker than it was at the start of the season. I take my chances and wrap my hand around his thigh, stopping his leg from bouncing. "I gotta say, I've been enjoying watching you limp around this airport."

Rocky narrows his eyes at me as I now shift in my seat, fighting the erection that's growing beneath my joggers. "Is that why you've been dragging me all around this god-forsaken airport?"

"No. Well, I mean... I really like airports, but watching you is an added bonus." I lean in to kiss his cheek before stopping myself, not knowing how much PDA he will be comfortable with, if any at all. Then I remember my hand is still wrapped around his thigh, where it seems to fall so naturally. But, as I start to pull it away he wraps his hand around mine and holds it there.

I'm about to suggest we go grab some ice cream from the shop a couple of gates down when the gate agent's voice sounds from the intercom, signaling that boarding is about to begin. Grabbing our carry-ons, I stand from my chair, but Rocky grabs my hand and tries to pull me back down. "Easy, *Garotão*. We don't need to crowd the gate. We might as well just wait here."

I smile proudly down at him. For a moment, I forgot he didn't know about this part of the surprise. "Nah, we get to be one of the first ones to board." I pull him to a standing position. "One of the first in line, Baby." He pinches his brows in confusion, and I huff a laugh while nodding to the gate agent. "Just come on."

Somehow, Rocky sneaks in front of me, so I reach around him and hand the gate agent our tickets, which I wouldn't let him hold onto. Once we get onto the plane, Rocky begins to walk toward the economy seats. Reaching out to grab his wrist, I stop his movements. "What? Come on, I don't want to hold up the line. What seats are we anyway?"

Nodding to the side, I grin ear to ear. "Right here."

Rocky does a double take, looking to the first-class seats, then to me, then back to the seats, before finally looking back at me slack-jawed. "Clay... you didn't?"

"Oh, but I did, Baby. And I don't want to hear a word

about it; this trip was for you, and I wanted to spoil you." I lean forward so my face is merely an inch away from his, and speak quiet enough for only him to hear, "Now close you're mouth unless you want me to find something useful to do with it." Standing up straight, I smile and motion for him to sit. "Hurry up now, don't want to hold up the line."

A flight from San Diego to Pensacola takes just under six hours, which is long enough for them to serve an in-flight meal. So, just over two hours into the flight, Rocky and I have both enjoyed our dinners, and I am now settling in to watch a movie while Rocky cracks open a book he got at the bookstore in the airport. I smile as I watch him get comfortable in his first-class seat.

I'm not going to lie, the seats did cost me a pretty penny since I booked them so last minute, but knowing that Rocky is ending his trip on an exciting note makes every dollar spent more than worth it.

Our seats are nothing overly extravagant, but they certainly aren't economy. Each first-class seat has partitions on three sides, with a retractable door facing the aisle. The partition facing the middle also slides away in case you'd like to chat with whoever is sitting next to you. Obviously, I've kept ours open the entire time, wanting to have an unobstructed view of Rocky experiencing this for the first time.

Not the last either, if I have any say in it.

*With both of our aisle doors closed, I lean my seat back as far as it will go, stretch my legs all the way out—being able to do that makes these tickets worth it in and of itself—and settle in to watch *10 Things I Hate About You*. I must have drifted off to sleep because a bump to my leg causes my eyes to open after what only feels like a few minutes, yet when I look at the screen in front of me, Kat and Patrick are already kissing in the school parking lot. However, that's not what shocks me the most because the nudge that woke me up was Rocky situating himself on the floor in front of me between my spread legs, and now he's staring up at me with that look that tells me he's up to no good.

Quickly, I look around the cabin to ensure no flight attendants are walking down the aisle because they can easily see over the partitions. Thankfully, there's no one to be found, and with the time-zone changes as we fly toward Florida, the cabin is now dark. A few overheard lights remain on, and I'm sure most of the passengers are either wrapped up in a movie or are asleep, but the fact still remains that we are on a plane filled with people just feet away.

And if he's about to do what I think he's about to do, I'm so. Fucking. Here. For. It.

Unable to help myself, I thread my hand through his jet-black curls. "If you're doing what I think you're doing, I literally might die right here in this seat."

Rocky tugs his bottom lip between his teeth before smiling. "You said you'd find something to keep my

---

* act ii: date @ 8 (feat. Drake) - 4batz, Drake

mouth busy, and…" he sighs dramatically. "I got bored reading, so I figured why not thank you for the trip."

"You don't need to thank me for anything, Baby. I did it because I wanted to." I don't want him to think he ever has to thank me with sexual favors when I do something for him just because I know it will make him happy.

Rocky's eyes soften. "I know you did, and I want to do this. Please let me."

There's an apprehensiveness to his tone, as if he thinks I'm really going to turn him away.

Never, in a million fucking years.

"Better be quick. Wouldn't want anyone to see us." The corner of his lips raise, as if he knows that's utter bullshit. We both know I'd love for someone to walk by, but I'm not particularly fond of getting put on the no-fly list, so my statement holds some weight.

"You love the thought of someone seeing your cock down my throat, don't you?" The second the question leaves his lips, my chest heaves in excitement because, yeah, I really fucking do.

I lift my hips slightly, allowing Rocky to pull down my joggers so they rest just below my ass, and when he sees my dick, already dripping with pre-cum at the tip, he licks his lips in anticipation. Before I even have the chance to speak another word, he has his hand wrapped around the base as he slides my length into his mouth. And for someone who has had very limited practice with someone else's dick, he shows not an ounce of hesitation.

I hiss a sharp breath when the head of my cock hits the back of his throat. Rocky slowly slides me out of his mouth before running the tip of his tongue along my piercing. I clench my teeth so hard that I'm surprised I don't chip a tooth as I fight the groan that wants to spill from my lips.

Knowing we need to speed this along, I tighten my grip on the back of his head. My eyes lock with his, silently asking permission for what I'm about to do. And with a slight nod, he opens his mouth.

I fuck his mouth fast, careful not to push too deep, knowing the sounds of him gagging on my cock wouldn't exactly be subtle. Rocky hollows out his cheeks while I slide in and out of him as he reaches up to cup my balls.

The fact that we could get caught any moment, coupled with the sensation of his mouth around me and his hands on me, is too much. It only takes a few more seconds before I press my hand over my mouth and cum down his throat.

And like the good boy he is, he swallows every last fucking drop.

Pulling off of me, he wipes his mouth with the back of his hand and rocks forward so he's in a crouched position. Rocky grabs the front of my shirt and pulls me forward. "I think I could get used to first class."

And with a quick kiss to my lips, he's climbing back into his seat. Leaving me completely and utterly speechless.

Miracles do *exist.*

CHAPTER 32
HIGHS AND LOWS

CLAYTON

A loud banging on my apartment door wakes me from my sleep. Groaning, I roll over to check the time on my phone.

7:45 a.m.

This better be fucking good. Rocky and I flew home Friday, and after a few delays at the airport in San Diego we didn't land in Florida until late. By the time we got our checked bags, found my car in the parking garage, and each made it back to our respective apartments, it was in the early hours of the morning.

As much as I wanted Rocky to spend all day Saturday at my apartment, the two of us both had schoolwork to catch up on, laundry to wash, and groceries to get. It's now Sunday morning, and I still feel exhausted.

Without answering the door, I already know who it is. Only two people would have the balls to show up at my apartment at this hour on a Sunday morning, and only one of those people would willingly be up this early.

The pounding continues and I roll my eyes. Throwing on a pair of black sweats over my briefs, not even bothering with a shirt, I pad down the hallway and through the kitchen and living room, rubbing my eyes. I'm five feet away from the door when I snap, "Good fucking Christ, Jackson. Would you have some fucking patience?"

Unlocking the front door, I throw it open, and his fist almost hits me in the face as he attempts to bang it against the door some more. "It's about time."

He brushes past me and walks right into my kitchen; you wouldn't know that just a few months ago, the guy blew apart his knee. Helping himself to my coffee grounds, he throws them into the coffee maker to brew us a pot. "Good morning, Jackson. Please, do come in."

Closing my front door, I sit on the kitchen stool as he moves about my kitchen as if it were his own. "Don't 'good morning, Jackson' me. I gave you one whole day to rest, and now I need to know."

Running my hands through my bed head, I sigh. "Need to know *what?*"

Jax looks at me deadpan. "You and Rocky. What happened last week?"

"Since when are you so invested in my relationships?"

"Ummm, since you actually fucking have one, even though the two of you like to act like you don't. Everyone sees it, Clay. You guys aren't as subtle as you think you are. Even Theo—"

He cuts himself off, as if he's said something he didn't mean to. Choosing to ignore the smart-ass remark about me having a relationship, I focus on the name he said just before he stopped talking. Jax spins around to grab a couple of mugs out of the cabinet. As he's pouring some of the delicious-smelling coffee into them, I ask, "Theo? As in Theodore Young? As in the athletic trainer?"

"Hmmm?" He pretends he didn't hear me as he slides the mug across the counter, but I'm not buying his bullshit. "Jackson…"

"Clayton," he counters.

"What have you been doing talking to Theo? You're not even playing anymore and he's not even you're physical therapist?"

Jax chews on the corner of his bottom lip, which he only does when he's feeling nervous. He opens and closes his mouth a few times as if he's trying to work up the courage to say something before shaking his head. "Nothing. I'm not. Don't try to change the subject." He points his finger across the counter at me. "Tell me what happened."

I look at my best friend for a moment and realize he doesn't look like his usual self. Whereas I look half-dead from a weekend full of travel and time zone changes, Jax looks… exhausted. His black hair is completely disheveled, and his bright blue eyes don't have any of their usual shine. There are dark circles underneath his eyes, and his clothes look wrinkled and worn. Like he's had them on for hours instead of just putting them on this morning.

But if there's one thing I know about Jax, it's that if he wanted to tell me something, he would, and if he's not ready, then there's no use in pushing him. He and I may share the same upbeat personality, but he's far more secretive than I'll ever be. Which I'd assume has a lot to do with the fact that he grew up with three younger and incredibly invasive brothers.

* Relenting, I take a long and slow sip of my coffee, Jax's eyes not straying from mine, before saying, "We hooked up."

"And?"

I knew that wasn't going to be the answer he was looking for. I've shared a lot about my relationship with Rocky to Jax. He's my best friend and brother, and I know I can trust him to keep my private life private. He's also one of the smartest people I know and has always encouraged me to stay true to my feelings, even when I confided in him my developing feelings for Rocky after his birthday party.

Sighing, knowing he's not going to drop it until he hears what he wants to, I finally confess the thing I've only said to myself. "I-I think he's the one, Jax."

"No shit. You think?" I pin him with a lethal glare and he chuckles as he holds up his hands in defense. "Sorry, continue."

"I've never felt like this about anyone in my life, man. I told him I love him, Jax."

Jackson's eyes go wide in surprise. "You did?"

"Yeah, I did. You know me… if I'm feeling something, I say it. We were just having this really special moment, and all of a sudden, everything I've felt for him since this whole thing started just felt so big, and I couldn't… I couldn't hold it in anymore."

"I'm assuming he didn't say it back."

I shrug and tell Jax the same thing I told Rocky,

---

* Beautiful Things - Acoustic - Benson Boone

meaning it wholeheartedly. "No, he didn't. But it's okay. He's not ready, and I wasn't expecting him to be. The way I feel about him isn't dependent on him reciprocating those feelings right away."

Jax's eyes soften as he asks, "How do you know? How do you know Rocky is it?" As I look at him, I get the feeling he's asking for himself just as much as he is for me.

I think about my answer for a moment before explaining, "For as long as I can remember, I've moved through almost every minute of every day with a giant weight on my chest. The expectations of everyone around me, of my parents... my father, of myself, feel so heavy sometimes it's almost debilitating. I've found ways to lighten the load, but it's never fully gone. But when I'm with Rocky... he feels like the drug for all my anxiety, Jax. All my panic. All of my fears. All of my *anger*. It's in the way he looks at me. The way he touches me. The way he speaks to me. The way he believes in me. It's just... *him*."

Jackson smiles softly at me from across the counter, but I notice the water that pools at his lower lids before he blinks it away. "Shit, man."

"Yeah." I huff a laugh. "Shit is right."

Jackson hangs out in my apartment for a few more hours as he listens to my stories about my week with Rocky's family. And the more I talk about my teammate, my partner, the man that I love... I know that, without a doubt, everything I just confessed to Jax is true.

Rocky is it.

Now, I just have to wait for him to realize it.

It's now Tuesday evening, and I was riding the high from spring break with Rocky all the way through our Monday morning practice and throughout classes today… that is until we just got our asses handed to us by Virginia State. And on our home turf, no less.

It wasn't that Rocky and I even played terribly, and it could easily be contributed to our fun-filled week in San Diego, but the fact of the matter is, Virginia's players just got off spring break, too. Sometimes you just get steamrolled, and there's fuck all you can do about it. Once you're too far behind in points in volleyball, it's extremely hard to recover.

And that's exactly what happened.

We didn't win a single fucking set. Not one.

As if that wasn't bad enough, Rocky got pulled to the side for an interview—of which I managed to avoid much to his despair—and the first thing I find when I pull my phone out of my bag in the locker room after I've showered is a string of texts from dear old Dad.

DAD

> You looked beyond sloppy in the first set, Clayton.

> Your hits weren't connecting as they should be. Clean it up. Don't be an embarrassment.

> I told you Rockwell Campos wasn't going to do you any favors.

> You have no chance of upholding the Aldrich legacy with a partner that does nothing but weigh you down.

> That match was a fucking disgrace. The two of you should be ashamed. We will discuss this later.

As I read each text, the grip on my phone tightens to the point that I worry it will shatter in my hand. I can feel my vision tunneling and my chest tightening. My eyes begin to well with tears as I recognize the all too familiar signs. "No, no, no. Not here. Not now."

Not wanting to do this here, I quickly turn off my phone and shove it to the bottom of my bag before throwing on my clothes. With my bag slung over my shoulder and my body fighting for air, I all but run out of the locker room. As soon as I round the corner I run square into the man who has quickly become my solace. But he can't see me like this.

I can't let him see me like this.

"Hey, thanks a lot for making me do—whoa, Clay. What's going on? What's the matter?" I hear the panic in his voice, but I can't stay here. I need to get home.

As he reaches to cup my face in his hands, I dodge his

grasp. "Nothing. I-I." My voice catches as it becomes harder to breathe. "I need to go."

I step around him and speed to my car, ignoring his calls for me to come back.

By some miracle, I manage to make it back to my apartment building. Feeling like the drive might have calmed me down for a moment, I realize I'm sorrily mistaken when I see the very cause of my impending panic attack standing in front of my building. One hand tucked into the pant of his suit, the other holding the phone to his ear.

"D-Dad?" I shake my head in disbelief as I walk up to him. "What-what are you doing here?"

He rolls his eyes and removes the phone from his ear. "Clayton, I've been trying to call you."

Fuck. "I haven't been able to check my phone. It's-it's dead."

Lies.

My fingers start to become numb as I flex them into fists at my side. If he sees me fall apart, I'll never hear the end of it. Aldrich men are stronger than this. We don't let the pressure get to us. We stand tall in the face of adversity.

"Care to explain what the hell happened out on that court?"

"You're here? You came to my game?" It's pathetic that the simple act of my own father driving a few hours to watch his only son play a sport he loves surprises me, yet here we are. But of course, this is the one game he chose to show up to.

"I had a meeting this afternoon with some investors in town. They knew you played for the school and had a game today, so they suggested we go watch it as a show of goodwill toward me. When it became clear all you were going to do was embarrass me, I was able to get them to leave early, and I came straight here."

And there it is. His being here had nothing to do with me. This trip was all about him.

Everything is *always* about him.

He pins me with his most disappointed glare, and I can feel chills begin to sweep over my body while a bead of sweat travels down my spine at his disapproval.

I need to get upstairs. He can't see me like this.

No one can see me like this.

I open my mouth to respond, but I can't get any words to come out. My dad continues to ramble on, but I don't hear a single thing he says because, over his shoulder, I watch as Rocky's car comes to a screeching halt in front of my building.

This cannot be happening.

Rocky cannot see this happening.

Before Rocky even closes the door of his car, I'm already in my building sprinting for the elevator with my dad calling after me just like Rocky did outside of the locker room.

But I know that all Rocky wanted to do was make sure I was okay; all my Dad wanted to do was ensure that I felt less and less okay.

As I finally reach the door to my apartment, I manage to unlock it before my vision fades to black, and I collapse right in the doorway.

CHAPTER 33
444

ROCKWELL

I pull in front of Clay's apartment complex, and before I even have a chance to get out of the car, I watch him sprint inside.

I run up to a man who's facing away from me, dressed in a suit—a very expensive suit. I round the man to face him, and I immediately recognize who I'm looking at. He's practically a carbon copy of Clay, just with wrinkles around the eyes and gray in his hair. "Tell me what you did. Now!"

"Rockwell Campos. How good it is to see you." He may look just like my Clay, but I can immediately tell he's nothing more than a goddamn wolf in sheep's clothing.

Disgust lines my face; this man radiates negativity. I drop my tone and practically growl, "What did you say to him?"

"Nothing that he didn't need to hear. Rockwell, you need to get seri—"

Snarling, I throw my hand up in his face, cutting him off. I don't want to hear anything this putrid man has to say. "You know what, it doesn't even matter." I look him up and down one more time as heat radiates through my body. "Clay may be a spitting image of you, but the man I'm falling for is *nothing* like you. You disgust me. Clay's soul isn't dipped in tar, like yours."

Not giving a shit what he has to say in return, I turn my back to him and jog into Clay's apartment building; I quickly realize I haven't been here yet and have no goddamn clue which apartment is his. There have to be hundreds of units in this damn high-rise.

I grab my phone out of my pocket and call the only person I can think of. Jax. He picks up on the first ring, and I ask in a panic, "What's Clay's apartment number?"

"Ohhhh, is this some kind of primal hunt thing? He may want to be chased longer… let me text him."

What in the fuck is he talking about?

"Jax! Now. I don't have time for this shit!"

"No kink-shaming here, Rockwell. It's apartment 444." Hearing the angel number brings tears to my eyes. *Protection*. That's what I hope this apartment was for him—an escape from being under his father's nose..

I hang up on Jax, pocket my phone, and start sprinting up the four flights of stairs. I run full speed down the hallway when I come to an abrupt stop at the site before me. The door to apartment 444 is wide open—Clay is lying unconscious on the floor.

*"Clay!" I gather my bearings and take the last few strides to reach him. Dropping down to the floor I begin

---

* Never Know - Bad Omen

shaking him as I scream out his name. What the fuck happened between outside and now?

I check for his pulse, and his heart rate is beating a hundred miles a minute; that's when it dawns on me...

He's in a full-on panic attack.

Brought on by his piece of shit Father.

Adrenaline is pumping through my veins as I pick him up and throw him over my shoulder. After making sure I hear the door to his apartment close behind me, I take him down the hall, which I'm assuming leads me to his bedroom. I know my assumptions are correct when I see piles of clothes scattered throughout the room as I walk through the first open door. It's not lost on me that this is not how I wanted to see his apartment for the first time.

I lay him down on the bed and start to strip him out of his clothes.

I whisper to him in the calmest tone I can manage, hoping something, anything, pulls him out of this, "*Garotão*, I have you." I pull his shoes and socks off, along with his pants. "You're safe now, Clay. Your Dad's gone." It's taking everything in me to keep my anger at bay at the mention of his dad, but he doesn't need that right now. He needs me to be calm and present.

Stripping out of my clothes as fast as possible, I head into the en suite bathroom to turn the shower on. Leaving the shower to warm up, I head back to Clay. I gently sit him up so I can start freeing him of his clothes. He is able to hold himself upright, and I realize that he's starting to regain some semblance of consciousness. His breathing is still erratic, but at least we're getting somewhere.

As we walk toward the bathroom, I continue to soothe,

"Clay, I'm going to get us in the shower, okay?" I see his head nod slightly.

Together we step under the stream of hot water in his oversized shower. Grabbing his soap, I start to clean his body gently while praising and affirming his psyche, "You're okay, Clay. Breathe for me. You're doing so good. Just breathe." He takes a shuddering breath and it kills me to see him have to fight these panic attacks all because of the person who raised him. The person he's always supposed to be able to turn to for support. But he's never had that. Every problem he's ever faced, he's had to face alone. Yet, despite all of that, Clayton Aldrich is a beacon of light. One that shines bright for everyone around him. "Come back to me, and we can bake all the cookies... I can't live without you, Clay. You have to come back to me."

I'm not brave enough to say this in English yet, so I take the coward's way out knowing he won't understand my confession, *"Acho que estou me apaixonando por você."*

Fuck that felt good.

Right as the words leave my mouth his eyes pop open, and I swear there's a slight curve to his lips. Maybe he finally put two and two together and the Portuguese makes him more aware that I'm here with him.

However, the smile quickly fades, and he begins looking at his surroundings like a scared, wounded animal, likely trying to make sense of how he got here and what's going on. All I want to do is make all of the hurt go away, so I ask, "What do you need? Tell me what you need."

"I-I need you to take it away. Take it all away. *Please.*"

CHAPTER 34
A MAYBE NOT-SO-MISERABLE MAN

CLAYTON

I watch Rocky's face as what I'm asking finally seems to register. His breath catches in his throat and his eyes widen. "Clay… you want me to—"

"Yes. Please, Rocky." He didn't finish that sentence, but he didn't need to. He and I both know exactly what I'm asking for.

*He takes my face in his hands, gently stroking my cheeks with the pads of his thumbs, wiping away any tears that may have fallen. His eyes search mine for a second, trying to figure out if this is something that I truly want or if it's the anxiety attack talking. Turning my head, I gently kiss the palm of one of his hands, all while keeping my eyes locked on his pools of green, silently reassuring him that this is what I want.

What I *need.*

---

*   Sweet Symphony - Joy Oladokun ft. Chris Stapleton

"I don't want to feel it. Any of it. All I want to feel is you. Make it go away, Baby."

He heaves a sigh of relief, as if me finally managing to string that many words together allows him to breathe just a little bit easier. With my face still in his hands, he tips it forward and places a deep yet gentle kiss on my forehead, and what normally feels like such an ordinary act of intimacy feels like anything but. I swear I can feel the caress of his lips all the way down to my toes.

His lips linger for a moment before he releases his hold on my face, turns the shower off, and pulls me through the bathroom and into my bedroom, not bothering to dry either of us off. Rocky spins me around so I'm facing him, and with his hands on my waist, he pushes me toward the side of the bed until the backs of my knees hit the edge. He gently pushes me so I'm sitting in front of him and he's standing between my spread legs. With a tenderness I've never seen from him, he reaches up and brushes my wet hair off of my forehead; when his fingers thread through my hair, I moan into his touch as the pads of his fingers gently massage my scalp. I can feel the exhaustion taking over my body. I haven't had a panic attack that intense in years, and even the mildest of ones make me want to do nothing but crawl into bed for twenty-four hours. But I want this more.

I want to let go. I want him to take care of me in the way I crave to be taken care of. I want this for me. For him. For *us*.

"You are beautiful, Clayton Aldrich," he whispers lovingly as he looks down at me.

"Hmmm," I groan in contentment. "I love when you say my name like that."

He huffs out a laugh. "So you've said."

With one hand on the center of my chest, he pushes until my back is flat against the bed. His fingers trail gently over the expanse of my body, stopping when they reach the tattoo on my collarbone that says "No risk, no story" in a thin script font. "When did you get this?"

"Beginning of sophomore year. Jax has the same one."

Rocky smiles softly. "You love him, huh?"

I do, without a doubt. So I answer plainly, "He's my brother."

Not needing any further clarification, the stroke of his fingers moves across the side of my rib cage, tracing the black ink that covers it. He reads the text written there, but phrases it as a question rather than a statement, "All we wanted was a place to feel like home?"

I shrug, the meaning behind this tattoo being a little more complicated than the first. "It's a lyric from the song 'Miserable Man.'"

"You really like that song or something?" A knowing look passes over his face, fully understanding that the quote means more to me than it simply being my favorite song.

But I don't want to get into that right now so I nod and answer, "Or something."

Rocky bends over and, much like he did to my forehead in the shower, places a soft kiss over the ink. And much like it did in the shower, his kiss sends a wave of rightness through my body. He hasn't even kissed me on the lips since we've been here, and yet, I feel more connected to him right now than I ever have.

Instead of righting himself, Rocky moves his head to the center of my stomach. While looking up at me, he whispers, "You are so much more than you think you are, Clay. You are capable." He places another light kiss on the center of my stomach and moves up until his face hovers over the right side of my chest.

"You are an incredible athlete."

Kiss.

He moves to the left side of my chest. "This heart… Shit, this fucking heart makes you one of the best people I know."

Kiss.

I feel tears well in my eyes as he moves to the base of my neck. "You make anyone you talk to feel like they're the most important person in the room."

Kiss.

"And this mouth." His lips hover on the corner of my mouth, and regardless of how much I want him to kiss me, how much I want to lose myself in him, I want to hear what he has to say more. "I love every single sound that comes out of it, regardless of how ridiculous you're being."

He kisses one corner before moving to the other, and for the first time since before our game started, I feel myself smile.

"And I love the way it feels on me." As much as I want to come up with some smart remark, I simply don't have the energy.

Finally, his mouth makes its way back up to my forehead, and he says the one thing that could have me fall apart right here, right now, if I let it. "You have so much to offer this world, Clay. See it. Own it. Recognize it. And don't let anyone tell you differently. Not now. Not ever."

His face hardens as his eyes search mine. "Do you understand?"

"I understand," I answer softly. Just when I think he's finally going to give me what I want, he stands in a rush.

Opening my bedside drawer, he smirks when he reaches in and grabs a bottle of lube. Squirting some in the palm of his hand, he reaches down and fists his cock. His hard cock.

I hadn't even noticed it until now, entirely too focused on the way his words were washing over me.

Rocky squirts some more lube on his fingers as he instructs, "Scoot back a little for me. Feet on the bed." His voice has dropped a couple of octaves, sending a wave of heat to my dick. I follow his instructions, and a look of satisfaction crosses his face once he notices me getting hard.

Positioning himself between my legs, he kneels on the bed. He rests one hand on the top of my knee before reaching down and rubbing his lubed fingers around my hole. Without much preamble, he shoves two fingers deep inside of me. My eyes close as I groan into the otherwise silent room.

"Uh-uh." His fingers don't move. "You look at me. Don't take your eyes off of me, Clay. If you want me to give you everything, you show me *everything*."

Looking him dead in the eye, I say with every ounce of confidence, beyond sure that I want this, "Fuck me, Baby. Fuck me, now." I want to feel him inside of me. Now.

"But—"

I shake my head. "I don't need it."

He looks at me for a moment before nodding and

removing his fingers. And in that moment I realize how much he trusts me.

Rocky leans forward, resting himself on the forearm that is pressed into the mattress next to my head, as he fists his cock with the other hand. I run my hands over his hips and grip his waist when I feel his head nudge against my entrance.

"Do it."

Without any further preparation, Rocky plunges himself deep inside of me. My back bows off the bed, as the two of us groan in unison. My jaw drops open as I savor every ounce of pleasure in the pain. Because this is exactly what I wanted. I wanted to feel nothing but him. Nothing but us.

Rocky stares down at me as I try to catch my breath, neither of us moving an inch. He repeats his words from earlier, and between the overwhelming sense of fullness, and the passion in his voice, a tear finally manages to escape. This one is so much different from the ones I shed in the shower only minutes ago. "So fucking beautiful, Clay."

Rocky pulls out of me, and in a fluid motion, his mouth crashes against mine as he slams his hips forward. Finally, the familiar tickle of his mustache against my lips makes my entire being feel like it's exactly where it's supposed to be. Nothing else matters if I don't have him.

Nothing.

As he continues to thrust in and out of me, the sounds of our wanton moans and the echos of skin slapping against skin fill the room. I haven't so much as touched my cock, and I know I'm not going to need to. Because regardless of how much I want this moment with him to last, the sensation of him filling me—coupled with the insurmountable love I have coursing through me for this man—is almost to much to bear. And before I even know what's happening, ecstasy races down my spine. I pull my mouth from his, and I come with a roar, my eyes locked on his the entire time. Calling his name like it's my every prayer and salvation.

Like he was waiting for my release, still deep inside of my ass, I feel his cock pulse inside of me as he comes. "Fuck! Clay!"

The two of us lay there for what feels like hours when in reality, I know it's only a few minutes. The sweat covering our faces and my cum between us causing our bodies to stick together as we catch our breaths.

"Thank you. For everything," I whisper softly, as he rests his head on my shoulder.

As his dick softens inside of me, his hand finds its way to my hair again, this time mindlessly curling the hair between his fingers. "You're welcome."

When it's clear neither of us is in any hurry to move, I say the only words I have the energy left to say, "I love you, Baby."

And even though I know he feels it too, I'm not expecting him to say it back. Instead, I do feel him smile against my skin as his body melts against mine. "So you've said."

CHAPTER 35

FINDING BOOKS?

ROCKWELL

It's the end of April, and the tournament is so close I can practically taste it. The end of our senior year is creeping up on us fast, and with that comes finals. With that being said, Clay and I are in the library studying our little hearts out. Correction: Clay has been studying his heart out; I've just been staring at him, admiring each vein on the top of his hand that's holding his pencil, the long thick lashes fanned over his cheeks as he reads, and wondering how I've gotten so lucky to be able to call him mine.

We've been living in our happy bubble, newly dating, winning games, and keeping up with schoolwork. Clay hasn't brought up whatever happened outside of his apartment with his father nor have I asked him to. He will talk to me about it if and whenever he's ready. I'm not going to lie, finding him unconscious on the floor scared the ever-living shit out of me. But once he came to, the light that showed in his eyes as he realized I was the one that was holding him—and what happened after—the way the two of us connected on an entirely different level was… it healed something inside of me that I didn't even know needed healing. Yet, there's still an ache inside of me. An ache so deep in my soul for him to have the love he deserves. I know I can give that to him, and so can my family.

"Where the hell is Jax at?" I ask, forcing myself to stay in the moment.

"I have no clue. He was supposed to be here twenty minutes ago."

I grab my phone off the table and send out a text in our ridiculous group chat.

ROCKY

Where the hell are you, Jax?

Clay grabs his phone off the table, too, not wanting to miss the opportunity to give his best friend shit.

GAROTÃO

Even computer geniuses like you need to study, Jackson. Chop chop.

Clay's text is nothing but jokes, but when I look over at him, he's staring into the distance, concern etched across his face. "I really hope he's okay. He's been acting off the last couple of months. I chalked it up to him getting hurt his senior year, but I think it's more than that." Clay doesn't need anything else to worry about on top of how his dad treats him, but that doesn't mean I want him to ignore the clear signs that something has been going on with Jax.

It's been the same old, same old as far as Charles Aldrich is concerned. When we win games, he leaves Clay the hell alone. But if we lose... or don't absolutely demolish our opposing team, I have to have a pick-up order ready at Delectable Desserts. Sometimes, I don't know if it's the baking or Nancy's sweet smile and Kevin's groans of annoyance that put Clay in a better mood.

Keeping him away from his phone is my highest priority after losses, though. It shouldn't be like this. A child shouldn't want to avoid their father for the fear of crippling anxiety taking over from a simple text message. A child shouldn't never speak or hear from their mother. As much as I'd love for my partner to have a relationship with their parents, I'll never push Clay to put himself in that position. Not to mention, I'll have a hard time ever laying eyes on Charles or Evelyn Aldrich again without saying something I shouldn't. I have no kind words for people who treat their child the way they've treated him.

JAX

Pulling into the parking lot. And fuck right off, Clay. You wish you were as smart as me.

Jax comes strolling in a couple of minutes later, looking a little better than he has the last couple of times I've seen him. I haven't known him well the past four years, always keeping to myself and avoiding people like him and Clay at all costs. But since I've been with Clay I've gotten to know his best friend a little bit better. Jax is usually chill and the life of the party, just like Clay, but where Clay is very much a "what you see is what you get" kind of guy, I know under that joking exterior, Jax is fighting some serious demons. I can see it in his eyes. What demons? I have no clue, and regardless of how close they are, I know Clay doesn't either.

He sits down beside Clay, setting his backpack onto the table with a huff. "Never thought I would see you using the group chat, *Rockwell*."

"I use it all the time now, *Jackson*, don't start your shit with me." I pin him with a glare before remembering why I had to get in the group chat in the first place. "And don't change the subject. Why the hell were you so late?"

A smirk lines his lips. "Unlike you two… I don't need to study. I had to install some new programs on my computer, and I got caught up watching…"

Clay tilts his head, and a knowing look crosses his face. "Watching what, Jax?"

"No one. It's none of your business."

Jax is a computer science major and probably one of the smartest fuckers I know. So, acting oblivious doesn't exactly suit him.

I goad him, making sure to keep my tone hushed. "Oh, so it's a person?" I look at Clay, and he's practically staring a hole through Jax's head. It's then I realize there's more going on that I don't know about. And based on the tick in Clay's clenched jaw, I'd assume he doesn't approve of whatever is happening.

Clay breaks his stare with a frustrated sigh. "I'm going to find the book that I need for my marketing class."

*Clay gets up and heads toward the back of the library. As I watch him go, his perfect ass filling out his dark blue joggers, an idea comes to my mind. But first, I peek across

---

* Daydreams - We Three

the table at Jax and ask, "Jax. Seriously, are you okay? Are you in some kind of trouble? I can help."

His face softens, and he responds with an exhausted sigh, "I'm fine, Rocky. I promise. I just have some shit going on. But nothing I can't keep an eye on." Taking him at his word I nod and stand from my chair. I don't know what, or I guess who, he's talking about, but it's not my place to prod.

"I'm going to help Clay find the book he needs," I say with a wink.

Jackson rolls his eyes. "Ugh, fine. Just make sure I don't have to hear it." I tilt my head back in a laugh and walk toward the shelves Clay disappeared between.

I see my *Garotão* and creep up behind him while he's busy staring at the books on the shelf. Pressing my front to his back, I rub my quickly thickening cock against his plump ass. Leaning into his ear, I whisper, "We could get caught… " I place both of my hands on his chest, rubbing and finding his peaked nipples, pinching them between my fingers. "There could be cameras. Could you be quiet while your cock is in my mouth?" If I've picked up on anything it's that my Clay is a little bit of an exhibitionist. The way he reacted when I played that recording for him all those months ago, how fast he came when we were surrounded by people on that plane, he gets off on the thrill. And when he's turned on, so the hell am I.

Clay nods eagerly, and I smile.

I start walking us to the opposite end of the aisle to hide us a little bit. I would never actually let us get caught, but I know just the thought that we might is enough for him. Satisfied with our position, I push his back into the shelves, hearing the huff of air that leaves his lungs right before I latch my mouth onto his. The kiss is rushed and heated, and soft groans are already coming from deep within him. I run my hands down his sculpted stomach, appreciating when they flex under my palms, just from my touch alone.

I pull away just enough to get my words out, mumbling into his pouty lips, "*Garotão*, you're not doing a very good job at keeping quiet. It's almost like you want us to get caught." We both know I'm right when I feel him smile against my lips.

My big, filthy man.

My hands find his hips, and now I'm the one groaning as I feel the dip of his deep V-cut through his shirt.

"On your knees, Baby." I fold like a goddamn lawn chair, not able to hit my knees fast enough.

My hands slide into the waistband of his shorts and pull them just low enough to pull his dick and balls out. "Are you leaking for me? Or is it from the thought of getting caught, that anyone in this library could hear or see you."

"C. All of the above. Now show me what that mouth can do. I think I've forg—" He shuts right the fuck up as I stick my tongue out, holding eye contact with him, and run my tongue around the crown of his perfect cock. I don't want to go slow this time though. I want to see how fast I can get him to come, and with the way he's pulsing between my lips, it's going to be very quick.

Still holding eye contact and smiling around his cock, I begin to bob up and down on his length like it's my one and only job. I didn't think I would like sucking dick as much as I do. And who knows, maybe I just like sucking Clay's dick. But it does bring me a sick sense of joy that

I'm able to be in control. I control when he gets to come. *Me.*

Clay begins fucking my face while I control the suction I have around his length. I gag as he hits the back of my throat, but that only seems to spur him on. The hushed grunts and the gagging alone are proof enough of what we're doing, and I'm fully expecting someone to come around the corner any minute.

My dick practically has its own heartbeat. It's painfully hard and leaking all over my shorts. I just hope it's not enough to be absolutely everywhere once this is over.

"I'm about to come, Baby." He grabs the sides of my head, gripping my curls above my ears, holding me right where he wants me. I swallow around his head, and that's what tips him over the edge.

His mouth drops open as the last little bit of his seed lands on my tongue. I pop off his cock, holding his cum in my mouth, keeping my mouth open so he can see his release resting on my tongue.

His eyes look feral as he says, "Swallow me, Baby. Swallow me like a good whore."

Yep, my dick's going to explode.

Hand in hand and completely bookless, Clay and I walk back to the table where Jax is smugly looking at us. "Didn't find the book you needed, I see?"

"Nah, got a little distracted," Clay says proudly.

Jax rolls his eyes. "You guys fucking suck."

Clay fucking snorts a laugh. "Yeah, he sure did."

CHAPTER 36
WHAT DO WE WANT MOST?

CLAYTON

It's the night before the start of championship tournament week, and Rocky and I have just arrived at the beach just down the street from campus. Students at Palm use our impending tournament as an excuse to throw a beach party—complete with the largest bonfire you've ever seen—every year, even though the majority of them won't even show up to watch a single game. But that's never bothered me any. It's always been a great way to connect with other people on campus, have a fun night out with the other guys on the team—even douche canoes like Chadwick and Prescott—and make memories I know will last a lifetime.

This year's tournament just feels extra special for a multitude of reasons. Not only is it my senior year, but it's the first championship tournament I'll be playing with Rocky. It's also the first championship tournament where I genuinely feel like first place isn't just within reach but in the palm of our hands.

Don't get me wrong, Jax and I played great together, but Rocky and I... we're unstoppable. His talent truly knows no bounds, and he knows exactly what I need, when I need it.

On and off the court.

Warmth blooms in my chest as I look over at him, dressed in a pair of black cotton shorts, white linen button-up, and black sandals as we make our way through the sand toward Jackson; he's standing several feet away from the obnoxious bonfire with what I'm assuming is a Jack and Coke in hand.

It's also safe to assume that he's the one in charge of the music at the moment because he's bopping back and forth with a buzzed smile on his face as the new country hit, "A Bar Song (Tipsy)" plays over the large wireless speaker. Rocky looks horrified as he turns to look at me. "Please tell me this is not some country version of 'Tipsy' by J-Kwon?"

I bark out a laugh. "Sure is, Baby."

He rolls his eyes. "Jesus fucking Christ."

I'm all smiles once we finally make it to Jax. "No Coach Taylor?" I ask.

"He left a while ago. Once the drinks came out he dipped. Didn't think it was a good idea to be around a bunch of drunk college students." I snort a laugh. He's probably not wrong. Jax opens the cooler next to him and asks, "So since the boss isn't here, what are you having? I've got beer, stuff for Jack and Coke's, Malibu..."

Rocky and I look at one another before I answer, "We're good, man. Got a big game tomorrow."

Jax shrugs before grabbing us each a bottle of water and closing the cooler. "I figured as much. Brought these for the two of you anyway."

I clap him on the shoulder and take our bottles of water, passing Rocky his. The three of us start shooting the shit, and I try to savor every moment. There are at least a hundred people milling around this part of the beach. Some are relaxing on beach towels, some are standing around the fire, and some are sitting in lawn chairs. There are people here that I talk to on a daily basis, and people here I've never seen once in my four years at Palm University—all of us so vastly different, yet all of us so similar. This is what I have loved about my years here at Palm. Experiences like these. The kind I'm not sure I'll be able to get once I'm out into the real world. Sure, if I make the Olympic team, volleyball will be part of my life for many years to come—hopefully with Rocky right by my side— but memories like these... of being surrounded by people who are in the same boat as you. People who have no idea what the next phase of life will bring, people who are trying to live their life to the absolute fullest with friends that became family in a city they love, and people who are trying to become the best versions of themselves all while being scared shitless that the best version still won't be good enough... It's something you can't get anywhere but college.

And when I look around at the smiles on everyone's faces, something suddenly feels like it clicks inside of me. Regardless of what happens this week, whether or not I win the championship, whether or not I make it to the Olympics, whether or not I finally make my dad proud...

none of it fucking matters. The only thing that matters is the person I've become here.

And I'm so damn proud of that person.

I've learned, I've laughed, I've cried, I've won, I've failed, I've *loved,* and I've grown. God, have I grown. I'm the man that I am today because of… *me.*

Nobody can take that away from me.

As if he can tell that I have just had some miraculous revelation, Rocky unashamedly rests his hand on my lower back and shoots me a mega-watt smile.

*We've been at the party for a little over an hour, and Rocky and I are currently playing a game of cornhole against Jax and Emerson, and considering how drunk Jax and his little brother are, it's no surprise that Rocky and I are winning. The glow of the fire lights our little area of the beach on the otherwise dark night, the sounds of the gulf crashing against the shore in the background intermingling with the sounds of music and laughter.

And just when I think the night couldn't get any better, I hear the shout of an all-too-familiar voice—the one I haven't heard since I left my apartment this afternoon to go to Rocky's.

"Irmão!" Liliana's voice cuts through the night, and all eyes turn to look at her. Joseph and Cassandra shake their

---

* Say You Won't Let Go - James Arthur

heads and smile as they all walk across the beach toward us behind a sprinting Liliana.

Rocky's eyes go wide and he drops the bean bags in his hands. "Lil?" he asks, his eyes ping-ponging between me and his family. "Mom? Dad? Wh—What are you guys doing here?"

In a few quick strides he reaches his sister and wraps her up in a giant hug before setting her down so she's facing away from me, but now I can see Rocky's face clear as day.

He looks so fucking happy.

Rocky grabs Lil by the shoulders. "You're here? How did you get here? When did you get here?"

Rocky hasn't explicitly said that he was upset that his family wouldn't be here this week. But as someone whose parents are actively uninvolved, I know how it feels to not have the people in the stands you want most. And after my week in California with the Campos' I knew that, win or lose, they would be who Rocky would want most.

Reaching up, Lil grabs her brother's forearms. "Clay flew us out here. We got here this morning. He picked us up from the airport."

Rock's eyes dart to mine as I stand still in my spot behind Lil, not wanting to intrude on their moment. But before he has the chance to say anything, his parents finally reach him and wrap him up in a hug. "You guys should have told me, I would have gotten my apartment ready. I—"

Joe cuts him off, "No need, son. Clay offered us his apartment for the week. Feels like I'm staying at the Ritz. Way nicer than your place."

Cassandra smacks him on the arm. "Joseph," she

scolds before looking lovingly back at her son. "We're so excited to be here, *filho*."

Rocky kisses her on the cheek. "I'm so happy you're here, Momma."

She whispers something in his ear before pushing him in my direction. As he makes his way over to me, I hear Lil ask Jax and Emerson, "What are we drinking, boys?" Followed by an "I think I'm in love" from Emerson.

Rocky clearly doesn't hear him because he has a smile plastered on his face once he reaches me. "Surprise," I say with a shrug.

Before I can blink, Rocky's grabbing me by the face and crashing his mouth to mine. In the middle of the beach. In front of people. In front of his family. Rocky is kissing me.

Not wasting a second, I fist the front of his shirt and kiss him back with everything I have. He snakes one hand around to the back of my head, threading his fingers through my hair just the way I like, and I moan into his mouth. He smiles against my lips and starts to soften the kiss, likely not wanting to get to carried away.

Jax and Lil are cheering with joy in the background while I hear Joe and Cassandra scream, "I knew it!" at the exact same time. Rocky and I both chuckle as we rest our foreheads against one another, gasping for breath. Quietly he says, "You brought them here."

"I brought them here."

"For me." It's not a question but a statement. As if he's now truly realizing the depths I will go for him.

"For you, Baby."

With our heads still pressed together, his eyes shine with the desire to say something. To say the words I've been dying to hear, and my heart feels like it stills in my chest. As if it's dying of starvation and all it needs to beat again is those three little words. "Clay, I—"

"What the hell is this?"

My hands fall from Rocky's shirt, and our faces part as the murderous voice I just heard registers in my brain.

He would be here. He would ruin this moment for me.

I step around Rocky as if I were shielding him from my dad's disgusted glare. He knew I was bisexual, and I knew he wasn't crazy about it, but if the look on his face is anything to go by, he's more than not okay with it than I thought.

Not even sparing him with a greeting, I ask, "What are you doing here?"

"You haven't been answering my calls." Rocky stiffens behind me as if that fact came as a shock to him. But it's true; I haven't spoken to my dad since the day of my panic attack. After that day I realized just how severely he negatively impacted my life. I've had him as a father for the last twenty-two years. And while it's true he hasn't always been as bad as he is today, those twenty-two years have accumulated to nothing but unyielding anxiety, doubts, and the desire to have the love in my life I know I deserve.

And over the span of *one week*, a family I had only just met, showered me with that love and then some. They made me feel wanted... cherished... whole. *Rocky* makes me feel whole. That is what a family should be. That is what *love* should be.

I cross my arms across my heaving chest, not providing him an explanation as to why I haven't picked up the phone, so he continues, "Called Taylor to see if he knew where you were. Told me you were here. Didn't think I'd show up to find you kissing your damn teammate."

I watch Joe stiffen behind my dad at the mention of his son. "You didn't answer my question. Why are you here?"

"Tomorrow is the first game of championship week."

I laugh incredulously. "You've come to one game all season, and it was only because your investors asked you to go. So I ask again, why are you here, Dad?"

His jaw clenches, realizing I'm not falling for his bull-shit. "I'm closing on a high rise in the city this week, and I needed to be here to ensure everything went smoothly."

Rocky scoffs behind me, but I don't even dignify Dad with a reaction. Because I'm not surprised. Not even a little.

But in typical Charles Aldrich fashion, he tries to side-step the fact that he's a lackluster father by zeroing in on the man behind me. "Is this why you've been distracted all season? Because of *him?*"

I open my mouth to respond, but he doesn't waste a breath. "I told you this whole partnership was a mistake. I told you he was going to bring you down. I told you that someone like him was going to be a waste of your time." I feel Lil step up next to Rocky, anger radiating off her in waves. "And instead of listening to me, you decide to-to what?"

Dad waves his hand at the two of us like he can't even come up with the words. The fact that his son is in a rela-tionship with a man he thinks is so below him is completely incomprehensible.

Joe takes a furious step toward my dad, but Cassie grabs him by the arm. Hurt and worry clearly etched on her face.

This is so not happening. I'm fucking done with this shit.

"You know what…" Dad's nostrils are flared, and his fists are clenched at his side. Ready to rage against the fact that I dare speak up. "I'm done, Dad."

"You're done?" he asks with a laugh. "Done with what exactly?"

"You. I'm done with you," I answer clear as day.

"You're done with me? I'm your father, Clayton. Everything you are is because of me."

"You see… that's where you're wrong. Everything I am is despite you. I am who I am because of me. Yes, I'll always be thankful for the opportunities you and Mom have given me, but that's not enough reason to hold on to what I hope we could be. Because it's useless to hope where you're concerned, Dad. I'm done with you acting like I'm not enough. I'm done feeling unworthy of love. I'm just *done.*"

I release a heavy exhale, my body finally feeling like it's shed the weight of a lifetime by merely speaking those words. Rocky's strong hand threads itself through mine, and I'm only reassured by my decision.

My dad chuckles humorously. "And what are you going to do, Clayton? You cut me out of your life, and I cut you off. Who do you think pays for all of this?" He holds his arms out at his side as if he truly believes he owns the right to my entire life, but he's wrong again.

So, I look at him dead in the eyes. Eyes that, in some ways, are an exact mirror of my own, but in others hold only the hopes and dreams of the father I wish I had, and answer him with unwavering strength, "Me."

<h1 style="text-align:center">CHAPTER 31
EVERYTHING</h1>

CLAYTON

"You?" my Dad asks, looking truly confused.

*"Yeah, Dad. Me. Have you bothered to check any of my accounts lately?" My lips curl up at the sides, knowing what I'm about to say will be the nail in the proverbial coffin. His brows pinch in confusion, so I continue, "There's nothing in them. Opened my own accounts two years ago. Ones you have no access to. Oh, I also got my real estate license two years ago. Was actually pretty easy. Don't know why it took you five tries to finally pass."

His face begins to turn a deep shade of crimson, and I listen as Lil stifles a laugh. "You know that building I live in? I own it. Used the money in my accounts to buy that one. The five buildings around it? Own those, too. Every dollar you've put into my account the last two years, I've

---

* Son of a Sinner - Jelly Roll

220

donated to various charities. Haven't used a dime. Call it intuition, but I had a feeling this would happen one day. Just didn't know when I'd have the courage to do it. You always wanted me to be someone. To achieve something. Well, I am, and I did."

Reluctantly, I let go of Rocky's hand and move toward my dad until we're toe to toe. "So, yeah, *Dad.* I'm done. I don't need you."

In a last-ditch effort, he snarls, "You'll have nothing without me."

"Wrong again." Joseph's deep voice sounds from behind Dad. "He'll have *everything*. Leave. Now."

Dad looks at Joe and Cassie, firm and unwavering, then over my shoulder at Rocky and Lil. My family. These people are my family now. "You heard him. Big Joe said leave. So, leave."

Without another word, and Dad's jaw agape, I turn on my heel and walk back to the man I love. Rocky pins him with one last glare before honing his eyes on me. A mischievous smile tugs at his lips as he asks, "Big Joe, huh?"

The music restarts in the background, and the rest of the party resumes. No one spared my dad another moment of their time. Which I'm sure only infuriates him further. "What can I say? Your Dad and I are basically best buds now. Jax better watch out."

Rocky tips his head back in a laugh before grabbing my hand. "Come with me."

Pulling me away from the fire and the crowd, Rocky leads us toward the lifeguard shack down the beach. It's painted in shades of bright blue, pink, yellow, and green, and I can see a slight glow coming from the window on the side. "Rocky, what's going on?"

He doesn't say anything and just leads me up the short ramp before pausing at the door, fidgeting nervously. "I wanted to do something for you. But then you flew my family here, and now it feels entirely inadequate."

I smile and plant a quick kiss on his lips, reassuring him, "Nothing you do is inadequate, Baby."

Slowly, he pushes open the wooden door, and I inhale a sharp breath. Inside the lifeguard shack, a large, white, fluffy duvet rests on the floor with a multitude of colorful pillows. Battery-operated tea lights are scattered throughout the floor, and a couple of strings of lights hang from the ceiling. "Rocky…"

"It's not a lot, but—"

I cut him off, "It's *everything.*"

His smile beams just as a crack of thunder sounds through the sky. There was no rain in the forecast, but Florida weather has a mind of its own. "Well damn," I say sarcastically. "Looks like it's about to storm. Probably will be stuck in here a while."

He pulls me through the threshold and slams the door closed behind me. "*Perfeito.*"

CHAPTER 38
PERMANENT WORDS

ROCKWELL

I'm waiting for the bomb to drop from Clay's dad showing up at the beach—uninvited. He usually sends Clay into an immediate panic attack, but as I stare at him, I realize he looks better than ever. Lighter. Happier. Yet, I feel the need to ask, just to make sure, "How are you feeling, *Garotão*?"

*Clay breathes a sigh of relief. "I've wanted to tell that man that he doesn't have power over me anymore for longer than you could imagine. So to answer your question… yeah, I feel great." He smiles softly as he looks at me, the twinkle of the lights I set up reflect off his brown eyes. I watch as his gaze rakes up and down my body. "But let's not talk about him. I want all my focus on you, Rockwell Campos."

I try my hardest to hide the blush I know is creeping

---

* THE WITHDRAWLS - Kae

up my neck. "I have one more surprise for you first." I stride over to the duffle I used to carry everything in here earlier today and pull out a prostate massager and a bottle of lube. I knew we would need the lube, but I'm hoping he's open to using the toy.

"Is that what I think it is, Baby?" The smirk on his lips, and the way his pupils blow wide, tells me he's more than okay with it. He bites his lips and stares at the objects in my hand a moment before finally asking, "Can you put it in me? I need to be stretched before you take me."

"Are you sure? You don't have to if you don—" He cuts me off.

He spins me around, plastering my back to the the blue wall so hard I'm surprised the surfboards stored up there don't come tumbling down on us. "You brought me here, Baby. So I intend on making the most of it." Clay's voice suddenly takes on that gravely tone that makes every hair on my body stand on end. Lowering his face to mine he adds, "That includes letting you fill me any way you see fit."

I whimper at the thought of getting to claim him again. He backs away from me slowly, and I follow him all the way to the fluffy blanket I have laid out for us. I throw the toy and lube down on the blanket and grab Clay's arms. "Raise your arms for me. I need to see you."

Doing as I say, he raises his arms, and I feverishly pull his shirt over his head. Once it's gone, I drop to my knees so I can get his shorts off. I run my hands down his stomach into his waistband, pulling his black athletic shorts down. I let out a whistle. "Scandalous, Clayton… No underwear." I mock a couple of tsks while dragging my eyes back up to his.

He smiles down at me, and I swear those damn dimples make my breath catch in my chest. I run my hands down his muscular thighs but stop in my tracks when I feel a piece of plastic wrapped around his upper thigh. My fingers graze over what I now realize is second skin, and I huff a laugh. Only he would get a fresh tattoo in the middle of tournament week. I'm just about to lecture him when I realize what I'm looking at. Permanently inked into his skin is the phrase, "*O amor não tem lei.*" My voice wobbles as I read it out loud.

When my eyes find his, he rubs his hand over my head, adoration lining his features, before translating the phrase I know all to well. "Love has no law, Baby."

"How di—Why did—When did you get this?"

"Your mom said it to me that day she was helping me bake in the kitchen while you were outside with Joe. I know that's when she knew about us, even though she never said it. Love doesn't have laws in your family's eyes. Without so much as batting an eye, they welcomed me with open arms and showed me what a family… what *love* is supposed to look like. I wanted to carry that lesson with me." I lean into his touch as his fingers thread through my curls. "Love doesn't have any rules. It's not dependent upon what the other person can give you in return. It doesn't matter who you are, where you're from, how you grew up, or who you thought you were meant to be. None of it matters. The only thing that matters is knowing in your heart that someone is meant to be in your life. That they're meant to change you're life for the better. That is love. Love has no laws. And *that* is what I feel for you."

I run my fingers over the beautiful words again. Suddenly, the familiar script registers in my brain. "Clay, is this my momma's writing?" The tears lining my eyes are on the verge of falling even before he answers. I already know the answer; she has always had the most beautiful handwriting.

"It is." The first tear falls but doesn't make it far before Clay brushes it away with the pad of his thumb. "Don't cry. I didn't do this to make you cry, Baby. I didn't want to make you cry."

I smile when a thought pops into my head. She only ever says that phrase in Portuguese. I don't think I've ever heard her say that in English. Not once. "Did she tell you what it meant?"

He's sporting a wicked grin. "Nope." He's sure to pop the P in a dramatic fashion. "I knew what she said. Just like I knew you admitted you were falling in love with me in the shower during my panic attack or when you started calling me Big Boy from the very beginning."

I pull my eyebrows together, truly confused. "What the hell? Did you translate everything after I said it?"

"No, Baby," he laughs. "I know Portuguese." My mouth drops open. To say I'm shocked is an understatement. However, now that I think back to when he was at my house, we all spoke Portuguese a lot, and never did he ask me to translate anything. I was so caught up in conversation I didn't even think to make sure he could understand what we were saying. Goes to show how often I've brought someone to my home. But lo and behold, this shithead knew what we were saying this whole time.

"You forget, Baby. I went to a prestigious private school. I learned how to speak three languages by the time I was sixteen. Portuguese happens to be one of them. I'm more than just good looks you know?"

I wrap my hands around the back of his thighs. It's not lost on me the dichotomy of the position that we're in. As Clay lays his soul bare, giving me a gift I couldn't have dreamt of in my wildest dreams, I'm the one kneeling at his feet. Finally ready and willing to give this man all of the love and happiness he deserves but has never gotten. And as the overwhelming feeling of our unrequited love blooms in my chest, I lean in, kiss his new tattoo, and ask, "Can we have some fun now?"

CHAPTER 39
PLEASURE SWITCH?

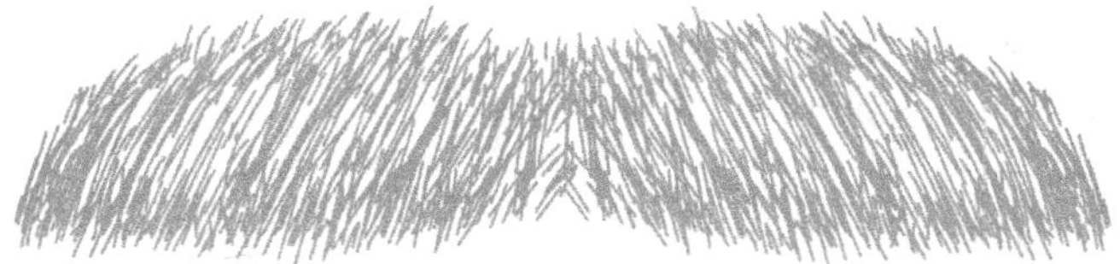

"**O**n the bed, *Garotão*." There's a crack of thunder in the distance. The storm sounds like it's getting closer.

I'd like to say I planned for the storm, but even the best weatherman can't seem to predict Florida's wild weather. Be that as it may, I'm not complaining about the impending storm. I know good and well that fucking in public would do nothing but get us arrested, and even though this is the closest we can get, I know it still turns Clay all the way on. We can pretend that someone will catch us all we want, but the oncoming downpour and cracks of thunder will ensure no one will hear us. "Let me see you. Pull those legs back."

*I lube the toy up and press the tip to his entrance, but

---

* Oh Nah (feat. The Weeknd, Wiz Khalifa, & DJ Mustard) - Remix - Ty Dolla $ign, The Weeknd, Wiz Khalifa, Mustard

he tenses in anticipation. I run my free hand up the back of his thigh while still holding the pressure on his tight ring of muscle, but I comfort him. "Relax, Clay. I've got you."

I keep massaging the back of his thighs. "The rains coming… What if they all come to this lifeguard shack to seek shelter?"

He relaxes just enough at that image that I can work the toy's tip in. I slide it in and out while paying close attention to his facial expressions. Feeling particularly brave, I lean forward and take the tip of his cock into my mouth, lapping at the pre-cum that's spilling from it. It's hard to believe that before Clay, I had never even been with a man. Now, with him, it feels like this is where I was always meant to be.

He lets out a whimper. "More, Baby. Please."

I start to work the toy faster, bobbing my head up and down his length. Once I get the massager fully seated inside of him, the groan that leaves his lips has my whole body vibrating with need.

Unable to take it any longer, I say the one thing I know he won't be able to deny, "Fill me up, *Garotão*."

He's up and has me flipped around before I can even blink. "You're already begging for my cock, Baby?"

He's spread out above me, elbows beside my head, rubbing his rock-hard cock against mine, the sound of our ragged breaths barely audible against the winds of the storm as it draws closer. "You were just begging too… Or have you already forgotten?"

With a playful smile on his face, he bites out, "Someone's feeling extra bratty today."

"Maybe," I shrug, "Or maybe I just like giving you exactly what you want. And you know you love it when

I'm a brat for you." A deep growl sounds from his chest. "I love to drive you wild, Clay. I need the sounds coming out of you to be loud enough for them to hear you back at the bonfire. I'm not going to be able to see that pretty face of yours while you fuck me from behind, so let go. Let go for me. I want control of your pleasure… at least for now."

We both know he's always the one in control. I know that's where he feels most comfortable, most likely to compensate for the utter lack of control he's had over his own life. But I want him to be comfortable with me. I want him to be able to let go. Just like he did the other night at his apartment

Just like he let go of his father earlier.

He moves his hands to the side of my head, still bearing all his weight on top of my body, and I sink into the comforting feeling of all that is Clayton Aldrich. With a ragged whisper, he confides, "Rocky, you're one of the only things that brings me pleasure in this life."

"More than volleyball?" I ask with a cheeky grin.

Clay tips his head back in a laugh. "Would you accept a tie?"

I smile up at him and smash my lips to his. I reach to the side of him where the remote is for the toy and hit the button to bring it to life. Clay's head falls forward with a groan. "Is that too much?"

He takes a deep breath, steadying himself. "No. It's perfect. Let me get you ready." He drops a dollop of lube on his fingers, and his rough fingers move around my hole. He gets one in before he quickly enters another, stretching me while he's coating his pulsing cock in lube.

I moan at his touch. *"Foda-me já."* His eyes burn with lust, fully aware of what I just said to him.

My favorite switch of his visibly flips as he commands, "Flip over, hands and knees. Now." I flip over the second his fingers slide out of me, but I don't even have time to miss them as his cock breaches my hole the next second. We both let out a feral groan. Somehow I have enough wherewithal to click the remote a couple more times, fully aware that the intense vibrations will have him coming in a matter of minutes.

His jaw is clenched as he pumps in and out of me. "Baby," he groans. "If you don't turn it down, I'm not going to last." I hit the button twice as the last word leaves his mouth, wanting to see him unravel.

I mumble into the blanket my face is currently smashed into, "Let me hear you. Let them hear you, *Garotão*. Use me."

"You want to be my little cock whore?" He's pounding into me at a punishing pace. "You want everyone to know what you do to me? That you drive me wild. That you know exactly what I need and when I need it?" I'm nodding my head against the blanket, and I hear his hand land on my ass before my body registers the sting. "Words, Rocky."

All at once, I turn the toy up to max vibration while clenching my ass around him. "Mmm, yes, *Garotão*, I'm your filthy little cock whore."

That tips him over the edge. He growls deep and low. A sound that's so very unlike the happy-go-lucky Clay the rest of the world is used to—a noise that will be ingrained in my brain until the end of time. "Fuck, Baby, I'm coming. Tell me you want my cum."

"*Preencha, Garotão.*"

He's so deep in me that I know nothing will ever

compare. And I don't ever want it to. As his body is over mine, he whispers in my ear, "You're going to keep my cum nice and warm, right where it belongs, while you fuck me."

He pulls out of me, pulling my ass cheeks apart and admiring his handy work. My body heats under his intense gaze. It's filthy and feral, and I fucking love it.

Once he's had his fill, I pull away and flip around. "Lay down for me."

Clay gets into position, and I kneel over him. "Are you ready for me?"

Grabbing my face, he kisses my lips fiercely. After a moment, his mouth moves against mine as he answers, "Yes, Baby. Fill me up."

I reach down and slowly pull the plug out of him, tossing it to the side. Lubing my cock up, then rubbing the head around his perfect little hole, I pause for a second as I look up at his face and appreciate his deep brown eyes, his jawline that's covered in just the right amount of stubble, and his hair that's always perfectly messy on the top.

And just like on the court, he knows what I'm thinking before I do, and he nods his head. "Please, Baby. Use me, take the lead." Fuck, I don't know how long I'm going to last.

I break through his ring of muscle and slowly slide to the hilt. Feral groans leave both of our lips in a beautiful symphony of filth. Lightening flashes outside with another crack of thunder right on its heels, and not more than a moment later, rain begins to pound against the roof of the lifeguard shack.

Clay's legs are up by his chest, and it gives me the

perfect angle to really drive into him, and even though he just came, his cock is still hard as a rock.

His refractory period really does need to be studied, but I'll circle back to that thought.

Breathlessly, I plead, "I want you to come without touching your cock."

To know that just the feeling of me being inside of him is enough to make him come is one of the hottest things I can imagine.

"Fuck me like you mean it then. Milk my prostate, Baby."

That's all I need from his lips to start ruthlessly pounding into him. His whimpers are enough to drive me up a goddamn wall. I can already feel the tingling starting in my thighs, and I try to slow up, knowing my orgasm is way too close for my liking. But Clay has no intention of letting me slow down. "Right there, baby. Yes, keep going. Yes."

"You want my cum, *Garotão*? Beg me for it."

"Please, Baby. Can your good boy have your cum?" The moment the words leave his delicious mouth, his dick starts erupting. The sight of his cum pooling on his toned stomach drags me over the cliff I've been dying to fall over. Stilling as deep as I can get, I pulse inside him. The two of us lay still for a moment. The sounds of our ragged breath and the torrential downpour are like a balm to my soul. Once I catch my breath, I swipe a curl off his damp forehead and press a soft kiss in its place.

I lay down beside him, and Clay settles his head on my chest while wrapping his leg and arm around me.

I tuck my chin, pressing another kiss to the top of his

head. He nuzzles in further and says, "I love you, Rock-well Campos."

Finally, I'm able to speak the words I've known for a while but have been too afraid to admit, and I can say with absolute certainty that nothing has ever felt more right. "I love you, Clayton Aldrich."

CHAPTER 40
LOVE IS...

CLAYTON

I'm floating on cloud fucking nine. For the first time in my entire life, everything feels… right.

*The immense weight I've felt lift off of my chest since I walked away from my dad Sunday night at the beach is unlike anything I could have imagined. I'm not going to lie; for the last four days, I've waited and waited for a wave of sadness, guilt, or disappointment over the fact that he's no longer going to be a part of my life. But it never came.

Then, I began to wonder if there was something wrong with me. I mean, what kind of person doesn't get upset that they are no longer going to have ties with their parents? The two people who are supposed to mean the most to you in this world. It's then that I realized they no longer mean the most to me.

---

* Nonsense - Sabrina Carpenter

No. The person that means the most to me is the man currently sitting across the locker room from me; head tipped back as it rests against the locker, eyes closed, as he listens to whatever noise is blaring through his headphones.

He means the most to me.

Rockwell Campos.

My heart now lives outside of my chest. It beats for him, and the life that the two of us will have together means the most.

I no longer have the desire to keep someone in my life out of some misguided sense of dedication simply because they are blood. And that's okay.

Rocky taught me that.

He has taught me what love and family are supposed to feel like. He taught me that I should never have to prove myself to earn someone's love. He has taught me that love is showing someone the most vulnerable parts of you; love is a "how are you?" text just because you want to check in; love is listening to each other's favorite songs even though you think they suck; love is a feeling of belonging; love is watching someone's eyes light up when they try your new chocolate chip cookie recipe; love is feeling safe enough with someone to let go; *love* is the feeling I get whenever I look at him.

And I want to chase that feeling for the rest of my life.

Like he always does, Rocky must sense my eyes on him because he cracks one eye open, and the corner of his lips turn up in a soft smile.

Sometimes, I can't believe I fell in love with a man with a mustache, but here we are.

I also never want him to get rid of it.

Rocky shoots me a wink before closing his eyes again, losing himself in his pregame playlist.

Regardless of how much I want to sit here and daydream about him and his fuckable face, I know we have a game to win. Rocky and I have been dominating all week long, not losing a single set. We're now set to play in the semifinal game against South Carolina, and *when* we win, we'll face off against Arizona State tomorrow. We lucked out big this year as hosts of the NCAA tournament, and having the city of Pensacola show up to cheer us on has only pushed us to dig deeper.

Throwing on my white jersey, I quickly shuffle out of the locker room to head toward Theo's office across the hall from the weight room.

However, the second I round the corner, I see Jax and Theo talking in the hallway just outside his office door. Actually, let me rephrase that. Jax has Theo pinned against the wall, his hands fisting the front of his blue Panthers polo. It looks like they're having a heated conversation, one that's already far too inappropriate for a student and a staff member. But it's only made more scandalous as I watch Theo's hands move to Jackson's waist just as Jax lowers his head and whispers something into Theo's ear.

Jesus fucking christ.

I clear my throat, reminding these two they're in an extremely *not* private hallway. Theo shoves Jax away from him with force. Okay, Theo has a decent amount of muscle underneath that polo because Jax isn't exactly a small individual. "Knee's looking good, Jackson. Just keep up the conditioning and you'll be set for next season."

I roll my eyes dramatically, letting them know I'm clearly not buying the bullshit. Wait.

"Next season?" I ask, looking at Jax.

"Yeah," he runs his hand through his messy black hair. "I was going to tell you after championship week was over. I'm using my fifth-year eligibility and coming back to play next year. I have some advanced-level coding and programming classes I could take, and I just wanted one more year to play. I'm not looking to make it a career, but I just—" He inhales a deep sigh. "I just wasn't ready to be done yet. I want one more year so I can end it my way. Ya know?"

I look at my best friend, then over at Theo, who has his eyes firmly planted on the ground. I know this could very well have just as much to do with him as it does Jax wanting to play, but he hasn't explained to me whatever the fuck is going on with them. Regardless of the fact that we all know that I know what I know. Jackson looks at me with pleading eyes, silently asking me to both understand and not confront him about this yet. And I won't. But for all intents and purposes Jackson Baker, is my brother, so I do want to make one thing crystal clear.

"That's great, man." I clap him on the shoulder. "I'm happy for you, really. You deserve to have a great final season. Just take it easy over the summer." My eyes look toward Theo, who has finally grown the balls to look at me. I may be talking to Jax, but my next words are directed toward him. "Would hate to see you get hurt. Again."

Theo pins me with a glare, but my stare doesn't waver. Understanding I'm not budging, he asks, "Did you need something from me, Clayton?"

"Yup," I answer with all of the sunshine I can muster. "Just need you to tape up my wrist quick. Tweaked it a little yesterday on a dive and figured better safe than sorry."

Trying to change the subject, Jax states, "You feel good about today?"

"Great." I refocus my attention on him as Theo spins on his heels to go into his office to get a roll of athletic tape.

"Don't, Clay. I've got it handled."

"Got what handled? I didn't say a word. Just telling you to take it easy over the summer, like the good friend I am."

His eye roll rivals mine. "There's just some... *stuff* we're trying to work out."

I huff a sarcastic laugh. "Like the fact that he's a staff member and you're a student."

"It's not like I'm eighteen years old, Clay. I'll be twenty-three in August." Jax shakes his head. "Not that it matters because nothing is going on. Not a damn thing." He speaks the last words as if they physically pain him to say.

"So you staying here an extra year has nothing to do with him?"

"Don't make me lie to you."

I hold Jackson's face in my hands, forcing him to look at me. "I'm here when you're ready to tell me. I have your back. *Always.*"

He nods in my hold, and I don't miss the way his eyes have suddenly glossed over. Then his voice cracks as he speaks softly, "I know." Before I can say another word, Theo comes back out, the roll of tape in hand. Jax clears his throat. "I'm going to go find my seat. Emerson said he was sitting by Rocky's sister, Liliana, and his parents. I'll see you after. Good luck, and kick some ass."

Without another word toward Theo, Jackson walks away, forcing me to sit through the most awkward five minutes of my life, alone.

Should have just stayed in the locker room staring at Rocky's fuckable face.

As South Carolina's player walks to the back of the court for what could be the final serve of the game, Rocky and I glance over at one another, all while getting in our ready positions, both of us knowing this could be the end of our collegiate career or the moment where everything changes. The sun is blaring down, Rocky and I are covered in sweat and sand, and the stands are full as they cheer us on—The Campos', Jackson's, and Emerson's voices roar above the rest. Hell, even Kevin and Nancy are here.

I have never felt more alive.

As much as I enjoy having a comfortable lead, *this* is the moment I live for. The one where everything is down to the wire.

It's our third match. South Carolina won the first set and us the second. We're now winning 14-13. If South Carolina misses this serve or we get a side out, we win. We'll be in the championships this time tomorrow.

This is it.

The whistle blows, and South Carolina's player throws it up in the air. Hitting the ball, the serve sails right toward my outstretched arms. Ready for it, I pass it up perfectly. Rocky's underneath it in a few quick steps, backsetting it to the number three position in the middle of the net. Seeing an open spot, I tip it over to the front right side of South Carolina's court, but one of their players is able to dig it up from the sand.

Two desperate passes later, the ball is floating over the net. I easily receive the ball and pass it up to Rocky at the net. He bump-sets to the right side of the net. My foot slips in the sand, so I'm not able to attack it like I wanted, and instead hit it with the heel of my hand, barely getting it over as the opposing player grazes the ball in an attempted block.

"Come on, Clay! You got this!" Lilliana's screams like a banshee over the announcer's voice as I gasp for breath, sweat pouring down my face.

I watch as South Carolina sets up for a line drive, but Rocky and I know what's coming. They've been doing it all game. As their player jumps up for an outside hit, Rocky readies himself tight against the right side of our net.

And just like I knew they would, instead of hitting line, they power tip right at Rocky.

"Five, five, five!" he says, just loud enough for me to hear him. In the span of two seconds, he's quickly setting to the middle, as I'm already mid-approach. And just as the ball crests the net, I make contact with the palm of my hand, sending it into the wide-open back corner of South Carolina's court.

The ball hits the sand, the whistle blows, and the crowd roars.

We won.

We're going to the championships.

Mine and Rocky's eyes connect, both simultaneously realizing what just happened. After everything that happened this year, after where we started, after defying all odds, the two of us are going to the NCAA championship.

In perfect unison, we take two quick strides toward one another. Not caring that anyone else is around, not caring about shaking hands with our opponents, not caring about what we should or shouldn't do or what people in the stands might think about two men kissing—we wrap our arms around one another and crash our lips together. I faintly hear the crowd silence for a moment before erupting in a roar of screams and applause.

But I don't give a fuck about any of that right now. All I care about is him. The man I love. My partner. My teammate.

My *everything*.

CHAPTER 41
DO NOT DISTURB

ROCKWELL

We just won the Semifinals.

I have Clay in my arms, and our lips are crushed together in the middle of the court. I hear the telltale sound of cameras shuttering as they take pictures of the two of us and wolf whistles coming from what feels like the whole crowd. Lil's voice booms through the commotion, "Get a room, you two!"

I pull away from him slightly to look into his dark brown eyes. Tears pool as he hits me with his signature beaming smile, dimples and all. "We did it! We're going to the finals!"

The words have barely left my mouth when he grabs the sides of my face, popping two more quick kisses on my lips. Far sooner than I like, he's pulling away and dragging me behind him toward the net to shake South Carolina's hands. They played a hell of a game, but we pushed harder. We played harder. And now there's only one game left.

Arizona State has had a similar run, their only advantage being that those two have played together for four years. Be that as it may, with the way Clay and I connect out on that sand, there's no way to tell we only became partners mere months ago.

The reporters on the sidelines are calling our names, and for the first time all season I can genuinely say I'm eager to talk to them, so I head over, leaving Clay up by the net as he chats with our opponents.

I stop at one of the reporters I'm familiar with, and she smiles ear to ear as she excitedly holds the microphone out toward me. "Rockwell, after everything that happened at the start of this season with your former partner, did you see yourself getting to the finals?"

*"This year has been nothing short of amazing. And as far as my old partner goes… I wish it wouldn't have been for the reason it was, but I'm so thankful the universe put Clay and I together on the court." I look over my shoulder at Clay, who's now made his way over to the photographers, but he must feel my eyes on him because he smiles over at me, and I can practically feel my heart swell in my chest.

Fuck, I love him so much.

"Oh. My. God. You two are precious," she squeals in excitement. "I told myself I wouldn't pressure you into talking about the kiss, but the look in both of your eyes just now…" she trails off as she places her hand over her heart in dramatic fashion.

---

* Loveeeeeee Song - Rhianna, Future

I'm still looking at him, unable and unwilling to pull my eyes away. "Clayton Aldrich is my partner in every aspect. He is the kindest human I've ever met, one of the best players I've seen, and the light that illuminates from him is truly magical to get to experience firsthand." I look back at her, and she has tears running down her face. "I'm sorry. I didn't mean to upset you…"

She waves her hand at me as she sniffles. "Back to volleyball before I'm a sobbing mess… What are the plans for the championship game against Arizona State?" Just as I'm about to answer I feel Clay brush up against my arm.

Looking way too mischievous for my liking, Clay wraps his arm around me and pops a kiss on my cheek before rambling to the reporter as if she asked *him* the question. "My boyfriend and I plan to keep that championship trophy here at Palm University, where it belongs."

I'm listening to him talk in pure awe. He has that boyish excitement that takes over when he's talking about something he loves, and it's something I don't think I'll ever tire of seeing. "Now, if there aren't any more questions, I would like to go celebrate with my Rock Man."

I roll my eyes and elbow him in the ribs. "Don't call me Rock Man."

Clay chuckles. "Hard limit. Got it." Then he leans down to whisper in my ear, ensuring no one else can hear what he's about to say, "However, I distinctly remember you once said that about me calling you Baby. Now you love it… hell, you've even begged for it."

He rights himself before I have a chance to respond quietly, so I don't say anything. Instead, I grab his face and crush our lips together. We kiss for longer than socially acceptable, but I know Clay's getting some kind of kick out of putting on a show. We're letting everyone know that he is mine and I am his.

I pull away breathless, then turn to the now blushing reporter and say the same words that are now forever marked on Clay's skin, "*O amor não tem lei.*"

Of course, the pictures of us kissing after winning the semi-finals have been plastered onto every social media site you can think of. People have shocked me, though; most have been nothing but supportive of us dating, not that I'm one to give much of a fuck either way.

Coach, of course, had no clue, but he didn't seem all that shocked either. He congratulated us in one breath and in the next went right back into going over the game.

The championship is tomorrow, and we just got back to my place. Clay's making something for dinner real quick, and then I'm sure we'll be cuddled up on the couch watching some rom-com in no time.

I'm sitting at my little kitchen table with my thumb hovering over the "post" button on the picture one of the reporters got of our kiss when I glance up at Clay. He's already smiling at me softly, love and adoration covering every feature of his face, yet he's the one who asks, "What are you smiling at over there, Baby?"

"About to announce to the world that I'm gay for Clay and dating some hot as fuck guy I know," I respond with a nonchalant shrug.

"Are you nervous about what people will say?" I

watch as his smile falls ever so slightly, his brows pinched with concern.

"No, *Garotão*. Anyone who doesn't support who I decide to love doesn't need access to me or my life. And I'll be happy to see them out. Matter of fact, I'll open the door for them."

I hit the post without another thought and put my phone on "Do Not Disturb."

We eat the soup Clay whipped up from the limited ingredients I had in the fridge, and I can't even lie, it's good as fuck. I've been groaning and moaning in appreciation since the first bite.

Clay gets up to put our dishes in the sink, and my eyes immediately spot the tent he's sporting in his pants, and I let out a whistle. "That things ready to go…"

"It's from you moaning like a goddamn erotic audio creator over my food. Leave me and my erect penis alone."

Right as those words leave his lips there's a knock at the door before it's being thrown wide open. I'm up and in front of Clay, ready to fight to protect him if need be. I immediately realize none of that is necessary, though.

"What the hell are you doing here, Lil? You couldn't text before coming over here?" I'm still standing in front of Clay, now more worried about hiding his boner than protecting him. I'm not trying to give my little sister a free show.

"You didn't answer, fuck face," Lil snaps.

Shit, I forgot I put my phone on "Do Not Disturb." I'm not used to family being close enough to just pop in. But that's besides the point. "What if we were fucking on the table? I know he wants to see my dick"—I point at Clay, who's now trying not to laugh—"but do you?"

The horrified look that takes over her face is worth the minor heart attack I just had. Clay's bent over, howling in laughter, but once he finally regains his composure and catches his breath, he asks, "Is there something wrong at the apartment? What's going on?"

"Nothing. I was bored."

One look at her face, and I immediately call bullshit. I know how to read my sister better than anyone. "Lilliana…"

"I just wanted to hang out with you two and give Mom and Dad a night away from me. I love them, but it's good to have a break from your roommates… especially when they're your parents." She looks down at her feet like she's ashamed before she continues, "I just… Seeing you guys this week and watching all of these students on campus… I feel like I should be further along with my life by now. I want to live on my own, but SoCal is outrageously expensive, and building my clientele hasn't been as easy as I thought it was going to be. I just feel like I'm free falling and stuck in one place all at the same time. I don't know how that's even possible, but that's how I feel."

"Move into my place," Clay says without a moment's hesitation. It takes him a second to realize what he just said before he looks over at me hesitantly.

Lil looks from me to Clay and then back to me. I wink at her, then turn to him. "I didn't think I would be having this conversation in front of my sister, but why the hell not." I shrug and ask Clay what I've been keeping bottled up for a while now, "Move in with me, *Garotão?*"

Tears are already lining his eyes like he can't believe I'm jumping on board so easily. But I want this. I want him in my bed every night when I go to bed and every morning when I wake up. I want his delicious desserts to cover my kitchen, and I want to hear him complain about how grumpy I get when I'm tired. I want it all.

Little does he know I've wanted this since the first night I had him in my bed.

"This can't be because I offered my place to Lil, though. I don't want to pressure you and take over your space. She can stay in my spare ro—"

I cut him off before he can say one more word. "The only Campos you'll be living with is me, Clayton. Plus, you said so yourself, this is the kitchen of your dreams. And you'll be right above your favorite store, so you can visit your BFF Kevin whenever you want."

He closes the distance between us, wrapping me up in his arms. "Yes. Yes. Yes." Clay pops kisses on my neck between each word. "I'll move in, Baby."

And like she has no self-control, Lil ruins the moment by fake gagging. "I'll throw up, please, for the love of god. No tonguing each other in front of me." She shivers dramatically, and I roll my eyes before she walks into the living room to flop on the couch. She quickly makes herself at home by grabbing the remote and turning on the TV.

She gives it a second before turning her head and smiling softly up at Clay. "Thank you."

I pry myself out of Clay's arms and hold his face to really get a read on him. "Are you sure you're okay with her moving into your apartment?"

He grins as he reassures me, "Of course, Baby. Lil is as much my sister now as she is yours. I think she could do great here."

"I'm sure my parents are going to love finally having an empty house," I joke, but a serious look crosses his face.

"I have a feeling they're not going to like being so far away from both of you." I give a slow nod because he has a point, but I pacify him with, "We'll cross that bridge when we get to it. All I care about right now is winning the championship tomorrow and having you in my arms... *and bed.*"

After tomorrow, all I have to do is graduate, and I'll be on my way to teaching and coaching, to making children's lives better and their futures as bright as they can possibly be.

The only thing that's up in the air is our biggest goal, the one that we want most while simultaneously being the one furthest from our reach.

The Olympics.

While that goal has always felt like a pipe dream, it was still that... a dream. But one thing I know for certain, is that no dream is out of reach with him by my side.

Clayton Aldrich.

CHAPTER 42
LEAVE IT ALL ON THE COURT

CLAYTON

This is the last time I'll wear the Panthers uniform.

This is the last time Rocky and I will don blue and yellow as teammates.

This is the last time our names will be called over the speakers as the announcers introduce us.

This is it.

This is *the* game.

I've played countless games during my career as a volleyball player, and I can count on one hand the amount of times nerves have truly shaken me to my bones. But none of those compare to the way I'm feeling today.

Anyone who's ever been in love with a sport will understand the complex mixture of emotions you feel during your very last game, regardless of the level of play.

You're buzzing with excitement at the possibility of taking home that championship trophy, yet dreading the start of the game because once it does, you know the end is moments away.

You've never felt prouder to stand on the court with your teammates while simultaneously experiencing a wave of sadness that's impossible to put into words.

But most of all, you try to take in every play, every cheer from the stands, every boom of the announcer's voice. All of it feels like it goes in slow motion, but before you know it, you've played the fastest game of your life.

Sure, we still have a chance to make the Olympic team. This might not be our last game together. But none of that is guaranteed. But what is guaranteed is this moment, right here, right now.

With Rocky.

With the number one on the back of my jersey.

With the Panthers logo adorned on my chest with pride.

Rocky and I sit side by side on our chairs, with Coach Taylor standing off to our right as the announcer introduces the opposing team and the coaching staff. Both of us sit in matching positions, elbows resting on the tops of our legs, heads hanging as we look down at the sand, getting in the zone while we wait for our names to be called. Today, though, we each have one hand wrapped around the other's thigh. Silently grounding one another, silently communicating everything we're feeling at this moment.

"And now for your home team, the Palm University Panthers!"

Rocky and I turn our heads slightly, and I'm met with the comforting sight of his deep green eyes looking back at me. The eyes that have now become a reflection of my soul. Who I am at my very being shines in his eyes. When I look at them, I'm at home.

He is my peace.

He is my strong side.

"Ready, Campos?"

"Ready, Aldrich."

"Great game, man," I say as I pull Arizona's other player in for a hug. None of us care about the fact that we're caked in sweat and sand. All four of us here are seniors, and opponents or not, we all absolutely kicked ass out there today. "You guys played amazing. I wouldn't have wanted to play against anyone else today."

He steps back and grabs me by my shoulders. "You two earned this. Now go celebrate."

*With that, I turn toward Rocky and yell at the top of my lungs, "WE WON, BABY!"

He's not within reach for more than half a second before the entirety of the men's sand volleyball team is piling on top of us, Jackson included.

Rocky and I are stuck beneath a pile of sweaty screaming men as the crowd roars in the background and the Panther's fight song plays over the speakers, and I can say without a doubt in my mind that I will remember this moment for the rest of my life.

---

* Work Song - Hozier

Finally having enough of their shit, Rocky groans, "Alright, enough. Enough. Let us go get our trophy."

The team piles off as they chuckle at his usual grouchiness. Rocky stands first, and he reaches down toward me. Grabbing his hand, he pulls me upright and into a searing kiss. His tongue fights for dominance with mine, and after a few moments I relent, more than happy to let him take over. I groan into him as his tongue explores my mouth, savoring the way he feels against me. We only part when Coach shouts, "Would the two of you get over here already! I'm about two seconds from taking this trophy home myself!"

I laugh against Rocky's lips, "Come on, Baby. We have a trophy to take home."

Our home.

The next thirty minutes pass in a blur as Rocky and Coach Taylor are subjected to an endless wave of congratulations and interviews with local and national news channels.

The majority of the students and opposing fan base have begun to clear out. It's only then that I see a familiar face standing alongside the bleachers, lurking in their shadows. Likely trying not to sweat through his five-thousand-dollar suit.

How long has he been here?

Why is he here?

I don't want him ruining this.

Tapping Rocky on the arm, I look in the man's direction. "He's here?"

"Hmmm?" It takes Rocky a moment, but he follows my line of sight and snarls, "What is your dad doing here?"

"Boys, I think we just have one more interview, and

then—" Coach Taylor stops mid-sentence as his gaze also lands on Dad's. Clearing his throat, he pulls his sunglasses off his eyes and sets them atop the brim of his hat.

As much as I didn't want to involve Coach Taylor, Rocky insisted we fill him in on what happened at the beach. He wanted to ensure that Coach Taylor knew Dad and I were no longer on speaking terms and to not provide him with any details about my life unless I said it was okay.

Coach Taylor didn't hesitate for a moment. He simply nodded and said I was doing the right thing. But it's when he said he was proud of me for standing up for myself that a sob caught in my throat. Never once in my entire life do I remember my own father saying he was proud of me. So when the man I have looked up to for as long as I can remember—the one who has never stopped striving to help me be the best I can be while simultaneously accepting me for who I am and am not—said he was proud of me, it quite literally felt like it stole the breath from my lungs.

I could see it on his face, though. He really was proud of me. But right now, when I look at his face, all I see is a simmering inferno ten seconds away from exploding.

"You boys stay here. I'm going to go have a chat with Charles."

Coach Taylor stomps off, and Rocky chuckles under his breath before mumbling, "Oh, shit."

My head snaps in his direction. "What do you mean, 'oh, shit'? What do you think he's—"

"You son of a bitch!" Taylor's voice booms, followed by a crack, and by the time my eyes land back on Dad, he's bent over, hands cupping his nose as blood begins to pool through his fingers.

"Oh, shit," I repeat Rocky's words as I take off in a sprint to the side of the bleachers.

"I think you broke my fucking nose! What the hell, Taylor?"

"You're lucky that's all I broke, you manipulative, money-hungry piece of shit." I stand next to Taylor as Dad stands up straight. His eyes go wide when he realizes I'm not about to come to his aide. "I don't know why you're here after the stunt you pulled at the bonfire the other night."

"I—"

"Save it," Taylor snaps. "They told me what happened, and I don't give a fuck about your side of the story. For years, I have watched you berate and belittle this man. Your *son*. You've not only done it to him but to your wife and everyone around you." Dad's eyes darken with rage as blood continues to pour from his likely very broken nose. "You were once a man I admired. Someone I called not only a teammate but a friend. But this"—he waves his hand up and down in my dad's direction—"this isn't someone I recognize."

I feel Rocky come up behind me, and he doesn't waste a second threading his fingers through mine. Dad's eyes dart toward the gesture before refocusing on Taylor.

"For four years, I haven't been able to say a word because I've been Clayton's Coach, but as of thirty minutes ago, he is no longer my player. And I'm not going to let you soil what should be another incredible day for him. So"—Taylor takes half a menacing step toward Dad—"you are going to leave now. And if you're not gone in the next fifteen seconds, I will not hesitate to break another one of your bones."

"Clayton…"

"Uh-uh. You don't talk to him. Leave, Charles. *Now.* Before I make you leave."

Without another word, Dad spins on his heels and shuffles through the sand toward the parking lot. I don't know when I'll see him again or if we will ever be able to mend our relationship, but I can say with complete confidence that I'm not upset as I watch him walk away.

Taylor sighs as he spins to face us, shaking out his hand. "Clayton, I'm sorry."

My mouth hangs open for a moment before an uncontrollable laugh bubbles from my chest. "Sorry? That was amazing! I mean, I know I should probably be appalled that you just decked Dad across the face, but that was totally epic."

"Yeah, Coach. That was totally badass. I just wish I would have recorded it," Rocky adds. Taylor huffs an incredulous laugh and rolls his eyes.

"Come on, you two. We have one more interview, and then the night is yours."

We've been at Jack's, a sports bar right off the beach, celebrating with friends, family, students, and members of the community for several hours now. "Sweet Home Alabama" is loudly playing as Emerson and Liliana down another round of shots. They're not the only ones, though.

There are more people in this bar drunk than not, with Rocky and I both being well on our way.

Liliana leans over and whispers something in Emerson's ear, and Rocky and I watch as his entire face turns a comical shade of pink. I look over at Rocky, laughing, only to find him clenching his jaw in irritation. I roll my eyes and pull him from his stool, not wanting him to get sent to jail for murder on such a special night.

"Come with me," I shout over the music.

Rocky looks from me to his sister. "I don't know if—"

"Baby, your parents are literally right there. They'll keep an eye on her."

He looks back at me deadpan. "You mean the same parents who are currently doing Jägerbombs with Jackson? Yeah, they'll do a great job."

I bark out a laugh as I watch Big Joe and Cassandra down their shots and make a mental note to have breakfast delivered to my apartment tomorrow morning for them. "Come on, ya big baby. Come for a walk with me."

I don't give him much of a chance as I pull him through the bar, with him mumbling and grumbling behind me. We're only walking through the sand for a few minutes before we're only a couple of yards away from the rising tide. Stopping, I toe off my sandals and set my phone, keys, and wallet on top of them. Rocky raises a brow at me and I just smile. Relenting, he does the same and grabs my outstretched hand. We walk until the cool, salty water is resting at our ankles. The sound of the waves crashing against the shoreline, mixed with the muffled music blaring from Jack's, is the perfect soundtrack to end the most perfect day.

Rocky and I stand hand in hand in the water as we

look out at the Gulf before us. "We really won," his deep voice says softly.

I turn my head to look at him. His dark curly hair blowing in the breeze, his full lips that I could never live another day without kissing, his emerald eyes that I could get lost in over and over again, and his walnut skin that I want to spend the rest of my life exploring. What started as a partnership by happenstance, one once filled with animosity and misunderstanding, is now filled with so much love that it has woven its way into the very marrow of my bones.

It's a partnership I want now and always.

"Yeah, Baby. We won."

EPILOGUE

ROCKWELL

SIX MONTHS LATER

Hand in hand with Clay, we walk out of the tattoo shop. A dull ache throbs over my heart from the ink I got, an exact replica of the one Clay got all of those months ago. The poor guy who was going to be tattooing me looked nauseous at the thought of matching tattoos, but once we explained what it meant and that it was my Momma's handwriting, I swear the big man shed a tear.

Running my free hand over my left peck, I smile into the abyss, daydreaming about everything that's happened over the last six months.

We have what is supposedly the iconic Jax Baker Halloween party tonight—or should I say Baker

Halloween party. He's passing the torch to his younger brother, Emerson, since he'll be living in the house when Jax is finally done with his fifth year.

I don't care who's hosting the party to be honest, as long as I get a night out.

I've been at the local high school teaching a couple of high-level elective history classes, and the rest are the juniors' mandatory classes. Most of my students are as equally obsessed with the subject as I am, and the ones who aren't, seem to be coming around as the year goes on. It has been so rewarding seeing them excel while simultaneously being a mentor for those who need it.

I love it. I truly do. However, my job still revolves around teaching hormonal and overly emotional teenagers, so it's safe to say I could use a drink… or five.

Clay and I pull into the parking lot of Delectable Desserts and our apartment. Clay jumps out of the driver's side and is around to open my door just as I grab my energy drink out of the cup holder. "What have I told you about opening my door, *Garotão?*"

I don't know why he feels the need to treat me like a princess, but I'd be lying if I denied the smile that spreads across my face when he does it.

"As long as I'm able to open your door, Baby, I will." He gives me a wink and starts up the stairs. Smile or not, I roll my eyes as he retreats.

"The last one in the shower is the bottom for the night!" I yell up the stairs at him, knowing damn well I'll be the last one in. He looks down at me, smirking, and takes off through the door when he finally gets it unlocked.

We park down the street from Jax's house, ensuring we can get out when we're ready and not be blocked in by a bunch of college kids who won't even be able to spell their own names. We can hear the music blaring from their house the moment we get out of the car. "Are we too old for this?"

He looks at me deadpan. "We're twenty-three, not fifty. Come on. Let's go have some fun." Excitedly, he pulls me down the street toward the Baker party that's already in full swing. The two of us intend to make the most out of this party because, in a couple of weeks, Clayton will officially be a member of the staff, and parties like this will officially be a no-go for him.

After I got hired at the high school, the staff caught wind of my collegiate career and offered me the position of head coach of their men's volleyball program. If everything goes to plan, I hope to start a sand team there as well.

Taylor pretty much forced Clay to come and coach with him at Palm, which I already know he's going to love. He has loved owning his own business and managing all of his real estate properties since we graduated, but it's clear to anyone with eyes that nothing will ever compare to the love he has for his sport. We still haven't heard from the Olympic team, but there are still three years until the next Olympics, and we have time. Taylor has us practicing against the guys whenever he gets the chance in order for us to keep our skills sharp.

As we're stepping onto Jax's driveway, he comes barreling out the front door. I'm not joking; he's full-on sprinting.

Right on his tail is a man in a mask. I stare as they run past us, trying to pinpoint why the man chasing after Jackson looks so familiar.

Then it hits me. I snap my head back in Clay's direction. "Is that fucking Theo?"

Clay's eyes follow them as they run down the street, and then he sighs heavily. "Sure looks like it, doesn't it?"

"Well, that's… interesting."

"Might as well leave them to it." Clay's voice is laced with apprehension, and I can tell part of him wants to intervene in the situation.

We finally step into the house. It's packed full of already drunk college kids, and I immediately spot Lil pressed against the kitchen counter by Dominic, the goalie for our hockey team. I've seen him a few times in passing but never said much to the guy. I know he's pretty good friends with Emerson, though.

Emerson's friend or not… he's about five seconds away from me shoving my fist through the side of his face.

"LILIANA CAMPOS!" I yell over the music, but she doesn't even pull away. He's leaned into her ear, whispering lord knows what.

Clay wolf whistles like the shit stirrer he is, and I snap my head toward him. "Get it, sister!" I slap his chest, and he just laughs at me. "Oh, stop; she's plenty old enough to let loose. Quit acting like a grandpa."

"I hate you," I grumble under my breath.

He pops an obnoxious kiss on my cheek. "Love you too, Baby."

Lil spots us as we approach them. "Oh hey, guys. Didn't think you old fuckers would be here," she laughs out. Her words slurred from the drinks she's already had.

I step up to Dominic and lower my voice to my most menacing tone. "You hurt her, and I'll fucking castrate you with a smile on my face."

"I'm more scared of her than you, man… but I would never hurt her. Scouts honor." He holds two fingers up and puts the other hand over his heart. I step back and roll my eyes, not bothering to dignify him with a response. Lil can hold her own, I have no doubt about it, but I'll always worry about her, regardless of where I am, how old she is, or who she's with. She's my baby sister, and I'll be damned if I let anyone or anything cause her any harm.

I grab one of my beers out of the fridge that we keep over here and head into the living room. As the two of us sit next to one another, watching the party unfold in front of us, I can't help but think back to the night of my birthday party. That night, I knew that my life would never be the same again. I knew then that I wouldn't spend another moment hating this beautiful man. A lot has changed since then, but one thing remains the same.

I hate him almost as much as I love him.

CLAYTON

"Rockwell, I swear on all that is holy. If you don't start pulling your weight, I'm finding a new partner."

"Like anyone else here would want to deal with you being their partner."

"Me?" I gasp. "I'm great. The best, actually. I'm the one that's been carrying this team for the last twenty minutes. You're a Division I athlete. Act like it."

Rocky scoffs, like he does at least a thousand times a day, and picks up the ball. Emerson and Dominic stand at the opposite end of the table, taunting him. He lines up his shot, and the ping-pong ball goes sailing across the table before sinking into one of the two remaining red cups.

My arms shoot up in the air. Rocky crosses his arms and raises a brow at me. "Thank youuuuu," I swoon.

"Kiss my ass."

"Hole? Gladly."

I lean in and pucker my lips. He tries to fight a laugh but fails and pushes his palm into my face. "Just shoot the ball."

And because I'm clutch as fuck, I shoot the ball across the table, my eyes never leaving Rocky's.

I know I made it because Emerson yells, "Horse shit!" at the top of his lungs before storming off.

"I'd take that kiss now, please."

He cups my face with one hand, hard enough to purse my lips, and grants me a quick but deep kiss. "Come on, *Garotão*. I need another beer."

As the two of us walk into the kitchen I see a group of people huddled up by the back door.

Correction: I see three guys and a girl.

Actually, let me be more specific: I see three guys who look identical, with skull face paint covering half of their faces, and a blonde girl who looks like every guy's wet dream in a skimpy fairy costume.

One of them leans in and whispers something in her ear, while the second one crashes his lips to hers, all while the third one runs his hand up her leg and beneath her skirt.

"Fuck sakes. Is this a party or an orgy?" Rocky groans

"God, I fucking miss college. Can we come back?"

"No." In the span of two seconds, he's opening the fridge, grabbing two beers, and pulling me out of the kitchen.

"Awwww, come on. I wanna watch. That was hot."

Rocky stops in his tracks and looks back at me, his pupils blown wide and his jaw clenched tight.

There he is.

"You want something to watch, Clayton?"

"Sure do, Baby."

His eyes narrow at me, but I don't back down. More than willing to play whatever game he wants to play. The corner of his lips turn up before he turns back around and pulls me up the stairs.

Rocky drags me down the hallway until we reach the guest bathroom. Pushing me inside, he slams the door closed behind us. Before I even have a chance to talk, he's pressed up against me, my back to his front. His hand snakes around and wraps firmly around my neck.

He shuffles us forward until my hips bump the edge of the vanity. With his free hand, he works open my pants and slides them down past my ass, my already hard dick springing free. I watch our reflection in the mirror, and he bends me forward until my forearms rest on either side of the sink.

Kicking my legs apart, Rocky leans forward so his lips dust the shell of my ear. Staring at our reflection, he looks me in the eyes and asks on a growl, "Ready to watch a show, *Garotão?*"

My smile goes wide, and I press my ass into him. "Show me what you got, Baby."

THE END

If you're not finished with these two, follow the QR code below for extended epilogues for Clay and Rocky.

ALSO BY S.R. CLARK AND TILLY RIDGE

Dive into book two of Palm University!

Side Out: An MM College Sand Volleyball Romance

<u>**Available on Kindle Unlimited!**</u>

I knew from the moment I saw him moving into the house down the street. I knew that a man like Jackson Baker was going to be the one to turn my world upside down. I saw it coming a mile away. But what I didn't see coming was finding out he is one of my patients at my brand new job. I know it's wrong. I know it's against the rules. I know it could destroy the white picket fence that's being thrust upon me, and yet... chasing Jackson Baker is a high I can't seem to quit.

Theodore Young. My neighbor. My Athletic Trainer. My every waking thought. My addiction. I should be spending my fifth year at Palm University--my second chance at the perfect senior year-- making memories with friends, being the team captain everyone is counting on, and setting myself up for a career after college, and yet, the only thing I can think about is him. Watching him. Touching him. Kissing him. He's everywhere and nowhere all at once. But it's not enough. Because he's not mine and I know I can't have him. And yet, whenever I look into his eyes I know…

THE GAME HAS ONLY JUST BEGUN.

****Side Out is an MM forbidden lovers, college romance. It will be book two in the Palm University Series.****

Hat Trick: An MMF College Hockey Romance

<u>Available on Kindle Unlimited!</u>

They're best friends. Teammates. They're each other's person.

And I'm, well… me. Dominic Foster and Emerson Baker are Palm University's star hockey players. They're in the prime of their life, and I'm in mine. I'm creating a life for myself, one that I'm proud of. And yet, I see it everywhere I look. Love. I see it in my parents, and in my brother and his new husband. A kind of love so loud I find myself wanting it with everything in me, and I refuse to settle for less. Which is why they're my new addiction. Both of them. Together. What started as a casual fling is quickly starting to feel like it could be more. But is it what I need? Is what they have to offer me, what I deserve? Will I even get a chance to decide before one of them blows the whistle on this entire thing?

Liliana Campos is… everything. She's a tornado of chaos and sass, with a fire burning so bright inside of her she could do anything, have anyone she sets her sights on. She snuck up on both of us when we weren't looking. She wasn't part of the plan. And yet, she feels like she was always meant to be here. She has the power to bring both of us to our knees. It's always been the two of us, but now, we have to decide if what the three of us are building together is something we should run from or hold on to. Because if one of us is done, all three of us are done. That's the rule.

The real question is, are rules meant to be broken, or…

Will we get our own *Hat Trick?*

Triple Threat: A Reverse Harem Halloween

Short Story

Triple Threat is free when you sign up for our newsletters. It's triplets and one lucky gal on Halloween night that is in this world of Palm University.

Dangerously Safe: A McDermott Empire Novel (Book One)

<u>**Available now on Kindle Unlimited and Amazon.**</u>

Harper Hayes is an introverted, curvy, curly-haired, coffee-loving bookstore owner. And now, she's officially all alone. She has no family, friends, or life outside her parent's bookstore. She's made it her mission to live the rest of her life alone, not willing to take the risk of loving and losing. Again. That is until the three giant men, cloaked in danger, came to steal her in the night.

Ronan, Mac, and Finn, leaders of the Irish Mafia in New York City, have been given the impossible task of keeping her safe. Little did they know that their lives would be changed forever the night they walked into the bookstore. They quickly realize they'd give anything to keep her safe. But from whom, and at what cost?

Dangerously Kept: A McDermott Empire Novel (Book Two)

<u>Available now on Kindle Unlimited and Amazon.</u>

After finally allowing herself to love again, Harper wakes up miles away from the men that have kept her safe, and in the hands of those determined to destroy her from the inside out. Unsure of whether or not she can rely on Ronan, Mac, and Finn to save her, Harper must find the strength to free herself. But if she does, how is she meant to face what comes next?

With a world of unknowns hanging in the balance, Ronan, Mac, and Finn know two things for certain. They are willing to burn the world down around them to get her back, and just as they own her heart, she owns theirs. They just need to figure out how to keep her.

The Prices We Pay: A Vittori Enterprises Novel (Book One)

<u>**Available now on Kindle Unlimited and Amazon.**</u>

As CEO of Vittori Enterprises, Luca Vittori has made his fair share of enemies both in the corporate world and in less . . . legal business. But with the help of his teammates, best friends, and family—Enzo, Dante, and Sebastian—no one has been a worthy opponent. That is, until they're forced to hire a new employee in the tempting form of Josephine Jenkins. The four of them rapidly have to decide whether or not their feelings for Josephine and one another are worth the risk.

Will love destroy everything they've built, or will it make it stronger?

Josephine Jenkins is a woman who truly marches to the beat of her own drum. After running from memories better left buried, Joe made a life for herself in New York City. She finally had the life she always wanted for herself. Everything was perfect . . . until she took a job at Vittori Enterprises. Upon her arrival, she quickly learns the four men who captured her attention have more going on behind closed doors than they lead on, and if she isn't careful, they could be the end of the life she so carefully crafted.

Is falling for them worth the price she'll have to pay in the end?

The Prizes We Win: A Vittori Enterprises Novel (Book One)

<u>**Available now on Kindle Unlimited and Amazon.**</u>

They're not just billionaire businessmen. They're The Horsemen. They've made enemies of their own. Enemies that are now her enemies. And after all of this time, after everything she's already been through, it turns out her ghosts aren't really ghosts at all.

The life Josephine Jenkins once thought she was building for herself is now long gone, and in its place is a life full of the unknown. And yet, it just might be the life she was meant to live all along.

Only one question remains.

Is she willing to risk it all to win the ultimate prize?

A life with the men she loves.

Masked & Mine: An MMF Dark Romance

<u>Available on Kindle Unlimited!</u>

@devils_sovereign : Marfa, but call me Mar.

I'm just your favorite devilish cam girl looking to showcase my assets to my loyal demons. I was encouraged to take on this new persona as a cam girl by one of my clients at my former place of employment, "Sins: In Sin City," and here I am thriving. Sins is the biggest and most reputable sex club in Vegas, and well, I just got fired yesterday. Not for anything I did, but because my father is the leader of the Russian Mafia. Now I'm stuck, needing to put my all into this cam girl gig if I want to survive living in Vegas.

@Untrained__Ghostt : Mack

To many, I'm known as a tattoo shop owner and artist by day, and in the words of my subs, a "drool-worthy" cam guy by night with the persona of Ghost from Call of Duty. Together with my partner, Percy, whom I met through TikTok, we have been camming for the best subscribers ever. Tomorrow we're meeting with the first person we are going to collaborate with. The first girl I've been with in years—let's see how this goes…

@Königoftheunderworld : Percy

I'm a marketing firm manager and a little bit of a control freak, but underneath the boring, my real self comes alive when I cosplay as König when camming with my partner, Mack. I've never been happier, and everything has been perfect, but the pessimist in me feels it's a little too perfect. I've been feeling a little apprehensive about sharing Mack, but I know it's been something we've both been wanting to dip our toes into. It doesn't, however, make me any less anxious about losing control.

Play the Game: A Dark Why Choose Romance

<u>Available on Kindle Unlimited!</u>

Taking candids turned into so much more...

Marriage never looked easy on the outside looking in, but with Simon, life had been better than ever. I found my soulmate in a man who cared for me, loved me feverishly, and protected me against all odds. But regardless of the love we shared for each other, our eyes often roamed to others. Even at night, when we spent time in each other's arms, we mused over the ideas of what it would be like to explore happily again, while remaining committed to each other.

But fear always held us back.

Then *they* entered the picture.

Nyx. Asher. And Rhodes.

men, but at the persistent pursuit from two players of the Vegas Rebels, she finds herself welcoming a little fun.

Nash Hayden, quarterback and number one draft pick, isn't used to the fast life. As he begins his new life, he finds his devotion to his father falters as his spirituality evolves, contradicting everything he thought he knew from his Texas upbringing.

Zamir Prifti, a wide receiver with Albanian mafia ties, does everything he can to hide the darkness woven into his soul. What he doesn't know is how far his family is willing to go to get him back.

Will Marcelo's unwillingness to share sever the connection they've formed?

Or will they learn to play together?

Taking Over the Dark: A Why Choose Mafia Sports Romance (Book Two)

<u>**Available on Kindle Unlimited!**</u>

Las Vegas

The City of Sin

What happens here, isn't what it seems.

Marcello has finally decided to share his life, his secrets, and his trust, with people he never saw coming. However, that trust is put to the test when Ellie and Nash disappear, and it all points to Zamir.

Will Marcello and Zamir be able to put everything else aside in order to save Ellie and Nash?

Or in the city of lights, will the darkness finally take over?

ABOUT S.R. CLARK

S.R. Clark is an indie author who lives in West Virginia with her husband, toddler, and hound dog. She writes romance books. She has a soft spot for characters who live unapologetically for themselves and who will lay down their lives for the ones they love. When she's not writing, she loves getting lost in a good book, cooking/baking, and exploring with her family.

Be the first to hear about updates, sneak peeks, and much more with my newsletter!

ABOUT TILLY RIDGE

Tilly Ridge is a romance author who resides in the middle of nowhere, Kentucky, with her husband, two kiddos, and two dogs. She loves to dabble in a variety of romance topics, themes, and subgenres, but you'll typically find her writing in the dark and polyamory sections of the shelves. Tilly can be easily identified by the pink slush clutched in one hand while her laptop is in the other, ready to write whenever the mood—or the character—strikes! In her free time, she enjoys playing sand volleyball in her local rec league. But what she finds most exciting is her podcast, Releasing Romance, where she shares her knowledge and experience about indie publishing, often bringing on guests to discuss the ins and outs of indie publishing from different professional points of view! This podcast is a passion project of Tilly's as she finds true joy in helping and educating others in a way that is easy to understand.

Join Tilly's readers group for exclusive BTS, art drops, first looks at pretty much anything, and even chapter-by-chapter releases of her ongoing projects at: <u>Tilly's Thots</u>

The newsletter is where the fun is, and maybe even a free ebook will hit your inbox after—along with a first look at the big news.

Find everything you'll need to stay connected at <u>https://www.tillyridgeauthor.com/links</u>

www.ingramcontent.com/pod-product-compliance
Lightning Source LLC
Chambersburg PA
CBHW071404300726
48976CB00006B/1976